INESCAPABLE DARKNESS

ALSO BY RAVEN WOOD

To see the most recently updated list of books by Raven Wood, please visit: www.authorravenwood.com

CONTENT WARNINGS

Inescapable Darkness is a bully romance intended for mature readers. It contains violence and graphic sexual content. If you have specific triggers, you can find the full list of content warnings at: www.authorravenwood.com/content-warnings

INESCAPABLE DARKNESS

RAVEN WOOD

ISBN 978-91-988025-9-7 (paperback)
ISBN 978-91-988025-8-0 (ebook)

Cover design by Krafigs Design

www.authorravenwood.com

For everyone who lives vicariously through fictional characters while still waiting for their own life to truly begin

1

ISABELLA

Be invisible. That is the rule that has been ingrained in me from the day I opened my eyes. It is the code by which I have lived my entire life, and the reason why I'm still alive. Now, abiding by it is more important than ever, because the very people who taught me that vital rule are out for blood. Specifically, mine.

"Listen up!"

I shift my gaze to the instructor, Ms. Saber, by the door. She is dark-haired and looks to be in her thirties, but her gray eyes are sharp enough to slice through steel. This is the first time our class has met her since we started at Blackwater University a few weeks ago, but everyone already seems terrified of her.

Since I was raised in a literal cult led by a dictatorial man who expects complete obedience, I'm not particularly intimidated by her. Rather the opposite. I quite like her, because she has a no-nonsense attitude and bold confidence but without being cruel. And that is a good combination.

"You're about to be tested on your ability to remain calm

while your instincts are screaming at you to panic," Saber continues. Twisting slightly, she raps her knuckles on the metal door behind her. "After you go through this door, line up along the edge."

Nervous tension ripples through the group. Not all first-years are present for this class. This morning, we were split into several groups so that there are only about fifteen people in each group. Based on that, I'm assuming that whatever we're about to do is going to take place in a rather limited space.

"The edge of what?" a guy to my left asks hesitantly.

I glance towards him.

Gods above, he looks so young. They all look so young. Most of them are probably twenty, since they enrolled at Blackwater right after high school. I'm only two years older than them, but because of everything I've done, I feel like I've been an adult since I was five.

"You'll see when you get there." Ms. Saber grabs the handle and shoves the door open. "Get to it."

The smell of chlorine wafts through the door.

Staying in the back half of the group, I follow the others across the threshold and into the room beyond. It's a large space, shaped like a rectangle. And just like the smell indicated, in the center of it is a pool.

While carefully moving towards the long side where the others are lining up, I study the water as well as our surroundings. Metal bleachers run along one side of the room, but they're deserted. In fact, the whole room is. The surface of the water is smooth as a mirror. Not one ripple disturbs it.

I flick my gaze around it again, trying to figure out what it is that they are about to do to us in order to induce panic.

The metal door bangs shut behind Saber as she enters the room as well. Everyone else has lined up along the edge of the pool. Since we didn't know that we would be getting into a pool, everyone is dressed in normal clothes. A few people glance down at their garments, as if they're worried that those will become too heavy when wet. I'm wearing a pair of jeans and a tight-fitting black t-shirt, and I've survived swimming in far worse attire, so I know that I'll be fine.

"Your mission is simple," Saber announces as she strides over to a panel by the wall. "Find your way out of the pool."

Several of my classmates furrow their brows in confusion while others quickly check to see where the pool ladders are located. I don't, because I already checked that the moment I walked inside. And the answer is that there are none. But the water level is only about a foot or so below the edge of the pool, so it will be easy to climb out of it anyway.

"When I say jump, you will all jump into the pool at the same time," Saber declares. "Anyone who does not jump will be immediately expelled."

That raises a few eyebrows, but before anyone can comment or ask questions, Ms. Saber barks the order.

"Jump!"

We do.

The mirror smooth surface shatters as all fifteen of us jump into the pool at the same time. Water splashes around us, and then the world is drowned out. Through the thick muffling effect from the water, I can hear the people around me moving, but I don't open my eyes.

I'm just about to start swimming back to the surface when another sound cuts through the water.

Metallic whirring.

I snap my eyes open in time to see a sheet of metal shoot

out from the wall behind us and quickly move towards the other side of the pool. It's low enough to run through the water, so it's blocking our way to the surface.

If I wasn't busy holding my breath, I would've snorted. So *that* is how they were planning to create panic.

And based on the reactions of the people closest to me, it's working. Their movements are jerky as they flail their limbs to get to the metal sheet. Dull clanging sounds echo through the water as several of them bang their fists against the metal. I shake my head.

Since I know that our instructors aren't actually trying to kill us, not actively anyway, I'm confident that there is a logical way to get out. After all, that was what she said the test was all about. Staying calm and thinking clearly while our animalistic survival instincts are screaming at us that we are going to die.

While swimming away from the panicking people, I scan the area before me. Everything is blurred by the water, and with the sheet intact, it's also dark. Except for three spots farther up ahead.

Light streams down in three perfect circles. One to the left, one to the right, and one straight ahead. Since there is no light in the pool, it must be coming from the ceiling in the room, which means that there are openings in the metal sheet. The one to my left is the closest one, so I start towards it.

About half of our group has figured out the same thing too. The others, however, are still thrashing around in blind panic. If I was a decent person, I would've tapped the ones I passed on the shoulder and pointed towards the openings. But I'm not a decent person. And helping people would only draw attention to me. Attention I can't afford.

Since the day I started at Blackwater University, all I have done is to quietly go to all my classes. I'm never late. And never too early. I never ask questions and only answer when someone speaks to me directly. I sit at the edge of a group when I eat, so that I don't stand out by eating completely alone, but I don't belong to the group either and make sure to rotate groups every day.

Then I go straight back to my apartment in the residential area where all of the other students live too. I never attend parties unless I'm directly invited, since refusing would draw attention. But I thankfully haven't been invited to one yet. I stay inside my apartment as much as possible. I barely interact with the rest of the first-years, and never with anyone in the second or third year.

And because of all that, I have managed to follow that one vital rule that will keep me alive. Be invisible. So I completely ignore the panicking students who are frantically banging their fists on the metal sheet and instead simply swim towards the closest circle of light.

When I get close to it, two other people are near it as well. Two guys.

The circle is only wide enough for one person to climb out at a time. The first guy to reach it immediately grabs the edges and starts hauling himself up. I reach the hole next, so I tread water while waiting for my turn.

A few seconds later, the second guy arrives beside me.

His features are blurred from the water, but I can clearly read the panic on his face. He must not be used to holding his breath because he looks about two seconds away from gulping down water in sheer panic.

Once the first guy is out, I start towards the hole.

Dull pain pulses through me, and the air in my lungs involuntarily escapes, as the second guy punches me in the stomach. Bubbles float up to the surface as my breath leaves me.

The punch shifted me away from the hole, which I'm assuming was the primary purpose of it, and the guy immediately swims up and grabs the edges.

I could've yanked him back down and snapped his fucking wrist for daring to hit me, but that would also draw attention, so I do what I have done from the moment I set foot on this campus. Nothing.

My lungs burn as I tread water, waiting for the guy to finish getting up. But I smother the panic like I have been taught to do and summon the incredible patience that has been my companion for most of my life.

I can wait.

I can take it.

I can endure it.

I repeat that over and over in my head until the guy has finally crawled out of the hole. Kicking my legs, I swim towards the rippling surface above.

Noise crashes back against my eardrums as I at last break the surface. I suck in a gasp, refilling my lungs. While blinking water out of my eyes, I reach up and grab the edges of the hole.

The metal is cold and slick underneath my palms.

Bracing myself on it, I climb out of the water and roll over so that I'm lying on my back on the metal sheet. My chest rises and falls as I drag in another few deep breaths.

"Well done, Johnson," Ms. Saber says from somewhere to my left.

I push myself up on my elbows to find her looking straight at me. After sucking in another breath, I give her a nod in acknowledgement of the praise.

"Class is finished when you've made it out," she continues, and then points towards another door that is set into the outer wall. "So go back home and change clothes before your next class."

"Yes, ma'am," I reply.

After pushing my wet hair out of my face, I get to my feet and start towards the indicated door. Water runs down from my entire body, leaving a dark trail on the metal and then on the stone floor beside the pool. I squeeze some water from my hair and then shake it out before pushing the door open.

Behind me, the sound of water splashing on metal echoes through the room.

"Well done, O'Malley," Saber says. "Class is finished when—"

But the rest of her instructions are cut off as I stride back out into the warm September air. I draw in a deep breath and tip my head up towards the sun for a few seconds. In this part of the country, the heat of summer will linger for a while yet. And right now, I'm thankful for it.

I glance down at my soaked clothes as I start towards the parking lot. I have a car, so I don't have to walk all the way to the residential area, but I'm not too thrilled about getting into my car in this state either. But it's better than—

A huff rips from my throat as I slam chest first into someone when I round the corner. Stumbling back, I snap my gaze up, an apology already on my tongue.

But my words falter when I take in the person standing in front of me. The *guy* standing in front of me.

He's tall and athletic, with an impressive array of lethal muscles but without being too bulky. His dark brown hair curls softly at the ends. It's perfectly styled and is swept back from his face, giving him a composed look that screams power and control. He has brown eyes and a face that is so fucking gorgeous that is should be illegal.

Dread spreads through my veins like ice.

It can't be.

It can't.

For one second, it feels as if time itself has stopped moving. The guy I bumped into is still looking down at his shirt, which is now wet from where I slammed into him, and all I can do is stare at him for this one moment that is suspended in time.

Even though my mind is desperately trying to deny the truth, I know without a shred of doubt that it's him.

I have never forgotten his face.

And I never will.

Because for the past six years, I have seen his face every time I close my eyes.

He was my darkest secret. My first and only act of rebellion. The source of my greatest confusion. The person who irrevocably shattered my world. The one who ripped painful feelings from me with just one look and one fucking sigh. And for the past few months, my biggest regret and the reason why the cult I was born into now wants my head.

This is the mafia prince I was supposed to have assassinated six years ago.

"Hey," he snaps as he looks up from his wet shirt.

Before his eyes are even halfway to my face, I have already schooled my features into an appropriately apologetic look. There are no traces left of the shock and dread that I really felt a second ago. No evidence that I recognized him.

And he won't recognize me either.

I have dyed my naturally auburn hair a dull brown and cut it so that it ends at my collarbones. The real color of my eyes is also hidden by brown contact lenses. And I have one of those neutral faces that are perfect for assassins.

I'm good-looking enough for people to treat me politely and with kindness. Because let's face it, everyone always instinctively treats pretty people better. But I'm not beautiful enough to stand out in a crowd. It's just one of those faces that make people offer me a smile when they meet me on the street but then forget me as soon as I'm out of sight.

Besides, this particular person only saw me for less than a minute six years ago in a dark room. So with the disguise added to that, there is no way he will recognize me now.

"Watch where you're…" he continues but then suddenly trails off when he meets my gaze.

His eyes go wide and his mouth drops open slightly.

Panic explodes in my chest like a cloud of cold poison.

"It's you," he blurts out.

"I'm sorry." I quickly run a hand over my face, ducking my head slightly as I pretend to push a few strands of hair out of my face. "I wasn't looking where I was going."

He just opens and closes his mouth a few times, utter shock pulsing across his features. I use the opportunity to quickly slip around him.

It takes all of my considerable self-control not to run the final distance to the parking lot. I keep my pace normal and resist the urge to look over my shoulder.

Be invisible.

Be invisible.

When I at last reach my car, I cast a quick glance back while opening the driver's side door to confirm that he has left.

My heart leaps into my throat when I find him still standing in the exact same spot, staring after me as if he has just seen a ghost. Which, ironically, is a very accurate description of who I am.

I slide into the driver's seat, my wet clothes sticking to the fabric and my soaked shoes squeaking. With my heart thudding in my chest, I fumble with the keys to start the car.

He can't have recognized me.

He can't.

It was six years ago, and I looked nothing like this back then. My hair, my eyes, even the way I carry myself is different now.

Starting the car, I throw it into reverse and then flick a glance up at the rearview mirror.

My heart stops.

A pair of blue-gray eyes stare back at me.

My *real* eyes.

Only a few minutes ago, I was trapped underwater. I didn't panic then. But I do now.

Terrible, searing panic crackles through my every vein as I stare at my own eyes in the rearview mirror. The brown contacts I wore must have washed out because I kept my eyes open for so long underwater. No one else was close enough to me to notice.

But *he* did.

2

RICO

I gasp and shoot up from the bed, my hand already closing around the gun in the drawer of my nightstand before my mind can catch up. My heart pounds in my chest and sweat trickles down my spine. Holding the gun straight, I flick my gaze around the room.

Only my dark bedroom stares back at me.

Reality trickles back in.

A nightmare.

Forcing out a long breath, I try to slow my thundering heart while I return the gun to my nightstand. The drawer closes with a soft thud. I draw a hand through my hair and then around the back of my neck, wiping away the beads of sweat. After dragging in another deep breath, I lie back down on the now rumpled sheets.

It has been months since the last time that nightmare plagued my sleep. But it's always the same. Because it's not really a nightmare at all. It's a memory.

Six years ago, I was sleeping in my bed back in the grand mansion my parents used to own when a flash of danger suddenly pulsed through my subconsciousness. I shot upright and snapped my eyes open.

And found myself staring down the barrel of a gun.

I opened my mouth to sound the alarm. But before I could, the person holding the gun pushed the muzzle of the silencer hard against my forehead. I still remember how cold it was as it dug into my skin. I froze. Remaining completely motionless on my bed, I slid my gaze up to the person standing next to it.

Even after all these years, I can still feel the shock that pulsed through me when I realized that it was a girl, a *teenager,* who couldn't be older than I was at the time. She was wearing black clothes and the room was dark, so I could barely make out her features. Except for her eyes. Light from the lamps in our garden outside the window shone through the gap in my blinds and illuminated her eyes.

For as long as I live, I will never forget those eyes. They were blue-gray. Cold. And hard. Like a merciless storm-swept sea.

And in that moment, I realized that I was going to die.

The silencer of her gun was pressed directly against my forehead. She could pull the trigger before I could even open my mouth to scream or lift my hands to try to fight her off. In hindsight, I know that I should probably have been terrified at that point. But all I felt was disappointment and bitter resignation.

Something, some kind of emotion, had flickered in her eyes then. But I never found out what it was because the faint sound of a gun with a silencer being fired came from down the hall. Then another only a second later.

At that point, I still hadn't realized that those two gunshots had been two other people executing my parents. All of my attention had been on the girl holding the gun to my own head. I know that I should probably have at least tried to fight back, but all I did was to sit there in my bed and hold her gaze.

Three seconds after that second gunshot, she made her own move.

Shifting the gun to the left, she fired right next to my head and down into the mattress instead.

A man's voice came from down the hall. "Dead."

It was followed by another man's voice. "Dead."

The girl kept her stormy eyes locked on mine as she called, "Dead."

Her eyes stayed on mine as she backed across the room, the gun still pointed in my direction. She paused for two seconds when she reached the door.

And then she was gone.

That was the night that everything changed. The night that a group of unknown people assassinated my parents. People that, even after six years, we still haven't been able to track down.

Until now.

She might not have betrayed any surprise at seeing me yesterday, but I know what I saw. I remember those eyes.

It makes no sense that she would be here. Since she was a part of the group who broke into our very secure house and killed my parents, she was already an incredibly skilled assassin when she was just a teenager. So there would be absolutely no reason for her to enroll at Blackwater. Not to mention that this is my state. *Our* state. It should be the last place she would want to be.

But I know that it's her. I know it is.

Pushing away the tangled sheets, I run a hand over the back of my neck as I sit up. I tap my phone. The screen lights up and informs me that it's only four-thirty.

If Eli had been here, I could've gone to him because he would've already been awake. Or maybe not anymore, since he actually sleeps through the night when he has Raina in his arms.

But Eli graduated this summer, so now I have become the de facto leader of the Hunter brothers and have to be the one to keep the degenerates Kaden and Jace from killing each other and everyone else.

With a sigh, I rake my fingers through my hair and then pick up my phone. Yesterday, after I snapped out of my stupor, I went straight to the admin office and requested all the information that they have about the mystery girl I bumped into. Which they complied with for the same reason that I can get away with practically anything at this university.

I don't expect them to have sent it over already, but I still check my email.

My heart lurches as I do in fact find an email from the admin office. With my pulse fluttering, I pull up the documents they have attached and read through them.

Isabella Johnson. She's twenty-two years old, like me, which means that she should have been a third-year and not a freshman. It's not the norm, but it's hardly rare either, so I can't nail her on that alone.

I scan the rest of the document.

She's from an average-sized Midwestern town where she went to an average high school that she graduated from with average grades. Then she worked as a cashier at a supermarket for two years before coming here. Her family is an average middle class family that has relocated to Canada for the next year due to her father's work.

No criminal record. No unexplained details. Nothing that stands out.

Everything about Isabella Johnson is just... average.

Except, I know that it's a lie.

It has to be.

Tossing my phone down on the bed, I stalk over to my closet and yank it open. After getting dressed, I grab my phone again and walk out the door. Kaden and Jace are both asleep, the doors to their rooms closed, so I simply walk down the stairs and right out the front door.

At this time of night, the air is pleasantly cool. I draw in a deep breath. My lungs expand, filling with air that tastes of summer mist and pine trees.

While I start down the street, I check Isabella's file again. She doesn't live in one of the freestanding houses, like we do, but she doesn't live in a dorm room either. Instead, she rents one of the apartments in the middle of the residential area.

Once again, average.

Most of the houses I pass are still dark. Only a few windows shine with yellow light, signaling that there are at least some other people apart from me who can't sleep. Or maybe they're training. I have never really cared enough about the other people on this campus to ask.

Once I reach the building that houses Isabella's apartment, I stop. Since it's technically still the middle of the night, the outer door is locked. There's a keypad next to it. I could get the code from the admin office, but none of them are at work yet. I blow out a breath.

Crossing my arms, I turn around and lean against the wall next to the door.

And then I wait.

At around seven-thirty, people start exiting the building. Most of them jerk back in surprise when they find me standing there, but no one dares to ask what I'm doing there.

They all just glance at me while they skirt past as if silently hoping that I'm not there for them.

Twenty minutes to eight, my target at last appears.

Just like everyone else, Isabella Johnson jerks back slightly in surprise as she strides across the threshold and finds me standing there.

I push off from the wall and approach her.

"You know who I am, right?" I say without preamble.

She frowns in confusion and glances from side to side, as if to check whether this is some kind of setup, before replying, "Of course."

I don't stop as I reach her. Instead, I continue pressing forward, forcing her to back up against the wall. Her brown hair ripples, brushing her collarbones, as her back connects with the wall. And when I'm standing this close, I realize one more thing about her.

She is slightly taller than the average woman. Not enough that she stands out. But it somehow feels like a victory in itself. Something that is *not* average about Isabella Johnson.

I'm moving until I'm standing barely a stride in front of her so that I'm crowding her space. Cocking my head, I study her face. The expression on her features is the same one that everyone has when they're cornered by me. Worried and apologetic. There is no hint of recognition, *real* recognition, in her eyes when she looks up at me.

"Who am I?" I press.

"You're one of the Hunter brothers. Rico." Her gaze flits around the area behind me again, the picture of nervous worry. "I'm really sorry for running into you like that yesterday. It was entirely my fault. Please. I'm sorry."

She sounds so… genuine. So truthful. As if she truly believes that the only reason I'm here is because I'm angry that she bumped into me when she walked around a corner yesterday.

But those eyes.

It's her. I know it's her.

She starts to slip around me.

Yanking up my arm, I slam my palm against the wall next to her head, blocking her path. She flinches. The girl who held a gun to my head six years ago wouldn't have flinched like that.

But it *is* her.

"Please, I'm sorry," she repeats, looking up at me with pleading blue-gray eyes that contain none of the cold hardness that they did all those years ago. "I can't be late for class."

I just stare her down in silence.

Indecision twists inside me like a nest of snakes.

Before I can come to a decision, Isabella slowly tries to edge away from the wall again. This time I let her.

After ducking under my arm, she pauses and wrings her hands before once more repeating, "I'm sorry."

Then she hurries away down the stone path that leads to the parking spaces around the back. Turning around, I watch her go.

She acts like a completely different person. And if it hadn't been for those eyes of hers, I would have believed that she was indeed someone else.

But I know that I'm right.

And I'm going to prove it.

I'm going to force her to reveal who she really is. That she is the incredibly skilled assassin who broke into my home six years ago and put a gun to my head. That she is a part of the group that murdered my parents.

And then I am going to get the answers I want. The answers that I need. The answers that my family has desperately been trying to find for far too long now.

Because my name is not Rico Hunter.

My name is Enrico Morelli.

And I officially died six years ago.

3

ISABELLA

Every nerve in my body was on high alert the rest of the day. I half expected Rico to show up and drag me out of class so that he could interrogate me some more. But he didn't. So I did what I have been doing since the day I got here. I faked my way through every lesson, making sure to never perform well enough to draw attention and never poorly enough to stand out either. Everything I did was average. Always average.

But as I sit in my car, driving away from Blackwater University and towards the city, my mind keeps drifting back to that encounter this morning with the officially-but-not-really-dead mafia prince.

After I bumped into him outside the swimming pool, I immediately gathered all the information I could about him. Turns out that that wasn't as difficult as I had imagined. Every single person on this entire campus knows who he is. Or rather, they know who he *pretends* to be. Rico Hunter.

When I first arrived, I did of course hear about the

infamous Hunter brothers. That the eldest, Eli, who graduated this summer, is seriously unhinged and has very little impulse control. That Kaden is an absolute psycho who might actually give Eli a run for his money in the unhinged department. That Jace is the out-of-control wildcard who spreads chaos everywhere he goes. And that Rico is the quietly powerful one who keeps them all in check.

I knew all of that from day one.

What I *didn't* know, however, was that Rico Hunter was actually Enrico Morelli, the heir to the Morelli mafia family who, according to all official documents, was killed along with his parents six years ago.

Tightening my grip on the steering wheel, I grind my teeth in annoyance at my own foolishness.

My decision to go straight home after class and to never interact with anyone outside my year really came back to bite me. If I had just seen him, even from a distance, I would've known immediately that it was him. But I hadn't expected to find him here, of all places. Which, in hindsight, is probably the reason why he is here. Just like me.

Shaking my head, I turn a corner and drive down a quiet street towards a parking lot that I picked out beforehand.

At least I'm reasonably sure that he believed me this morning. Well, *reasonably sure* might be a bit of a stretch. But since he let me go and also hasn't hunted me down today, I *hope* he believed me at least.

Slowing down, I drive into the parking lot. It's only half full, so I park close to the exit and then turn off the ignition. I flick a glance up at the rearview mirror, meeting my own eyes. My blue-gray eyes.

Because Rico has now seen me with that eye color, I

couldn't go back to wearing my brown contacts. That would've been too suspicious. So I went to class without them today. Only a few of my classmates noticed that my eye color had changed, and when they remarked on it, I went with the simplest explanation. Brown eyes are more common, so I figured it would be a better color for an assassin, but wearing contacts every day has become too much of a bother. They accepted that explanation without issue.

Blowing out a breath, I shove open my car door and climb out. After locking the car behind me, I start down the street and through a slightly rundown part of the city. Houses with flaking paint stare me down as I walk.

I heave another sigh and shake my head at how complicated my life has suddenly become. Because of Rico. Or Enrico, I suppose. But calling him that feels... wrong somehow. Maybe because I am the one who killed that person six years ago. Or maybe because if I call him Enrico, even just in my own head, I'm practically admitting that the very average student Isabella Johnson, who knows nothing of the Morelli tragedy, is not real. And one of the most important aspects of getting away with lying is to believe your own lie. So, Rico it is.

Quiet voices drift up from the street ahead where people are walking. Before I can reach it, I turn left into a deserted alley instead. The golden afternoon sunlight barely reaches in here because of how narrow the path between the two buildings is. A few empty bottles lie discarded by the gray concrete wall on my right, and the entire place smells of spilled alcohol and piss.

No one ever comes here. Well, except for the drunk college kids who sometimes pass through here when they drink the town dry during their initiation week. Or some such thing. Since I have never actually attended a real university, I'm not sure what it is that they do. I simply scouted out the alley for a couple of weeks to make sure that it was as deserted as a place could get inside a busy city.

I check over my shoulder before walking up to the door that is set into the red brick wall on my left. There is no one in sight, so I quickly get out my lockpicks and pick the lock on the rusted metal door. The hinges creak slightly as I pull the door open and slip inside.

Daylight barely makes it in through the grimy windows, but it's enough to illuminate the space in part at least. I skirt around a pile of broken wood and make my way towards the metal box at the back.

By my best guess, this place has been abandoned for years. It looks like someone started renovating it, hence the wooden planks and bag of plaster and the scattering of mismatched tools, but then ran out of money before the project could even get off the ground.

Crouching down in front of the decently sized box, I unlock the padlock I put on it and open the lid. A black duffel bag takes up most of the space inside. My go-bag.

I unzip it and push aside the stacks of cash and passports and ID cards until I can reach my encrypted cellphone.

After I let Rico live six years ago, I descended into an absolute spiral of mad panic. I knew what the others would do to me when the news broke that the parents had been killed but not the son. However, to my complete shock, all the news crews reported that both the parents and their sixteen-year-old son had been killed. But I still feared that the truth might come out one day, so I started building my own network and recruiting my own assets separate from the ones that were provided by the Hands of Peace.

Sitting back on my heels, I scoff quietly to myself at that name while I turn on the cellphone.

The Hands of Peace. As someone who was born and raised inside that cult, I know firsthand that the last thing they bring is fucking peace. All that they, all that *we*, have ever left in our wake is death and destruction.

The screen lights up. I scan my thumb print and then type in my password. It takes another few seconds for it to load. Once it's finished, I find a notification on our dedicated messenger app. Just like I expected.

My heart patters in my chest as I open it and read the message.

No signs yet.

I release a long whooshing breath.

After I spared Rico's life, I started setting up my own communications network. I knew that the truth would one day come out, and that I would be in deep shit then. After all, no one betrays the Hands of Peace. In that cult, you only have two options. You obey. Or you die.

I was hoping against hope that they would never discover what I had done that night, but if they did, I would need to run before they could kill me. And then stay hidden. So over the years, I hired skilled people who would be able to help me accomplish that, and to help me scan both the digital and the physical world for signs that a Hands of Peace strike team was closing in on me.

Thankfully, there are no signs of that at the moment.

I send back 'Received' and then close the app before turning off the phone again. Reaching into my pocket, I pull out the freshly charged powerbank I brought and swap out the other mostly drained one. After plugging it into the phone, I zip up the bag again and then close the lid.

A faint click sounds as I lock the box with the padlock again.

Then I push to my feet.

Making these trips into the city is risky. I would've preferred to keep my go-bag with me in the apartment I rent on campus. But that's dangerous as well. I'm pretty sure that the university staff has keys to all residences, for emergencies or whatever, and I don't want to risk them searching through my apartment and finding the bag. So keeping it in a secondary location is better.

After all, I'm Isabella Johnson, an average student with nothing to hide. And my apartment needs to reflect that.

I rake my fingers through my hair, pushing some dull brown strands out of my face, and then start towards the door. I need to get back to Blackwater before my absence is noticed. Earlier, I didn't have to worry about that, because there was no one there who kept track of me. But now, there is. That damn mafia prince that I really should have killed.

Shaking my head, I slip back out onto the street and lock the door behind me again.

Rico is going to get both me and himself killed if he doesn't stop investigating me. The Hands of Peace know that he is alive, but they don't know where he is yet. And they don't know where I am either. Both of us are at the top of their hit list. Rico because they're embarrassed that one of their targets is still alive, and no one embarrasses the Hands of Peace. And me because I disobeyed their orders, and no one disobeys the Hands of Peace either.

If they find out that both of us are at Blackwater, we will be dead within the next two days. And if Rico keeps going down this path, word might get back to them. So I need to make him lose interest. I need to make him believe that I'm not who he thinks I am.

I know that he will be coming at me hard now.

But no matter what he does to me, I won't give in.

I will never break.

4

RICO

"Stop with the incessant fucking drumming!"

I blink, pulling my mind away from my churning thoughts and back to the present. Across the table, Kaden's dark eyes are locked on me. Then he shoots a pointed look down at my left hand. I follow his gaze. And find that I am indeed drumming my fingers repeatedly on the polished wooden tabletop.

Kaden raises his eyebrows expectantly.

I flash him a grin and continue drumming.

"You have five seconds to stop that before I pin your hand to the table with a knife," Kaden warns, his voice dead serious.

While still tapping the table with my left hand, I use my right to quickly slide out my gun and knock it against the wood from underneath the table. With that grin still in place, I raise my eyebrows as well and challenge, "Oh really?"

He shifts his weight, casting a glance under the table to find me aiming the gun between his legs. Amusement lights up his normally so cold brown eyes, and he chuckles. I flash him another smile before returning the gun to the holster.

And then I actually do stop drumming my fingers on the table.

"Thank fuck," Kaden says, and draws a hand through his straight black hair while leaning back in his chair. "It was like having two Jaces there for a while. And just one Jace is still one too many."

Jace, who had been busy shoveling pasta into his mouth while we were threatening each other, at last pulls his attention away from his dinner and narrows his eyes at his brother.

"First of all, fuck you very much," he says around a mouthful of food. Then he swallows before stabbing his fork in Kaden's direction. "Secondly, there could never be two of me because I'm strictly one of a kind. A special limited edition, if you will. And thirdly, if there were two of me, we would be a fucking delight."

I laugh while Kaden shakes his head in exasperation. Jace, apparently satisfied with his comeback, grins at us both before once more attacking his mountain of pasta. I slide my attention back to my own plate too, but only end up picking at it.

"It's that girl though, right?" Kaden says. "Isabella Johnson. She's why you were drumming your fingers like a restless banshee, isn't she?"

Slumping back in my chair, I blow out a long sigh and admit, "Yeah."

After I confronted her outside her apartment building yesterday morning, I haven't done anything else about it. I have been waiting six years for this. For a chance to finally get some answers. And now that it's here, I don't want to screw it up.

Kaden's dark eyes, those eyes that always seem to see far

too much, are locked on me. "What can we do to help?"

"Yeah," Jace adds around another mouthful of pasta. "Just say the word and we're in."

"I was actually considering—" I begin right before Jace shoots up from his seat.

"Incoming," he snaps.

Kaden and I whip towards the window that he's staring through. My hand is already resting on my gun, and Kaden has a knife out while Jace has snatched up a bat that he had left lying on the couch earlier. I know that we give Jace a lot of shit for being loud and reckless and for having a terribly short attention span, but he's actually much more aware of his surroundings than most people assume.

I narrow my eyes at the black Audi A8 that stops in front of our house.

"Isn't that one of the boss man's cars?" Jace says.

Once again, much more aware than people assume.

"Yes," I confirm.

I slide my gun back into the holster as I watch Andrea climb out of the car. He is wearing a dark suit, as usual, and couldn't look more conspicuous if he tried. Jace and Kaden flick uncertain glances at me.

"Has something happened?" Kaden asks as we watch Andrea walk up to our door.

I shake my head. "I don't know."

The sofa cushions let out a faint huff as Jace tosses his bat back down. Kaden slides his knife back into its sheath as well. Then we start towards the door. Andrea might be many things, but he is never a threat. Not to me anyway.

We reach the door before he does, and I push it open right as he walks up to it.

"Is something wrong?" I ask before Andrea has even come to a halt.

His features are blank, as always, as he meets my gaze. "Mr. Morelli has ordered me to bring you to him straight away."

"Is something wrong?" I repeat, hard authority bleeding into my voice this time.

Discomfort flickers briefly in Andrea's brown eyes. "Please just get into the car, sir."

Which means that he has been ordered not to say anything. I force out an annoyed breath and then turn to grab my shoes.

"Do you want us to come with you?" Jace asks as I put my shoes on.

I straighten and open my mouth to respond, but Andrea speaks before I can.

"The invitation was for you alone," he says, still only focused on me.

After shooting him a hard look, I shift my attention back to Kaden and Jace. Both of them only look back at me, waiting for my answer. Even though they know what the repercussions would be if they came with me despite not being invited, they would still do it if I asked them to.

My heart squeezes in my chest.

Jace, Kaden, and Eli might not be my brothers by blood, but they are my brothers in every way that counts.

"It's alright," I tell them. "I'll see you later."

They hold my gaze for another few seconds before giving me a nod. I nod back and then follow Andrea down the path and towards his car.

The ride away from Blackwater is a silent one. If Andrea has been told not to share anything before I arrive, there is no point in asking. So I just sit there, watching the fields and woods flash past the window until they're replaced by grand buildings.

Andrea stops at the security checks, just like all cars need to do, before we arrive at the main mansion. He parks right outside the path leading up to the front door, and then walks around the car and opens the door for me.

"He's in his study," Andrea says as I climb out.

I nod. Without another word, I start up towards the door while Andrea returns to the car. The engine hums as he starts it and then drives away to park it properly. I run my gaze over the immaculate garden and then up over the elegant three-story mansion made of dark wood.

How many years has it been now since the last time I was here? I used to come here all the time when I was younger. But since that night when my parents were murdered, I have only been here less than a handful of times.

Seeing it again opens an empty pit inside my chest. This used to be a second home to me, and now I feel as if I'm a stranger, looking in through the windows and seeing someone else's life instead of my own.

I smother that terribly detached feeling and draw in a deep breath as I close the final distance to the door. It's opened by one of the household staff. She nods at me as I stride inside.

The inside of the house makes me feel even worse.

It's gorgeous, full of dark wooden furniture and paintings and historical objects that make it feel as if someone has just plucked the whole building from the rolling hills of Italy and dropped it here. It makes memories crash over me. Wonderful memories that are now tainted with death and destruction. Memories that now feel like a part of someone else's life.

I block out all those emotions and instead keep my spine

straight and my chin raised as I stop in front of the polished wooden door to the main study upstairs. After drawing in a bracing breath, I raise my fist and knock.

"Yes," a strong voice comes through the door.

And just hearing it almost shatters my composure again. I take an extra second to pull myself together once more before I open the door and step inside.

The study is just as I remember it. Dark wooden bookshelves line the entire wall next to the door, and two leather armchairs are positioned by the hearth on the left wall. Straight ahead, red light from the setting sun spills in from the windows and illuminates the grand desk in front of them. And the man sitting at it as well.

Federico Morelli, patriarch of the Morelli family and leader of the biggest and the most influential and dangerous mafia family in this entire state, is seated on the ornate chair behind the desk as if it were a throne. As always, he is wearing an impeccable bespoke suit. His once dark brown hair is now peppered with gray, but his brown eyes have lost none of their sharpness.

They light up, which is a very rare occurrence, when his gaze finds mine.

"Enrico," he says in that familiar rumbling voice.

A small smile lifts my lips. "Hello, Grandfather."

The chair scrapes against the dark wooden floorboards as he stands up and rounds the desk. Another pang of warmth mixed with pain and emptiness sears through my chest as he places his hands on my shoulders and gives them a squeeze.

"How are you, my boy?" he asks, his eyes searching my face. "You look troubled."

Federico Morelli has always been terrifyingly perceptive and shrewd, so I grew up with a grandfather who could read my emotions better than my parents. I got better at hiding things from him over the years, but I have apparently lost some of that edge now. Since I don't want to admit what I'm really feeling when I'm back in this house, I go with a version of the truth.

"I'm just worried," I say, trying to read answers in his eyes too. "No one is supposed to know that I'm alive, so we can't be seen meeting like this. It's the reason why I have been living with the Hunters for the past six years, after all. So the fact that you brought me here like this must mean that something big has happened."

"They're back," he says. "Word through the underworld is that the people who murdered Riccardo and Elsa have finally resurfaced."

My heart jerks in my chest. Both at hearing the names of my parents and also at realizing that my grandfather knows about Isabella. Thankfully though, I'm too stunned to reply, because when he keeps speaking, it becomes clear that he in fact doesn't.

"They have somehow figured out that you're still alive," he says, and he squeezes my shoulders a little harder. "And word is that they're now hellbent on finding you and finishing the job."

Indecision flashes through me. I know that I should probably tell him that I have already met one of them. But I just can't bring myself to do it. In fact, I can't even make up my own mind about how I feel about Isabella.

On the one hand, I kind of hate her and I should want to kill her on sight because of the part she played in my parents' murder. But on the other hand, I'm also grateful to her for sparing my life. And I don't know what to do about those conflicting emotions. All I know is that I need answers. From her.

"How close are they?" I ask, because I need to say something else, otherwise I will change my mind and confess that I have already found one of them.

"As far as we know, they're not in the state." He releases my shoulders but keeps holding my gaze with serious eyes. "Yet."

"Can we track them?"

Anger flickers in his eyes. "No. These people, they're…" He shakes his head. "They're ghosts. Just like they have been for the past six years."

That anger in his eyes lights the burning rage in mine as well.

At first, this was just supposed to be a temporary solution. Because of how easily these people had managed to get through the security at our house and all the way into our bedrooms, we knew that they might succeed if they realized that I was still alive and came back to finish the job. So Federico decided that I should keep pretending to be dead and stay with the Hunters. Just until they could catch the people who did it.

But then weeks turned into months and months turned into years, and there was still no trace of them. They just appeared one night, killed my parents, and then vanished like ghosts. Federico has had his people searching for them for six years, but it's as if they never existed. So my temporary identity as Rico Hunter became semi-permanent as the years went by.

But I'm not a Hunter. And at this point, I'm not even sure if I'm a Morelli anymore either.

"It's time, Enrico," he says. "It's time to stop pretending."

An unexpected flash of panic crackles through my veins.

And I can't even identify why. All I know is that I'm not ready to come back yet.

"They already know that you're alive," Federico continues. "So it's time for you to return home as Enrico Morelli and take your rightful place as my heir."

"No." The word is out of my mouth before I can even think it through properly.

My grandfather raises his eyebrows in surprise.

I desperately scramble for something to say. For some kind of explanation that will make sense to him. That will make sense to me too.

"I want to finish out my senior year," is the absolutely ridiculous explanation that I at last manage to blurt out.

He narrows his eyes in disapproval. "You are not an assassin. You are Enrico Morelli, sole heir to the Morelli empire. You do not need to finish anything at Blackwater University."

"No, I know," I confirm while frantically trying to figure out a better explanation for why I need to stay. One that does not involve telling him about Isabella or about my own jumbled emotions or the strange rootlessness I feel. "That's not what I meant."

"Then what did you mean?"

"They might know that I'm still alive, but they don't know where I am." Relief floods my chest when the words are out of my mouth. Yes, that was a much better reason. One that he will accept. "If I come back to live here, they will find me straight away. But they'll never even consider that I might be staying at Blackwater. So then you and your people will be able to find them while they're searching through the city."

He runs a hand over his jaw, a considering look on his face. "Hmm."

I wait in silence, not wanting to push too much.

"That's an excellent point," he says at last.

I resist the urge to heave a sigh of relief and instead just nod.

He nods too, but more to himself than to me. "Yes, you will stay at Blackwater for now. I will keep you updated on the progress of finding these people, via the Hunters, so as to not draw attention. And you will do the same." His gaze locks on mine again. "If you see or hear anything that indicates that they might have found you, contact me straight away using the emergency number."

"I will."

Guilt twists inside me. It's so potent that I could almost taste it on my tongue when those two words rolled over it.

But I won't tell him about Isabella until *I* get the answers that I need. And besides, I know that she is not here to finish the job. She has been living at Blackwater for weeks. If she wanted me dead, I would be already. In fact, if she wanted me dead, I would have been dead six years ago. But for some reason, she spared my life.

And I need to know why.

5

ISABELLA

Loud bangs echo across my apartment. I'm on my feet and reaching for a gun before I have even fully registered the noise. But my fingers only meet an empty nightstand. I panic for a second before remembering that I left all of my guns in my go-bag. Students at Blackwater are not allowed to bring their own guns to campus. For obvious reasons. But it's still irritating. Especially when someone is pounding on my door at five o'clock on a Saturday morning.

I'm pretty sure that I already know who it is, but I stay alert anyway as I sneak up to the door and look through the peephole.

An exasperated sigh escapes my chest.

Just as I suspected, I find Rico standing there on the other side. The two Hunter brothers are there with him too.

I briefly debate going to the kitchen and grabbing a knife so that I can just butcher them all right there in the corridor, but that would certainly draw attention, so I dismiss the idea quickly. Instead, I adopt a worried and slightly terrified expression as I unlock the door and then open it.

The moment it starts to swing open, Jace grabs the edge of the door and yanks it up fully. I stumble a step back as if in shock while I sweep my gaze over the three of them.

Heat flickers to life inside me as I take in the sight of Rico standing there in the middle. He's tall and muscular. In fact, all three of them are. But it's his face and the way he carries himself that sets him apart.

Objectively, they're all attractive. Jace in an effortless just-rolled-out-of-bed way with his messy brown curls and his glittering brown eyes. And Kaden in a sharp and severe way, like an ice sculpture, with his cold dark eyes and straight black hair. But Rico… Rico is something else.

He was already gorgeous when I saw him back when he was sixteen years old. But now, when his body has filled out completely and his features have sharpened from the transformation of going from teenager to man, he's fucking *devastating*.

His dark brown hair, which curls a little, lies perfectly styled as if not a single strand dares to disobey by being out of place. And he is standing in a way that makes effortless power roll off his lethal muscles and pulse through the air. So intense that I can almost feel it. Everything about him exudes dominance. As if there has never been a question that the world should bow at his feet.

"Isabella," he says.

A ripple rolls down my spine. Fuck, I like the way he says my name. He rolls the last two syllables over his tongue as if he can taste them.

I almost slap myself. Gods damn it, I need to focus. How would a normal person react?

"Y-yes?" I managed to reply in an appropriately scared voice.

"I will give you one chance to willingly return what you stole from me."

"I… what?" I frown at him. And this time, I don't even have to fake the confusion.

He holds out an expectant hand, palm up. "Hand it over, and beg for forgiveness." He nods towards the apartment over my shoulder. "Or we're going to come in and take it back ourselves. The first option will be a lot more pleasant than the second."

At last, my mind catches up. I almost laugh out loud. Damn, he's clever, I'll give him that. Accusing me of stealing so that he has an excuse to search through my apartment. It's a good plan. And it might have worked. If not for the fact that there is absolutely nothing for him to find.

All of my equipment, anything that would've proved that I'm not who I pretend to be, is safely stashed away in my go-bag downtown. And everything in this apartment, from the clothes in my closet to the shampoo in the bathroom, has been bought specifically to fit the persona of Isabella Johnson. He can look through it all with a fine-tooth comb and a magnifying glass if he wants to, but he won't find anything incriminating here.

While carefully hiding the smug victory that pulses through me, I shake my head and stare back at him with wide eyes. "Wait. No. I haven't stolen anything."

A satisfied grin curls his lips. "Option two it is."

Before I can reply, he strides across the threshold. I'm forced to scramble backwards lest I be mowed down by his muscular body. Jace and Kaden follow him.

I back across the floor as the three of them move into my

apartment as if they own the place. Though, given how everyone talks about the Hunter brothers, I suppose they do more or less own this entire university. Or at least, they believe that they do.

"Wait," I continue while Jace pulls the door shut behind him. "Please. I haven't stolen anything."

Rico only gives me a knowing smile before jerking his chin at the other two. "Search it."

Kaden and Jace give him a nod. Since I know that I'm supposed to be acting worried right now, I run after Rico while Jace starts going through my living room and Kaden starts on the kitchen. Pots and skillets clank against the floor as the psycho unceremoniously pulls them out of the cabinets. I flick a glance towards the couch where Jace is tossing all the cushions on the floor.

They won't find anything, but cleaning up this mess is going to be a real fucking drag.

"Wait," I call again, because that seems the right thing to say, as I hurry after Rico. "Please."

He ignores me as he simply stalks right into my bedroom. Light floods the space as he turns on the lamp in the ceiling. I skid into the room right before he reaches my bed.

"I haven't—" I begin but then break off abruptly as he yanks the cover off my bed. Blowing out a sigh, I finish with, "Stolen anything."

With his back to me, he just tosses the pillows to the floor and then lifts up the mattress to check underneath it.

Leaning my back against the wall next to the door, I just stand there and watch him search through my bed. I think I have protested enough to make me seem normal at this point, so I remain silent as I study him.

His muscles shift underneath his tight-fitting t-shirt as he shoves the mattress aside and checks the bedframe. I make note of how easy that move seems to him. If worst comes to worst and I end up having to fight him one day, I need to make sure that he never manages to grab me or ends up on top of me. I might be more skilled than him, but in a battle of raw strength, I will definitely lose.

When he doesn't find anything in the bed, he continues to the desk. Papers rustle as he goes through the drawers. Then he checks underneath it and behind it as well.

Out in the living room, the sound of books hitting the floor echoes through the air and mingles with the clanging noises from the kitchen.

Once again, Rico's search comes up empty. He slams the desk drawer shut before straightening and turning around to face me. But there is no anger in his eyes when he meets my gaze. Only shrewd calculation.

He moves on to the closet. I remain by the wall, tracking him with my gaze, as he yanks out all of the clothes that were hanging inside the closet and throws them on the floor. Fabric flutters and hangers clatter as they land in a pile.

That search naturally reveals nothing either, but he still checks every wall of the closet and behind it too before shoving the doors shut. Then he stalks over to my dresser. He yanks open the first drawer.

I already know what he will find there, so I just continue watching him from where I'm standing by the wall.

Rico slowly reaches into the drawer and picks something up. Then he turns to me and holds it up into the air.

It's a pair of black lace panties.

Part of Isabella Johnson's persona is that she likes wearing sexy underwear even though no one ever sees them.

I know that a normal person would be embarrassed by

what Rico is doing, but it's difficult to blush on command. So instead, I clear my throat and glance away to fake a similar reaction.

"This is what you wear?" he says. It sounds like something halfway between a question and a statement.

I just keep my eyes on the ground as if I'm too embarrassed to look him in the eye.

"Look at me," he orders.

Drawing in a breath, I raise my eyes and meet his gaze.

My heart flips in my chest at the way he is watching me.

While still holding those black lace panties, he rakes his gaze over my body. I'm wearing a t-shirt and a pair of hot pants, but I suddenly feel like I'm completely naked before that searing gaze.

"This is what you wear," he repeats. "Underneath that?"

"Yes," I reply. And now my damn cheeks are heating, but for a slightly different reason.

He watches me in silence for a few seconds while a smile ghosts across his lips. But all he says is, "Interesting."

Then he goes back to searching the drawers. But this time, he doesn't do it quickly and efficiently as he did with the rest of the room. Instead, he picks up each pair of panties and each bra and holds them up for me to see. I know why he's doing it. He's searching through it all in the most humiliating way possible in order to force me into trying to stop him so that I will reveal that I'm not as average as I pretend to be.

I don't take the bait.

Resting my back against the wall, I just stand there and watch him go through my entire underwear drawer.

His dark brows furrow slightly when he gets no reaction from me. But he continues his search. Once he's done, he straightens again and shoves the final drawer shut.

"You're a very meek and obedient one, aren't you?" he mocks. Leaning his hip against the dresser, he crosses his arms and drags his gaze over my body again before locking a commanding stare on me. "I fondled all of your underwear, and you didn't protest once."

"You're a Hunter."

"Meaning?"

"I've been told that if I'm ever unlucky enough to find you on my doorstep, I should just let you do whatever you want."

A smirk curves his lips. "Is that so?"

Pushing off from the drawer, he leans down and picks up a pair of panties that he tossed on the floor earlier. These ones are a dark purple color. He spins them around his finger as he saunters up to me where I'm still standing against the wall.

Every instinct inside me is telling me to fight. To slam the side of my hand into this predator's throat and put him on his knees before he can swallow me whole. But I smother all of those instincts and instead just straighten so that I'm no longer leaning against the wall at least.

Rico stops a single stride in front of me. Even though I'm slightly above average height, he still towers over me. I tilt my head back and meet his gaze. That wicked smirk still plays over his lips as he watches me.

From outside the room, thuds and clanks sound as Jace and Kaden continue going through the rest of my apartment.

With a knowing glint in his eyes, Rico holds up the purple lace panties in front of my face. Then he drops them on the floor between us. His eyes remain locked on mine.

"Pick it up," he commands, the complete authority in his voice vibrating against my skin.

I hold his gaze for another second while suppressing the overwhelming urge to crush his windpipe.

Then I slowly lower myself to my knees.

Since he is standing so close to me, I barely manage to accomplish the move, and end up kneeling with my back and the soles of my feet pressed against the wall. My fingers curl around the lace fabric, squeezing it far harder than necessary. Then I start pushing myself upwards again.

A strong hand lands on my shoulder, shoving me back down on the floor.

"I told you to pick it up," Rico says. "I never said that you could get off your knees."

I have to close my eyes for a moment to regain the grip on my self-control. Then I tilt my head back, and now I truly have to crane my neck, to meet his eyes. Challenge dances in them as he stares me down.

My face is level with his cock, and he is standing so close that the rough fabric of his pants would brush against my nose if I didn't keep the back of my head pressed against the wall behind me.

He holds out his hand. "Offer them to me. Use both hands."

Gritting my teeth, I keep my eyes locked on his as I cup the panties in my palms and then hold them up to him. He leaves me sitting like that for another second before picking up the scrap of lace.

"Open your mouth," he orders.

A flash shoots up my spine, and I barely manage to hide the emotion before it flickers over my face. Instead, I use all of my considerable self-control to keep a neutral expression on my features as I slowly open my mouth.

Rico balls the purple lace in his right hand while locking his left around my jaw. With that damn challenge still dancing in his eyes, he holds my gaze as he slowly pushes my panties into my mouth.

The fabric scrapes against my tongue and the roof of my mouth as he forces all of it behind my teeth. His fingers dig into my skin as he pushes up with his left hand, making me close my mouth with the panties still inside.

"No protests?" he asks, that mocking tone lacing his voice again.

Since I now have my own panties in my mouth, I couldn't have answered him even if I wanted to. Remaining motionless there on my knees before him, I just continue holding his gaze.

He takes his hand from my jaw and instead reaches for his belt.

My heart skips a beat as he unbuckles it.

But all he does is to slide the leather belt out of his pants. Breathing through my nose, I sit there as he loops the belt around my neck once while holding the ends of it in each hand. He moves his hands outwards, tightening the belt around my neck. Then he pushes his hands against the wall, holding my head trapped firmly against the concrete wall behind me. My chest rises and falls as I fight down labored breaths through my nose.

"Still no reaction?" Rico baits.

I just stare up at him, my face a blank mask, while I calculate in my mind the moves I would use to put him on his back right now. It would only take three of them. Three moves, and then I could be sitting on his chest with my hands wrapped around his fucking neck, ordering him to beg me for his life.

It takes everything inside me to keep that neutral

expression on my features and to stop him from seeing those murderous thoughts on my face.

Victory lights up his warm brown eyes.

The sight of it sends a pulse of panic up my spine. I know that I kept my face emotionless, which means that he couldn't have known what I was really thinking. So why is he looking at me as if I have just proved something to him?

Before I can figure it out, he releases his grip on the belt. The smooth leather drops down to rest on my shoulders. Since I still have those damn panties in my mouth, I suck in a deep breath through my nose.

Rico reaches forward and draws his thumb over my lips. Pressing firmly, he makes me part them for him. The move is strangely erotic, and my clit throbs unbidden as he slides his thumb along the inside of my bottom lip.

I open my mouth wider for him. His lips lift in a half smirk as he grabs the panties in my mouth and pulls them out. I draw in a deep breath, a full breath at last, as he lets the purple lace flutter to the floor beside me.

For a few seconds, nothing else happens.

Then Rico nods down at the belt. "Put it back on me."

Reaching up, I unwind the belt from around my neck. After repositioning it, I start sliding it back into his belt loops. The ones at the front of his pants are easy, but once I reach the back, I have to rise up onto my knees and circle his hips with my arms. In order to reach the other side, I'm forced to practically press my face against his crotch.

Rico chuckles softly.

I clench my jaw while I continue working and imagine the sound he would make if I cut off his cock. The buckle clinks faintly as I finish fastening it.

Once I'm done, I tilt my head back and meet Rico's gaze again. "Anything else?"

"Yes." He draws a hand along my jaw, almost lovingly. "But we'll get to that another time."

Before I can respond, he simply turns around and strides back into the living room. I force out a long breath to calm the storm inside me before I climb to my feet at last. Even though Rico has barely even touched me, I somehow still feel messy and rumpled. I run my hands down my white t-shirt a few times before walking into the living room as well.

Utter chaos meets me there.

A fresh wave of anger crashes over me as I sweep my gaze over the mess that these damn men have made in my apartment. Everything that could be pulled out of a drawer or cabinet or shelf has been pulled out and is now scattered across the floor. Cleaning all of this up is going to take the whole bloody weekend.

I walk into the room just in time to see Kaden shake his head at Rico, presumably telling him that he didn't find anything either. Jace just shrugs as well.

"Find what you were looking for?" I ask.

Rico turns to me. Those intelligent eyes of his glitter with unspoken threats as he strides back to me. Wrapping a hand around my throat, he pins me to the wall. I let him.

"No." He strokes the side of my neck with his thumb, which sends an involuntary shiver down my spine. He smiles like the fucking mafia prince he is. "But I will."

Without another word, he abruptly takes his hand off my throat and turns around before walking out of my apartment with the two Hunter brothers on his heels. I heave a deep sigh of both relief and annoyance as the door closes behind them.

Then searing hot panic shoots through my chest. Because I

suddenly realize where that look of victory came from. Realize the gigantic fucking mistake I made.

Rico had me on my knees with a belt around my neck, cutting off my air.

A normal person would have panicked.

But I hadn't. I had remained completely calm and just stared up at him with hard eyes. And that is something only a person who has been trained to withstand advanced interrogation tactics would do.

Oh fuck.

6

RICO

She might not have fought back and proved that she is indeed a skilled assassin, but she sure proved that she is not as normal as she pretends to be. No regular first-year would just sit there, looking as calm as a fucking millpond, while I cut off their air like that.

Part of me had wanted to just yank hard on the belt and crush her windpipe in retribution for my parents' murder. But she isn't the one who killed them. Instead, she *spared* my life. So the other part of me had wanted to... what? Thank her? Shove her up against the wall and kiss those damn troublesome lips of hers?

Six years.

I have been thinking about, dreaming about, this girl for six years. And now that I finally have her, I can't even decide what to do with her. All of my emotions are too tangled up. I hate her, but at the same time, I—

"You okay?"

Snapping out of my churning thoughts, I turn to find Jace looking at me from the corner of his eye. A hint of concern etches his brows, though he tries to hide it behind a casual expression.

I rake a hand through my hair and draw in a deep breath of temperate morning air. It tastes of mist and pine trees. To the east, the sun is just barely crawling over the horizon, smearing the sky with a splash of red.

"Yeah," I reply as we continue away from the cluster of apartment buildings and towards the section with free standing houses. "I suppose I didn't really expect to find any concrete proof anyway."

"If she's as good as you say, I doubt she would just leave it lying around," Kaden adds from my other side. As usual, he's twirling a knife in his right hand.

I heave a sigh. "Yeah."

"I could try to torture it out of her." Kaden meets my gaze casually and lifts his shoulders in a nonchalant shrug. Even with the motion, he doesn't miss a single spin with the knife. "If you want."

My mind drifts back to Isabella's emotionless features as I tightened the belt around her neck. I shake my head. "No. I have a feeling that she has been trained to withstand extensive torture."

A true psychopath smile spreads across Kaden's mouth. "I can be very persuasive."

On my left, Jace snorts. "I think you mean obsessive, overzealous—"

"I could always demonstrate my skills on *you,* little brother, if you like."

"Come try it. I would crush your skull with one swing of my bat before you could even get within three feet of me."

"And where, exactly, is your bat now?"

"I don't—"

Both of them abruptly stop bickering as we round the corner of a building and walk out onto the main street that runs through the entire residential area.

At the house in front of us, five people stop speaking as well and whip around to face us. The temperature seems to plummet several degrees as their gazes lock on ours.

The Petrovs.

They outnumber us at Blackwater this year. Since Eli has graduated, we're down to three now. And Mikhail and Anton Petrov have been joined by two of their cousins, bolstering their numbers to four.

Surprise flickers through me as I scan the group of hostile Russians who have now stopped halfway to their car.

No, not four. There are *five* of them.

Standing next to the four guys is a girl. Both Mikhail, who is a senior like me and Kaden, and Anton, who is a second-year like Jace, are tall and athletic. This girl is not. She is slim and barely reaches their collarbones. But despite the difference in physique, there is no mistaking that they're related. Her hair is the same shade of blond as Mikhail's, and she has the same gray eyes as Anton.

She has to be their sister.

Even though it's the only explanation that makes sense, the realization still shocks me. Not only because it has been weeks since the semester started, and we haven't even noticed that there was a fifth Petrov on campus. But mostly because she has none of that menacing energy that all the other Petrovs have. I know from experience that both Mikhail and Anton are tough. And word is that the two brown-haired twins, Maksim and Konstantin, are a force to be reckoned with among the first-years as well.

But this girl... She just looks so fucking *breakable*.

Mikhail snaps something in Russian, and shoots a commanding stare at the girl. But she doesn't move. She's just staring at us with wide gray eyes, looking like a deer caught in a headlight.

Next to me, Kaden has gone preternaturally still. Like a predator who has just caught the scent of that deer. He has even stopped twirling his knife. A slow smile spreads across his lips.

Suddenly, I wish I had brought my gun. Technically, students at Blackwater are not allowed to have their own guns. But my grandfather forced them to make an exception for me. I normally just keep it in our house, so that I won't draw unnecessary attention, but now I desperately wish that I had brought it with me. Because one look at Kaden's face tells me that shit is about to go down.

"What's this, Mikhail?" Kaden says with that sadistic smile still on his mouth. The question is clearly directed at the eldest Petrov, but his eyes are locked firmly on the girl. "You have a little sister? You've been holding out on me."

Hatred crackles like ice across Mikhail's face. He takes a step forward, angling his body so that he is shielding his sister. "If you come within six feet of her, I'll kill you."

Kaden's smile only widens.

It sends a ripple through the other three Petrovs as well, and they subtly shift their positions.

Yeah, I really, *really*, should've brought my gun.

Jace and I exchange a quick glance. His gaze shoots towards the twins for a second. I dip my chin a fraction before flicking my gaze to Anton. Jace gives me a barely perceptible nod as well.

Kaden isn't paying our silent communication any attention. His eyes are solely on the Petrov girl. I don't know whether to laugh or to groan in exasperation as he cocks his head. He looks like he has just found a shiny new toy. A toy that he won't stop playing with until he breaks it.

Then, just as Jace and I had predicted, he takes a step forward.

All hell breaks loose.

I dart forward, slamming my fist into Anton's side before he and Mikhail can trap Kaden between them. To my left, Jace engages the twins.

A huff rips from Anton's chest as my fist connects, but he recovers quickly and spins around to swing at me. I duck and twist before ramming my elbow into his back. He stumbles a step forward. Shifting position, I kick towards his knee, but he manages to jump back in time. I press the advantage.

Pain explodes behind his eyes as I manage to land a punch to his jaw hard enough to snap his head to the side. He blindly throws his forearms up, blocking my next strike. Shaking his head as if to clear it, he suddenly twists down and slams his leg up in a kick towards my side. I yank my arm down to block it.

A dull ache pulses through my bones as his boot connects with my forearm. I quickly shift my hand, aiming to grab his ankle. But he yanks his leg back down before I can.

All around us, the sounds of punches and kicks have been echoing through the warm morning air. But now, everything goes deadly silent.

Anton and I break apart at the same time, both of us snapping our gaze up to the people around us.

"One more step, and I'll slit her throat," Kaden announces, his voice dripping with cold threats.

"You move one muscle, and we'll break his arm," Maksim retorts.

I whip my head from side to side. Alarm shoots through me as I take in the scene.

On my right, Kaden is holding the girl trapped with her back pressed against his chest. He has one hand around her arm, keeping her immobile. The other is holding a knife across her throat.

Mikhail is standing two steps away, staring at them with a mix of hatred, horror, and panic in his blue eyes.

On my left, Jace, who was fighting two opponents at the same time, is down on one knee. Konstantin has his hand around the back of Jace's neck while Maksim is forcing his arm up behind him at an angle. Jace is clenching his jaw hard, the only outward sign of pain he is showing. But I can tell from the position of his arm that if they force it a little higher, they will in fact break it.

For a few seconds, we all only stare at each other while deafening silence pulses through the air.

"If you don't tell your cousins to get their fucking hands off *my* little brother, you're about to watch your sister bleed out on the street," Kaden declares, his voice so cold it could've sheared through a block of ice.

"If you don't get your fucking knife away from my little sister, I'll—" Mikhail begins before he's cut off.

"I said, lower his fucking arm!" Kaden yanks his knife high up, pressing the flat of the blade hard underneath the girl's chin and forcing her to tilt her head back. "Now!"

The twins shoot a panicked look at their cousins, and when Mikhail jerks his chin down, they lower Jace's arm a bit. They don't release him completely, but Jace at least stops clenching his jaw against the pain.

"We trade back, and then call it a day," I announce.

It's more of an order than a suggestion, but Anton replies anyway. "Agreed."

Mikhail snaps an angry look towards his little brother. Anton only shoots a hard stare back until the eldest Petrov forces out a long breath.

"Fine," Mikhail agrees.

They all turn to Kaden. A cold smile lurks on his lips.

"I'll release her," he agrees. "In exchange for my brother. And a name."

"What?" Mikhail says.

Kaden, who is still forcing the girl to crane her neck with his blade, looks down and meets her gaze. "What's your name, little doe?"

"You fucking—" Mikhail growls, but he is interrupted before he can finish cursing him to hell.

"Alina," the girl replies. Her voice is soft, but to my surprise, there is no tremor of fear in it. "My name is Alina."

Wicked light shines in Kaden's cold eyes, and he smiles even wider. Then, without warning, he yanks the knife away from her throat and shoves her towards Mikhail. The twins immediately release Jace as well and step back. Jace rolls his shoulder and straightens while Mikhail catches Alina by the arms before she can slam into his chest.

For a few seconds, no one moves.

Then Mikhail jerks his chin. "Get in the car."

The other four Petrovs quickly close the distance to the waiting car and climb inside. Mikhail remains where he is, his furious eyes locked on Kaden, until they're all in the vehicle. Then he spits on the ground before Kaden's feet and stalks to the car as well.

Kaden slips two throwing knives into his left hand, his eyes locked on Mikhail's back.

"Don't," I say softly.

He flexes his fingers but thankfully doesn't throw the blades.

A thud sounds as Mikhail slides into the car and slams the door shut behind him. Then he revs the engine and drives off. I blow out a long sigh as I watch them go.

Why did the Petrovs have to decide that *this* was the year that they were going to try to knock us down from our throne? I have enough to deal with because of Isabella. But now, I apparently need to make sure that Jace and Kaden don't get themselves killed by the fucking Russians too.

I glance at my two brothers-in-arms. Tension ripples around them like waves in the air. If they spend the entire day in our house, they will self-destruct. Or maybe burn it down. Or both.

No. No sitting around at home. Tonight, we need to blow off steam.

7

ISABELLA

Loud music and the smell of alcohol, perfume, and sweat hit me like a brick in the face the moment I step through the door. Drawing my eyebrows down, I glower at the sea of drunk assassins-in-training who fill the entire ground floor of the house. And probably upstairs too, if the thumping sounds coming from the smooth wooden ceiling are any indication.

As I squeeze my way through the crowd, I curse Rico not once but twice. The first time because of the bloody mess he made of my apartment this morning, which took me the entire day to clean up. And the second time because while I was throwing out some of the stuff that Kaden broke in the kitchen, I ran into a couple of girls from my class, who invited me to this party. I tried to politely decline, but they insisted. And if I had kept refusing, that would've drawn attention, so now I have to at least put in a short appearance.

All because of Rico fucking Morelli.

"Isabella," someone calls from my left.

Pushing my way out of the group blocking the hallway, I

find myself in a kitchen with one of the girls who invited me. Carla. She has curly brown hair that has been pulled up in an elaborate style, and her brown eyes sparkle, almost as brightly as the gold-shimmering dress she's wearing, when her gaze finds mine.

"You made it!" she continues, a bright smile on her lips.

I almost wince. She's actually really nice, and it's not her fault that I can't be a normal person, so I wipe any trace of annoyance from my features and smile back. "Yeah, thanks for inviting me."

"Of course." She closes the distance between us and runs her hands down my arms and then gently draws her fingers over the fabric of my dress. "Gosh, you look gorgeous!"

I'm wearing a dark purple dress that hugs my chest and then flows out slightly from my waist before ending at my mid-thighs. It fits the persona of Isabella Johnson perfectly. Though I have to admit that I don't hate it for myself either.

"Have you gotten anything to drink?" Carla asks.

Before I can even reply, she grabs a red plastic cup and fills it to the brim with whatever pink bubbly mix of alcohol is in the bowl next to her on the counter.

"Here," she says, handing it to me. "Do you—"

A bang sounds from another room down the hall.

She whips her head in that direction, and lightning flashes in her eyes as she bellows, "I told you not to touch the fucking cabinets!"

Snatching up a huge kitchen knife, she spins it in her hand with incredible precision as she starts stalking out of the room. Right before she reaches the door, she seems to remember that I'm still there, because she turns around and flashes me an apologetic smile.

"We'll talk later, yeah?" she says.

"Yeah," I lie.

I have no plans to be here that long. But Carla is apparently satisfied with my answer, because she strides away to threaten whoever opened those cabinets without her permission.

Once she's gone, I set my cup down with the other full ones on another counter. Drinking dulls my senses. And dulled senses are dangerous.

Leaving the kitchen behind, I slip back into the crowd in the hallway. After some careful maneuvering, I manage to get through the worst of it and find myself in a slightly less packed spot by the doorway to the living room. I stop at the threshold, leaning once shoulder against the wall while looking in through the open doorway.

Lots of people are sprawled on the couches and armchairs while others are dancing on the open areas of the floor. The ones seated by the grand dining room table on the other side of the room appear to be playing some kind of drinking game. Playing cards are scattered across the dark wooden surface and a guy claps his hands together in victory and laughs before pointing at a girl sitting across from him. She shoots him a look that promises vengeance before picking up her cup and drinking deeply from it.

Laughter and chatter mingle with the thumping music and fill the room, making it vibrate with life.

I have to grip the doorframe hard with one hand as a sudden stab of pain spears right through my chest.

Sucking in a breath through my nose, I try to swallow past the sudden onslaught of regret and disappointment and… *longing* that crawl up my throat.

I wonder what that would be like. To be a real person with real friends who do stupid shit just because it's fun.

Even before I had to hide from the Hands of Peace, I was never a real person. I'm just a collection of the people I've had to be in order to complete my missions. All I've ever done is to put on mask after mask in order to blend in. Isabella Johnson is just the latest one in a very long line. So why do I suddenly feel so sad about it?

As if my subconscious had summoned them, my eyes suddenly land on three people seated on one of the dark blue couches.

Rico, Kaden, and Jace.

Though I suppose that Jace is not exactly *sitting* on it. He alternates constantly between standing up, sitting down, and leaning forwards. The red plastic cup in his hand moves with his motions, and what looks like beer spills from it with his jerky movements. Throwing his head back, he laughs loudly at something a guy on the couch opposite him said. Then he abruptly leans to the side, running his hand over the thigh of the girl who is sitting on the couch's armrest beside him. Reaching up, he wraps his hand around her jaw and pulls her face down to his. She slides her fingers through his messy brown curls as she kisses him back with equal fervor.

Apparently, he's always like this. He drinks too much, parties too hard, talks too much, gets into fights too easily, laughs too loudly. And if rumors are to be believed, he has already fucked his way through half of Blackwater, even though he is only a few weeks into his second year, because he always gets bored and loses interest in everyone very quickly.

Even from all the way across the room, I can feel the restlessness inside him vibrate through the air like shockwaves. Part of me wonders where it comes from. The other part is just thankful for any distraction that pulls him away from helping Rico come after me.

Kaden, on the other hand, sits beside him like an ice sculpture. But his normally so expressionless eyes are now constantly flicking through the room as if he is searching for something. Or someone.

A flash of panic shoots through me when I realize that it might be me. But then his cold gaze slides directly over me, and he doesn't react.

I relax slightly as I shift my attention to the final person on the couch.

Rico.

He is sitting at the other end, one elbow propped up on the armrest and his chin in his palm. From my place partially hidden behind the wall, I study his expression. He is staring across the room at something to the left of where I'm standing.

I narrow my eyes.

No, he's not staring at anything in the room. He's lost in thought.

And he looks…

Panic, and another stab of pain, sears through me.

He looks like he's feeling exactly what I felt a few minutes ago.

Pushing off from the wall, I abruptly stride along the hallway and away from the living room.

I can't be here. I can't watch this damn guy sit there and look like that.

In all my life, I have only ever spared one person. Saved one person. Him. And I know exactly why I did it, even though I refuse to admit it to myself.

For the past six years, I've thought about this guy. Wondered what he was doing. What his life was like. If he had somehow recovered from his parents' murder and had gone on to live a happy and full life despite it all. For six years, I've been living vicariously through him. Through the life I imagined for him.

Rico Morelli. The one life that belongs to me.

Shaking my head, I blindly try to push my way through the crowd.

I should never have come here. My feelings for that damn mafia prince are already complicated enough as it is. I don't need to add even more to the weird connection I feel to him.

A huff escapes my throat as I slam into someone's chest.

"Hey," a man says, sounding more surprised than angry. "I haven't seen you here before."

Looking up, I find a blond guy with green eyes and a lean athletic frame blinking at me. He's objectively attractive, but I have already stayed far too long. I need to leave. Now. Where the fuck is the door again?

"Wow," he says. Reaching up, he draws his fingers over my cheekbone. "Your eyes are very pretty."

It takes everything I have not to slap his hand away and instead press out, "Thanks."

I scan the hallway behind him and realize that I walked the wrong way when I left the living room. The front door is behind me. Fuck, I'm not usually this unaware of my surroundings. But seeing Rico like that threw me off more than I want to admit.

The guy slides his hand down my throat and over my collarbones while he flashes me what I think is supposed to be a seductive smile. "You know, there are some empty rooms upstairs."

"I was actually on my way home," I reply while starting to turn around.

He grabs my arm. "Oh, come on—"

My hands shoot up, and within the span of a few seconds, I've grabbed his wrist and pried his fingers from my arm. He lets out a strangled noise of pain as I twist his wrist back so far that I almost break it. Another whimper spills from his lips as he shifts his body along with my movements to ease the strain on his wrist.

"I said *no*," I growl at him. "Now fuck off."

In the drunken chaos, no one around us notices. I just reacted on instinct, but I'm hoping that this guy won't remember me tomorrow as I quickly release him. Spinning on my heel, I start towards the front door.

And come face to face with Rico.

A knowing smile curls his lips as he meets my gaze. "So, the cat does have claws."

Alarm crackles through me. Oh fuck. He wasn't supposed to see that.

Rico jerks his chin, silently ordering the blond guy to leave. He scrambles away immediately, cradling his wrist.

Suspicion swirls inside me as I flick a glance towards the guy. "Did you send him? Did you tell him to try to hit on me like that?"

Narrowing my eyes, I turn back towards Rico. But I forget the rest of what I had been about to say, because the damn mafia prince has moved so close that my chin almost hits him when I turn my head back. I blink, edging a step back. Rico presses forward.

My back hits the wall with a thud that is lost in the music and chatter around us.

"No," Rico replies. Ruthless power pulses from his muscular body as he stops right in front of me, his brown eyes locked on me. "In fact, I will be paying him a little visit later. Because you're mine. And no one touches you except for me."

My heart flips at the dark protectiveness in his words. And at the heat in his eyes as he stares at me. I can't tell for certain, but I'm pretty sure that it's not only from anger.

I lick my lips.

His hand shoots up, and he draws his thumb over my bottom lip, following the same path my tongue just did.

And for one ridiculous moment, I desperately wish that I was just a normal girl. That I could just drink that entire cup of pink sparkly alcohol that Carla gave me earlier and then take this criminally gorgeous man up to a bedroom and run my hands through his rich brown hair and trace the contours of his hard muscles and then fuck his damn brains out just because I want to. Just because I also want to be a real person who makes real connections and does real stupid shit. Even if only for a moment.

Rico slides his fingers from my lips and down my throat before trailing them across my collarbones in almost exactly the same way that the blond guy did. But this time, the reaction it produces is completely different. Instead of wanting to break his wrist, I want him to move his hands lower.

He doesn't. His hand remains resting lightly at the base of my throat. But he does raise his other hand, slowly drawing it up the side of my thigh.

A shudder of pleasure threatens to roll through me, and I barely manage to suppress it.

While keeping his eyes locked on mine, he slides his hand up my bare thigh, pushing the dark purple fabric of my dress up as he continues towards my hip.

"Why aren't you pushing me off like you did with him?" Rico asks. Though, given the sheer amount of authority in his voice, it's more of a demand.

Gods above, I want him to rip my dress off and fuck me hard against this wall just so that I can feel alive for one fucking second.

Pushing down that absolutely insane impulse, I remind myself that Rico is an enemy who will get me killed if I don't manage to fool him.

"I've already told you," I reply, making my voice the absolute opposite of his. Submissive instead of dominant. "You're a Hunter, and no one refuses you anything."

He lets his hand drop from my thigh. The loss of it leaves me feeling strangely empty. His other hand, however, remains resting lightly at the base of my throat.

"I see you, you know," he says, and the seriousness in his tone and on his features sends a spike of alarm through me. He runs an assessing glance over my body before meeting my eyes again. "Living a life that doesn't belong to you."

A chill snakes down my spine.

It suddenly feels as if he can see through me. See through all of my masks and right down into the soul that I'm not even sure I actually have.

However, before I can figure out what to say, he takes his hand off my throat and lets it drop back down by his side. Then he takes a step back and jerks his chin in the direction of the front door.

"Go," he says, his voice suddenly strangely empty.

My brows knit in surprise and confusion. He's letting me leave? Just like that?

But I'm not one to miss opportunities when I'm handed them on a silver platter, so I quickly slip away from the wall and start towards the door. The crowd swallows me immediately.

However, before I reach the front door, I turn around and glance back at the hallway.

Rico is still standing there.

Looking more lost than ever.

8

RICO

Annoyance flits across Mr. Hansen's face as Kaden, Jace, and I stroll into his training hall. All the first-years standing on the padded mats stop sparring and glance hesitantly between us and their instructor.

"Hunter," Mr. Hansen says, keeping his tone carefully neutral. "Do you need something?"

"We figured we'd help some of the first-years," I reply.

"Did you now?" he grumbles.

Coming to a halt, I raise my eyebrows and shoot him a pointed look. "What was that?"

Tension crackles between the concrete walls like lightning. Some of the students even suck in sharp breaths. Because no one talks back to the teachers at Blackwater.

No one except us.

As per my grandfather's decree, the Hunter brothers are untouchable. It was easier to make all of us untouchable than for him to try to explain why only I was beyond reproach without revealing my true identity. Eli was the one who mostly used those privileges, but I'm not above pulling rank in order to get what I want, so I intend to make full use of them now.

Mr. Hansen looks like he wants to teach me a lesson, or three, in humility. But no one disobeys orders that have come from the mafia king Federico Morelli himself, so in the end, he just swallows down his annoyance and grunts.

"I said, *alright*," he amends it to. After a somewhat stiff shrug, he motions at the rest of the room. "Knock yourselves out."

Shock bounces from face to face as the group of first-years stare at us. Though, not *all* faces.

At the back of the room, Isabella rolls her eyes from where she probably thinks I can't see her.

The first-years have been split into several groups for the lessons this morning, so not all of them are here. But my target is.

And so is Kaden's. His dark eyes dance with anticipation as he sets course straight for Alina. The blond girl blinks in surprise and then glances from side to side, as if hoping that someone will intervene. Naturally, no one does.

Her cousin, Maksim Petrov, is also in this class, which is why Jace decided to tag along as well. The promise of brutal revenge rolls off Jace's shoulders as he stalks forward, cutting off Maksim's path to Alina.

I leave them to their own schemes as I stride through the group of stunned students with my gaze locked on Isabella.

"First Eli interrupts my class to spar with that bloody lunatic Raina," Mr. Hansen mutters under his breath, not realizing that I can still hear him. "And now the whole lot of them have come to do the same bloody thing. Damn entitled children."

Since I have more important matters to deal with right

now, and since I do understand his frustration, I let his muttering slide and instead continue across the room.

"Alright, that's enough dawdling," Mr. Hansen barks at his students. "Get back to work, the lot of you."

The room lurches back into motion. Within seconds, the sound of punches and kicks striking flesh once more echoes between the gray concrete walls as the rest of them go back to their sparring practice.

"I didn't realize that your skills in hand-to-hand combat were so bad that you needed to take lessons with the first-years," Isabella says as I come to a halt in front of her. Then she blinks, as if belatedly remembering that she is supposed to act meek and obedient around me. Clearing her throat, she quickly adds, "I'm sorry. I forget myself."

"No, you didn't." I flash her a sharp smile. "Quite the opposite. You finally showed yourself."

She throws her arms out in a show of exasperation. "Look, I don't know what it is that you want from me. But whatever it is, just tell me so that I can do it and then you can leave me alone."

"You know exactly what I want from you."

"No, I don't kn—"

I slam my fist straight towards her cheek.

She yanks up her left arm, blocking the strike perfectly, while throwing an expert retaliation punch towards my throat.

I leap back, barely managing to avoid it.

For a moment, we just stare at each other from across the padded mat.

Then a grin spreads across my lips.

You can fake a lot of things, which I know from

experience. But it's very difficult to suppress reflexes that your body has spent years developing.

Even from two steps away, I swear I can hear Isabella's heart thumping in her chest. Can hear her cursing herself in her own head. She knows what a reflex like that means. And she knows that I know what it means.

I lunge at her again.

This time, she's much slower in blocking, and I manage to get in two strikes to her ribs. She winces even though I'm pulling my punches, which leads me to believe that she is faking those reactions too.

For quite a while, we spar there at the back of the room. I keep pushing her away from the others. Keep trying to surprise her with quick kicks and fast punches so that she will reveal more of those instincts. But she doesn't slip up again. After that first instinctive block, she fights like a mediocre first-year. It annoys the fuck out of me.

I feint a hit towards her side and instead crouch down, drawing my foot along the floor and taking her legs out from underneath her. She crashes down back first on the padded mat and blinks as if disoriented.

Dropping down as well, I straddle her body and settle my weight on her hips. A very convincing look of fear, that I don't believe for a second, shines on her features as I raise my fist as if to hit her. She yanks her hand out to the side, frantically tapping out and surrendering.

Irritation burns through me. Fucking hell, I *know* that it's her. I know that she's just pretending. What the hell do I have to do to make her reveal it?

"Please," she begs, flicking a desperate glance between me and the fist I still have raised.

A harsh laugh rips from my throat, but I lower my hand. "You really are a great actress, aren't you?"

"I don't know what you mean." She stares up at me with pleading eyes. "Please. I'm sorry for crashing into you that day outside the pool. Just tell me what you want me to do and I'll do it."

"Stop pretending. I know who you are. And you know who I am."

"Of course I know who you are. Everyone knows who you are."

"Say it."

"Rico Hunter."

I slam my palm against the mat next to her head. She flinches, but the reaction is delayed by half a second, as if she had to tell her body to perform the movement instead of just reacting to it.

Taking her chin in a firm grip, I force her to keep her eyes locked on mine as I say, "Stop lying. I know you can feel the connection between us. I can see it in your eyes."

She wiggles underneath me. And as if to reinforce my words, a jolt shoots through my body when her hips grind against mine. It makes blood rush to my cock.

Another wave of rage crashes through me because this girl is making me fucking crazy.

I want to strangle her.

But at the same time, I feel like her entire soul is calling to mine. As if there is a part of me that only she sees. Only she understands. And I fucking know that she feels it too.

"Please, I submit." She taps her hand against the mat again and again, declaring defeat. "I submit."

I want to grab her by the shoulders and shake her. Because I know that she isn't submitting. Not yet, anyway.

When I at last make her surrender to me, fully and completely and for real, she will know it. Know in the depths of her very bones that she has no other shelter but me. That I alone am what stands between her and utter destruction. That she has no other choice but to obey my every command. That she is *mine*.

And then… then she will give me the answers that I need.

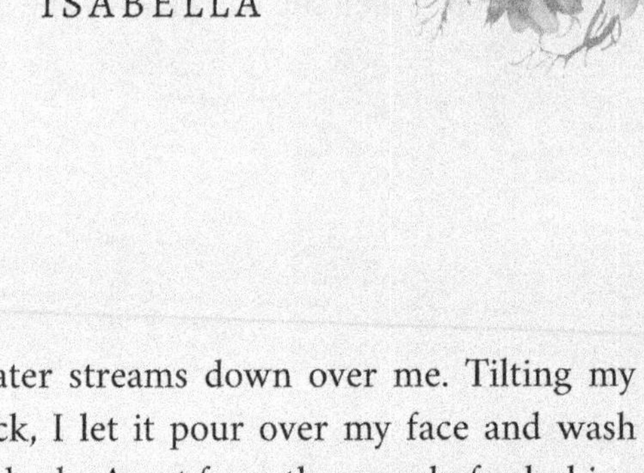

9

ISABELLA

Warm water streams down over me. Tilting my head back, I let it pour over my face and wash down my body. Apart from the sound of splashing water coming from my own shower, the shared shower room is silent around me.

I took my time undressing in order to make sure that everyone else in my class had mostly finished showering by the time I got in. Thanks to the Hands of Peace, I have quite the collection of scars and burn marks and other evidence of past injuries on my skin. I know that I'm not exactly the only person with scars at this university, but it's better to avoid unnecessary questions if I can.

Dragging my feet like this means that I will have to practically inhale my lunch before our next class, and just standing here under the rushing water isn't exactly helping my now tight schedule either. But after that damn sparring session with Rico, I need to get my head back on straight.

I know you can feel the connection between us.

That's what he said. A connection between us. He wasn't

just demanding that I tell him who I really am. He told me that there is a *connection* between us.

With my eyes still closed, I draw my hands over my face and then through my wet hair while heaving a deep sigh.

If he only knew how right he is about that. About our connection. If he only knew how much I feel like I know him. How much I feel as if I'm seeing myself mirrored in his eyes.

Opening my eyes, I turn off the shower and then shake my head.

Gods above, this guy is going to be the death of me.

Maybe I should just bolt. Maybe I should just leave Blackwater and set up a fake life somewhere else. Far away from him.

But as I squeeze water from my hair, I discard that idea. I considered it that day when I first ran into him, but decided against it then too. Now that he has seen me, now that he knows that I'm here, he is never going to let me go. If I were to run, he would hunt me to the ends of the earth. And that would certainly draw the attention of the Hands of Peace. My only option is to make him believe that he is mistaken. That I am not who he thinks I am. But that is apparently going to take a hell of a lot more work than I had hoped.

I turn around and take a step away from the wall lined with now silent showerheads.

Shock pulses through me.

Actual, *real*, stunned surprise clangs inside my skull as I stare at the open doorway leading to the rest of the changing room.

Rico is standing there.

He is leaning one shoulder against the doorframe, and his arms are crossed over his broad chest as he watches me.

I suddenly become acutely aware that I'm entirely naked.

His gaze slides up and down my body. Not in a leering way. In an assessing way.

Ice spreads through my veins, because I know what he sees. What I have been hiding underneath my clothes. Not only the scars and burn marks, which are proof that I have been in a lot of fights and have been trained to withstand torture, but also the fact that I am incredibly fit.

It's one thing to pretend to be mediocre at everything here when I'm wearing clothes. But naked, there is no hiding that my sleek legs and arms, and everything about me, is made up of lean muscles.

Fuck, I need to try to salvage this somehow.

"What are you doing here?" I blurt out, using my very real shock to make my words believable. While covering my private parts with my arms, I lean to the side and try to glance around him towards the changing room beyond, but he's blocking the entire doorway. "Where is everyone else?"

"Gone," he replies.

I take a few steps forward. Rico remains where he is, leaning against the doorframe with his arms crossed. My gaze flits towards the small metal hooks set into the wall next to him, where we hang our towels while showering. Mine is now missing, which means that the rack is now completely empty.

Rico runs his eyes over my body again, and then jerks his chin at me. "Where did you get those?"

I don't need to look down to know what he means. The scars. The burn marks.

"Abusive father," I reply. It's true enough.

He is silent for a while, holding my gaze as if trying to read any lies in my eyes. But since it is more or less the truth, or a version of it anyway, he doesn't find any. When he realizes that it's true, a spark of fury lights in his eyes.

"If you give me a name and an address, I can have him dead within the week."

Another wave of genuine surprise pulses through me. He offered to kill someone for me. And that fury in his eyes... He is angry that someone hurt me. Strange emotions twist through my chest at the realization. No one has ever been upset that someone hurt me before.

A small and pathetic part of me wants to tell him. Tell him exactly where he can find the Hands of Peace and then let him and the rest of the Morelli family deal with my problem for me.

But the world doesn't work like that. If I tell Rico who I am, he *might* let me live. But the patriarch Federico Morelli himself? Not a fucking chance. I know exactly what he does to his enemies, and since I was a part of the group who murdered Federico's only child, I am the Morelli family's enemy number one. If Federico learns who I am, all I will get is a very agonizing death.

"I appreciate the offer," I say, surprising myself when I realize that I actually mean it too. "But that's a score I need to settle on my own."

Rico sucks his teeth, but then nods in acknowledgement.

With my arms still covering as much of my body as I can, I move closer to the doorway. Rico remains firmly in the way.

"Can you please move?" I ask. "I need to get changed before lunch ends."

He says nothing. Only continues watching me. I once again try to glance around him, hoping against hope that someone else will come in and tell him to get the hell out of the women's changing room. But I know that it's useless. Even if someone were to come in, they would never dare to kick Rico out.

I edge another step forward. "Please move."

"Make me."

It takes great effort not to visibly grind my teeth. Instead, I summon my dwindling reserves of patience and give him a pleading look. "Please, I—"

He moves like a fucking viper.

Just like that first strike in the sparring room, my instincts are screaming at me to move, to block, and to hit back. This time, however, I manage to smother them and instead just jerk back as if in panic when Rico comes for me.

Within the span of a few seconds, I end up on my back on the cold shower room floor. The suppressed instincts might be fake, but the huff as I hit the floor is real since I don't try to catch myself.

Before I can roll over, Rico steps up beside me and puts his boot on my throat. He pushes down slightly, putting pressure on my windpipe and pinning me to the floor.

His eyes are hard as he locks them on me. "Fight back."

I wiggle on the cold wet floor and weakly try to push his boot off my throat while croaking out, "Please, I—"

"Fight back. I know you can."

"Please—"

"Do it!"

A brief flash of anger shoots through me. Why does he have to be so fucking persistent? Why can't he just accept my lies like everyone else does?

He puts more of his weight on my throat, trying to force me to panic. And I know that I should. I'm naked, lying on my back on the floor while a ruthless mafia prince has his boot on my throat. Any normal person would have panicked. But all I can think about is the four moves I would use to get out of this while also snapping his neck.

"Touch yourself."

I'm yanked out of my murderous thoughts by his unexpected demand. He eases the pressure on my throat slightly.

"What?" I blurt out.

He jerks his chin towards my pussy. "Touch yourself." Then his eyes harden even more as he locks them on me again. "Or fight back."

If I didn't need to keep up the pretense, I would've snorted and rolled my eyes. I know exactly what he's doing. Direct threats obviously didn't work. So now, he's trying to humiliate me instead. But he has no idea who he's dealing with.

I keep my eyes on his as I slide my right hand down to my pussy. His boot is still on my throat, so I can't see what I'm doing. Not that I need to. With my gaze locked on Rico's now utterly stunned face, I start stroking my clit.

He blinks, as if he hadn't actually expected me to do it.

Then he flicks a glance down at my hand, and another emotion surges up in his eyes. Something like hunger. Or maybe jealousy.

Closing my eyes, I continue stroking my clit.

I only make it three more seconds before the boot disappears from my throat. I let out a yelp and snap my eyes open as Rico yanks me up from the floor. The sound of naked flesh hitting stone echoes through the large shower room as Rico shoves me up against the wall. His left hand locks around my throat, trapping me there, as he closes the distance between us.

"Fine," he says, and there is a roughness to his voice now. "If you don't want to fight back, then at least tell me to stop."

His brown eyes, now burning with fire, sear into mine as

he puts his right hand on the side of my ribs. It's warm against my chilled skin. Especially compared to the cold stone wall behind my back.

I stare back at him, my mind still trying to catch up, as he slowly starts sliding his hand down to my hip.

"Tell me to stop," he says.

A ripple of pleasure courses through me as he caresses my hipbone.

His eyes remain locked firmly on mine. "Tell me to stop and I will."

My skin prickles as he traces his fingers gently down my thigh.

"Tell me to stop." This time, it's an order. A command to do as he fucking says and tell him to stop.

I don't.

While I try to tell myself that it's because I can't reveal who I really am, I know that it's complete bullshit. Telling him to stop wouldn't reveal any of my true skills. It wouldn't even ruin my fake identity as Isabella Johnson. Begging him to stop would even be perfectly in line with what she would do. So it has nothing to do with my need to keep up any sort of pretense.

The real reason why I'm not telling him to stop is because I don't *want* him to stop.

Desperation bleeds into his eyes. "Tell me to stop." A plea this time. As if he knows that if we don't stop now, it will ruin us both.

But I don't tell him to stop.

And he doesn't stop either.

His fingers skim the inside of my thigh. My heart thumps in my chest as he trails them higher. He keeps his other hand around my throat, pinning me to the wall with effortless strength.

A gasp rips from my lungs as his knuckles brush against my pussy.

He pauses, his eyes searching my face. Waiting for me to tell him to stop. I don't.

Shifting the position of his hand, he draws his thumb around my clit.

Pleasure crackles through my veins like a lightning strike, and a small moan slips past my lips.

Rico draws in an unsteady breath, as if that tiny moan was something monumental.

His thumb traces my clit again, more firmly this time. It sends another ripple of pleasure through me. He does it again. Apparently using only the reactions on my face as a guide, he shifts into a rhythm and strength that is perfect for me.

Gasping in a breath, I rest the back of my head against the stone wall as pleasure builds exponentially inside me. I stare up at the ceiling, but I can feel Rico's eyes still studying every expression on my face. My heart hammers against my ribs.

While still rubbing my clit with his thumb, he brushes two fingers over my entrance.

I drag in a shuddering breath.

He slowly pushes one finger inside me.

A needy whimper escapes my throat, and I wiggle my hips.

As if he can read what I want from that alone, he adds the second finger.

My heart feels like it's going to burst as he starts pumping his fingers while also teasing my clit with his thumb at the same time.

Another shudder of pleasure rolls through my body, and I

squirm against the wall. Rico tightens his hand around my throat slightly. Not enough to cut off my air. But just enough to remind me of who is in charge. A subtle show of dominance.

My pussy throbs.

Tension builds inside me, thrumming through my soul like a thunderstorm.

And for the first time in a long time, I feel alive. I feel like a real person. Because I'm not doing this as part of a mission or any other type of necessity. I'm doing this solely because *I* want to.

He pumps his fingers in a strong commanding rhythm while continuing to inflict that sweet torture on my clit. I moan, throwing my head from side to side.

It feels as if my body is going to shatter from the pent-up tension.

Rico slides his hand higher up my throat, locking it directly under my jaw and forcing me to stop moving my head. I squirm against the wall while another moan tumbles from my lips. My pussy throbs.

I fucking love his dominant hands on my body.

He curls his fingers slightly on the way out.

And pleasure explodes through my veins.

My legs tremble as the orgasm crashes through me with the force of a tidal wave. Incoherent moans drip from my lips and I once more try to throw my head from side to side, but Rico keeps his hand locked around my throat. As my legs continue shaking, I realize that his hand is the only thing keeping me on my feet.

I suck in desperate breaths as pleasure washes through my limbs.

And through it all, Rico's gaze remains solely on my face. Studying every expression and every emotion.

Once the final ripples have faded out, I blink repeatedly to clear my head. My chest is heaving.

When my vision is once again clear, I'm met with a sight that almost stops my heart.

Rico is staring at me as if I'm the most incredible thing he has ever seen.

It sends a spike of panic through my spine.

Then he blinks, and the expression is wiped from his features so fast that I'm not even sure if it was ever there at all. In its place is another emotion. Contempt.

Before I can react, he abruptly releases my throat.

Since my legs are still unsteady, and I didn't have time to brace my weight, it sends me crashing down on my knees. Dull pain pulses through my legs as I hit the cold floor in front of Rico's boots.

After dragging in a deep breath, I look up to meet his gaze. Only that vicious contempt is visible on his features as he stares me down.

"You're pathetic," he says, his voice hard.

It's clearly directed at the fact that I didn't fight back earlier, so I reply, "You're a bully."

He draws his hand along my jaw and under my chin in an almost loving gesture while giving me a sweet smile laced with lethal threats. "And you're a liar."

Then he turns on his heel and stalks out, leaving me sitting there naked on my knees. Alone. And with my emotions even more tangled than before.

10

RICO

The house is not silent when I return. Afternoon classes have already started, which means that both Kaden and Jace should still be on campus. Confusion and alarm swirl through me.

With my body on high alert, I gently close the front door behind me and sneak down the hallway. A clinking sound comes from inside our combined kitchen and living room. Drawing myself up by the open doorway, I glance inside.

Relief crashes into me. But it's quickly exchanged for exasperation and confusion.

While heaving a deep sigh, I rake my fingers through my hair and walk into the room. "What are you doing here, Golden?"

Jace jerks up from where he was sprawled on the cream-colored sofa. From the doorway, I had just been able to see his messy curls spill over the armrest.

Twisting around on the couch, he meets my gaze from across the backrest. He holds up his hand, raising one finger. "One, don't call me that." He narrows his eyes at me while raising a second finger. "And two, I could ask you the same thing."

His words are slightly slurred, as if he has been drinking.

When I round the couch, my suspicions are confirmed as I found a half-empty bottle of whiskey on the low table in front of the sofa.

I nod towards it. "Day drinking, huh? Aren't you supposed to be in class?"

"Fuck off," he mutters, and swipes the bottle from the table.

For a moment, I consider… doing something. I know that their father would be livid if he found out that Jace was skipping class to instead get drunk on the couch. He gave Eli one hell of a beating when he found out that he had skipped an entire course his first year just because he was bored. But Jace has always been like this. Restless. Seeking chaos. However, it seems to have gotten worse since he started at Blackwater.

Standing there by the armrest, I watch him pour some more whiskey into his glass. Indecision swirls inside me.

"I would offer you one," Jace says. "If you weren't being such an insufferable mother hen right now."

A laugh rips from my chest. I huff out another exasperated chuckle while jerking my chin. "Just move over, asshole."

While still holding on to the glass and the bottle, he scoots over on the couch without spilling a single drop. Which I have to admit is a rather impressive feat.

After setting down his glass, he reaches for another one and starts pouring. I slump down on the pale cushions next to him. They let out a huff as my weight lands on them.

Jace silently hands me the second glass and then puts the bottle down on the table before picking up his own glass.

"Wanna talk about it?" I ask.

"Nope." He casts me a glance from the corner of his eye. "You?"

"No."

He nods and then just holds his glass out towards me. I clink mine against his.

And then we drink.

My insides feel like they're all twisted up, and my head is even more of a mess. And all because of Isabella fucking Johnson.

Tilting my head back, I rest it against the cushioned backrest while my mind drifts back to what I did to Isabella in that shower room just now.

I didn't mean to take it that far. Yes, I went in there with the intention of scaring her. Of making her panic and force her to reveal her skills. But I didn't mean to do... *that.*

And I meant what I said to her. If she had told me to stop, I would have. Immediately and without question. So why didn't she?

Why didn't she tell me to stop?

Doing that wouldn't have revealed any of the skills that I know she's hiding. Quite the opposite. Asking me to stop would have added even more credibility to the idea that this weak persona she's portraying is the real her. So why, in all hell, didn't she tell me to stop?

Guilt snakes around my heart, squeezing it like a cold snake.

Isabella is a part of the group who murdered my parents. And what did I do? I drank in the sight of her coming all over my hand. Drank it in desperately. Like a man dying of thirst.

Lifting the glass to my lips, I drink deeply and shake my head at myself.

What kind of son am I?

I *enjoyed* watching her climax. Enjoyed watching her eyes flutter as pleasure ricocheted through her. And I fucking *loved* hearing those incoherent moans spill from her lips as I made her come. Especially knowing that I was responsible for it. It was the most glorious thing I have ever experienced.

So what does that make me?

I drink deeply from my whiskey again.

Raking a hand through my hair, I heave a deep sigh.

Fuck, I should just hand her over to my grandfather and be done with it. It's the right thing to do. He would make her tell us where the others are, and then we would get revenge for my parents. Bloody vengeance at last.

The sight of Isabella's naked body flashes before my eyes. The sight of those scars. And burn marks.

I squeeze my eyes shut as a wave of pain and anger crashes over me.

Abusive father, she had said. And she had both sounded and looked so sincere that it had to be the truth. But then again, she is an excellent liar, so it's hard to tell. But still. I can't help but wonder if it might be true. Did her father abuse her that badly? Is that why she became an assassin? To get revenge on him? But then why did she join those other people to murder *my* parents? And why did she let *me* live?

Opening my eyes, I heave another sigh and then down the rest of the alcohol.

Jace wordlessly reaches for the bottle and refills my glass before setting it down again. But he's not looking at me. Instead, he just keeps staring at the black screen of the TV in front of us.

I trace the bottom of my glass with my finger while I try to sort through the twisted mass of tangled thoughts and emotions inside me.

Why is Isabella even here at Blackwater? Why is she not with those other assassins?

There are too many questions. And I want answers. I *need* answers.

If I hand Isabella over to my grandfather, he will get those answers for me. But I don't want him to know some of those answers. Some things I want her to tell me and only me. And that's why I can't give her up to Federico.

Or at least, that's what I tell myself.

But deep down, I know why I haven't ratted her out. Because if my grandfather got his hands on her, he would torture her until she told him where the others are. And the thought of that makes it feel like burning steel is being shoved down my throat.

She spared me, which means that I owe her my life. That's why I can't let them torture her.

Lie, my mind whispers.

I close my eyes again.

I know that it's a lie. That it's not the real reason why I can't stand the thought of Isabella being tortured.

But this time, I let myself believe it. Let myself desperately cling to that lie.

It's only because of my debt to her. Yes. Only that.

Because the alternative would be far, far worse.

11

ISABELLA

I shoot upright, my hand reaching for my gun, before I once again remember that I don't have one. Rolling out of bed, I sneak into the kitchen and grab one of the knives before hurrying over to the door. The faint scraping sound of someone trying to pick the lock continues from the other side.

My heart hammers in my chest as I edge forward to cast a quick glance out the peephole. If the Hands of Peace were here to kill me, they would most likely be coming through the windows, not the front door. But it might still be them.

A strange mix of relief, exasperation, and amusement pulses through me when I see who it is that's trying to break in.

Rico.

Of course it is.

That man never gives up, does he?

Sprinting back to the kitchen on silent feet, I return the knife to its proper place before darting into my bedroom.

The faint clicking sounds of the lockpicks continue for

another few seconds. Then everything goes silent as I quickly climb back into bed and lie down as if I'm sleeping. Another few moments of silence. Then the unmistakable sound of a key being inserted into the lock sounds from the front door.

I almost laugh. If he had a key, why even bother trying to pick the lock? Was it because he needed to prove to himself that he could? In that case, he failed epically.

Dread seeps through my veins as another possibility crosses my mind.

Rico doesn't strike me as a man who is in any way incapable. Does that mean that he *wanted* me to hear him fiddle with the lock so that he could see what I would do?

Fuck. Was I *supposed to* hear that? Would a normal person have heard it too? Would staying in bed as if I'm asleep in fact be a dead giveaway that I had heard it but was pretending not to?

Indecision flashes through me.

Fucking hell, this damn man is making me question everything.

The front door is pulled open.

Making a split-second decision, I quickly roll out of bed and instead draw myself up by the wall next to the doorway into my bedroom.

Rico is too smart to fail at picking the lock. It must have been done on purpose. To set a trap for me.

At least, that's what I gamble on as I grab the nearest hard object and wait for Rico to walk through the door.

The nearest hard object turns out to be a book on physics. Not exactly the best weapon ever, but at least it's a thick book.

Faint footsteps sound from my living room. My heart patters in my chest, and I hope that I have gambled correctly, as Rico draws closer.

The moment he steps across the threshold, I swing the book straight at his face.

He ducks while his forearm shoots up, slamming into my wrists and pushing my arms upwards so that the book smacks into the wooden doorframe above his head instead. His fingers lock around my wrist, keeping it trapped there. I try to yank it back while he twists towards the other side to flip the light switch.

Yellow light floods the room.

"Heard me picking the lock, did you?" he says as he turns back to me.

"The dead could've heard you picking the lock," I reply while relief washes through me. I did indeed gamble correctly.

Amusement flickers in his warn brown eyes before his gaze lands on the book that's still in my hands. While keeping my wrist trapped against the doorframe with one hand, he uses the other to pluck the book from my grip. Another burst of amusement blows across his face as he holds it up and arches an eyebrow at me.

"Seriously?" he says. "A book?"

"A *physics* book. I was kind of hoping that it might have its own gravitational pull that would make it hit your face even harder."

A laugh rips from his throat. A genuine laugh. He seems almost startled by it, because he blinks as if in surprise. It makes me feel weirdly smug that I manage to draw such a sound from him.

Then he clears his throat and at last releases my wrist before setting the book down on my dresser. I pull my hand back and rub my wrist with my thumb while studying his face. All previous traces of amusement are gone. Replaced by only grim determination.

I see his move coming, but I slow my reaction enough to make it seem like I didn't. He lurches forward as if to grab me. I leap back, making him barely miss me. But that was of course why he executed such a dramatic move. While I'm deliberately off balance, he darts forward and gives me a shove. I topple backwards, landing on top of my bed.

The mattress bounces underneath me as I make a show of trying to scramble backwards. He grabs my ankle, yanking me back, and then climbs onto the bed.

Once more, I find myself lying on my back with Rico straddling my hips. This time, however, he grabs my wrists and pins them to the mattress on either side of my head.

My heart thuds hard in my chest. And it's not just from the brief burst of activity.

Having him dominate me like this, in my *bed*, makes my mind drift back to what his commanding hands did to me in that shower room. Heat pools in my stomach, and my clit throbs in response. And I'm suddenly desperate to feel like that again. To feel alive like that again. I wonder if he felt it too, back then.

And because I can't help myself, I make a show of trying to wiggle out from underneath him while very deliberately grinding myself against him.

His eyes shutter for the briefest of moments, and he clenches his jaw.

Shock and amazement pulse through me. He felt it. He must have. Is he actually as desperate as I am for anything that will make him feel alive? Anything that will make him feel real?

No, he can't be. Because as opposed to me, he is already a real person.

I try to search his eyes, but there is no trace left of that brief flash of heat. It must only have been a purely carnal reaction, one that most humans would have in a situation like this. Nothing more.

"You're going to answer some questions now," Rico says, keeping my wrists in a firm grip while he locks commanding eyes on me. "Or this is going to be a very long night for you. Understood?"

"Yes," I breathe, adding a hint of worry to my voice.

"Six years ago… Why did you do it?"

My heart lurches into my throat, but I keep a confused mask firmly on my face. "Six years ago? Six years ago, I was in high school! I did a lot of stupid shit. Just like everyone else. Why did I do *what*?"

"Fucking hell, Isabella!"

My name on his tongue sends a ripple through my body.

"Enough!" he snaps. "Enough with the lies. Enough with the pretense. I'm so fucking tired of it. Just answer my bloody questions."

"*You're* tired?" I yell back. "*I'm* tired! I'm tired of constantly being ambushed and attacked and threatened. I'm tired of you harassing me every single day and bombarding me with questions that I don't even understand. I'm tired of you calling me a liar and trying to force me to tell you something when I have no fucking clue what you're talking about!" My chest heaves in anger as I stare up at him. "I'm so fucking tired, Rico!"

Deafening silence rings inside the room following my outburst.

Rico watches me, and for a single second, doubt blows across his features.

At last. At last, he is starting to doubt whether he's right about me.

Then he wipes all traces of it from his face. Releasing my wrists, he reaches behind his back and pulls something from his belt. It clanks metallically as he shifts it in his hand. Light from the lamp above glints in a pair of handcuffs.

"Hold out your wrists," he orders.

I slowly lift my hands from the mattress and hold them out above my chest. Rico quickly snaps the handcuffs shut around them.

When I thought about being handcuffed in bed a few weeks ago while I was practicing some self-care with my own fingers, this was not exactly what I had in mind. But oh well.

In one fluid motion, Rico climbs off me and straightens on the floor next to the bed. I sit up and swing my legs over the edge of the bed while he pulls out something else from his belt.

Black fabric flutters in the air as he tosses it at me.

"Put it on," he commands.

I catch it awkwardly with my shackled hands and hold it up in front of me. It's a black hood.

"A bag over my head?" I say dryly and roll my eyes. "How very mafia of you."

His eyes sharpen. "What was that?"

Panic crackles down my spine. Fuck.

Lifting my shoulders in a nonchalant shrug, I keep that dry amusement on my features as I reply, "I said, how very mafia of you." Before he can comment on it, I hold up the hood and let out a huff. "You know, sometimes I wonder if you and the rest of your brothers haven't in fact *already* started working as hitmen for the Morelli family. Even though you haven't even graduated yet." I move the hood towards my head. "You sure act like it at least."

Then I pull it on, hoping that I convinced him with my careful twist of words to explain away what I actually meant.

Since the bag is made of thick material, I can't see anything with it on. But I can hear him as he moves closer. His hands appear on my arms a moment later, and he pulls me to my feet. After tightening the strings of the bag around my neck, presumably so that it won't fall off, his hands disappear again.

I expect him to move to my side and grab my upper arm so that he can lead me to wherever it is that we're going. But he doesn't.

My stomach lurches, and I let out a yelp in surprise as he grabs me by the hips and throws me over his shoulder instead.

"What the hell?" I grumble.

He lets out a dark laugh. "You wanted mafia. I'll give you mafia."

12

RICO

She is silent the entire car ride. All she does is to sit there in the passenger seat in the t-shirt and hot pants that she apparently sleeps in, with her handcuffed hands in her lap and that black bag over her head. She does, however, rub her thumb on her palm and twist her fingers together, over and over, in a decidedly nervous way. And then, as I park the car at the edge of the woods and look over at her, for the second time ever, I feel a sense of doubt.

What if I'm wrong?

She had sounded so sincere back there in her apartment. The frustration, the *desperation*, had been so real when she screamed back at me that she couldn't take being ambushed and attacked like this anymore.

What if she really is just a random girl who simply happens to have the same eye color as the assassin from that night? What if I have done all of these awful things to someone who is completely innocent? The thought opens up a pit in my stomach.

I run my gaze over her body again. She is sitting as stiff as a board, still nervously wringing her hands in her lap.

That seed of doubt grows a little larger. What if—

No. Shaking my head, I force those thoughts away. It *is* her. She even said that thing about how it was such a mafia move to put a bag over her head. Though I suppose her explanation did make sense. Everyone knows that the Hunters work for our family. But it doesn't matter. Because it *is* her. Otherwise...

Shaking my head again, I shove aside any lingering sense of doubt and then open the driver's side door. Isabella remains sitting in the passenger seat as I throw the door shut again and stride around the car. She flinches slightly as I open her door.

Calculated. All of it is calculated.

I reach over her and unbuckle her seatbelt before grabbing her arm.

"Let's go," I order as I pull her out of the car.

She staggers out and then stumbles along beside me as I lead her into the forest. It's pitch black. Only the headlights from my car break up the darkness and illuminate our way as I walk Isabella to a tree a short distance into the woods. Grabbing her by the shoulders, I turn her around and then move her so that her back is pressed against the tree trunk. She sucks in a shuddering breath from underneath the dark hood.

A faint click sounds as I unlock her handcuffs. Walking up behind her, I pull her arms back behind the trunk and then lock the handcuffs around her wrists again. It traps her completely to the tree.

Then I stride back so that I'm standing in front of her

again. After loosening the strings on the bag, I yank it off her head.

She blinks against the bright headlights that are now shining directly in her eyes. In those blue-gray storm-swept eyes that I will never forget for as long as I live. It's her. It is her.

Once her eyes have adjusted, she flicks her gaze around, taking in her surroundings. Dread washes over her features as she looks back at me again.

"Please," she whispers.

"Six years ago," I begin, my voice hard and merciless. "Why did you do it?"

She yanks helplessly against the handcuffs trapping her to the tree. "Why did I do *what*?"

"Where are the others?"

Confusion and desperation shine on her entire face as she stares back at me with big pleading eyes. "*What* others? Please, Rico—"

"Why are you here now?"

"Because you're an obsessive lunatic who can't even see that he's wrong!" she screams back at me with such force that a bird flaps away in panic a short distance from us. Then her mouth drops open, and alarm crackles over her features instead. "I'm sorry." Desperation bleeds into her voice as she shakes her head. "I'm sorry. I didn't mean that. Please don't hurt me."

I want to scream in frustration. Because she's so fucking convincing. This damn girl is making me question everything. My memory. My intelligence. My skills. Everything. She's making me question everything and she's driving me fucking crazy. Because *I am right*. I know it.

"Answer my questions," I order. "Or I will leave you here."

"I don't—"

"Indefinitely."

Her eyes go wide. Flicking a terrified glance at the forest around her, she licks her lips and then swallows. Visibly. When she speaks again, her voice is back to that soft pleading tone. "Please don't."

"Answer my questions. Why did you do it? Where are the others? And why are you here now?"

Tears well up in her eyes. "I don't understand what that means. Please. I will answer whatever questions you want, but I don't understand what you're asking! So please, just tell me what you want me to say and I'll say it."

Again, that seed of doubt tries to sprout in my chest. I stomp it down, grinding it underneath my boot until it's nothing but dust.

I let out a harsh laugh and flick a cold glance up and down her body. "Fine. Have fun out here. I *might* come back tomorrow night. If I do, you'd better have some answers for me then. Or we'll do this the next night too. And then the next. And the next."

Fear floods her features as she looks down at her bare legs and feet, and then out at the silent trees around her. Metallic rattling echoes into the forest as she yanks against her handcuffs again.

"No, wait!" she calls.

I just turn around and start walking back to my car.

"You can't do this," she yells after me. "Rico! Please. You can't do this."

I keep walking.

"Rico! Please. I'm begging you. Don't leave me here."

Opening the car door, I slide into the driver's seat while Isabella continues begging me not to leave her. I just throw the door shut and make a sharp U-turn on the road. And then I drive away.

A *short* distance.

Once I'm certain that Isabella has seen me drive away in the direction of Blackwater, I park the car on the side of the road and turn it off. Sneaking into the woods, I silently move through the trees until I'm back where I left Isabella. She's still standing there, handcuffed to the tree, but she's not shouting anymore.

Quietly lowering myself to the ground, I settle down to watch her.

And then I wait.

And wait.

After about an hour, she sits down as well. Because her hands are shackled behind the tree, it leaves her arms in a slightly awkward position. She shifts several times before apparently finding a comfortable spot. And then she just sits there.

Another hour passes.

Two.

Once we're coming up on three and a half hours since I left her there, that seed of doubt in my chest has grown so large that I can no longer ignore it.

Surely, if she was the assassin from that night, she would have done something at this point. Would've picked the lock on the handcuffs and walked back to her apartment. Or something. Anything.

But she's just sitting there.

Unless that is actually proof that she is the assassin? Would a normal person just sit there like that?

If only I could see the expression on her face. Then I might be able to read her emotions. Is she sitting there with a defeated and hopeless look on her face? Or a calm and composed one? Because of how dark the woods are, it's impossible to tell.

I rake my hands through my hair with quick angry movements. Fuck. She's messing with my head again. She has been messing with it for the past six years, and finally meeting her in person has only made everything worse. Not better.

Except, it might not be her. Did I just handcuff an innocent woman to a tree and then—

A jolt shoots through me, interrupting my tangled thoughts, as Isabella stands up.

She turns her head as if looking carefully around the area.

And then she simply *walks away* from the tree trunk.

Stunned shock pulses through my body as I stare at her. But I don't dare to move in case I accidentally make any noise and give my presence away. I need to see what she's going to do now.

The handcuffs are lying discarded on the ground next to the tree. I look from them to Isabella as she lifts her arms above her head, stretching out her muscles.

My brows furrow in confusion as she walks deeper into the woods instead of towards the road.

She disappears behind a bush. Then the sound of something like a thin stream of water hitting dry leaves drifts through the air.

I blink. *Oh.* She's peeing. I fight the urge to look away, even though I can't see her.

After a few moments of silence, she reappears from behind the bush again. I narrow my eyes at her as she walks back to the tree.

Utter incredulity clangs through my skull as she picks up the handcuffs and then locks herself back in.

For almost half a minute, all I can do is stare at her.

Then the shock gives way to another feeling. Victory. I've got her now. No normal person would free themselves from the tree, go and pee, and then lock themselves back in. Not unless they were trying desperately to convince someone that they're much less skilled than they really are.

Silently rising to my feet, I get ready to stalk up to her and confront her about it. But I hesitate before I can take the first step.

I've been at this for two weeks now. Two weeks of almost constant harassment. Of threats and humiliation and blackmail. And she still hasn't said anything. No matter what I do, she never breaks.

And every time she says or does something even slightly incriminating, she always has a perfectly reasonable explanation for it.

Standing there in the dark woods, watching Isabella sit down again, I'm suddenly struck by an overwhelming sense of futility. She is never going to break. I should just kill her and be done with it.

My heart squeezes tight again.

I can't kill her. Because I still need those answers.

But maybe I have been going about it the wrong way? Maybe there is another way, a smarter way, to get her to tell me what I want to know?

I furrow my brows, but shelve that line of thought for later. Because right now, I have an incredibly stubborn secret assassin to confront about her strange actions.

Locking herself back in?

I can't wait to find out how she plans to explain away this one.

13

ISABELLA

My gaze snaps to the left as I catch movement from the corner of my eye. Dread pools like ice water in my stomach as Rico strides out from the darkness, coming straight towards me.

"Let me get this straight," he says, a mocking note to his voice that hides none of the threats beneath it. "You free yourself from the handcuffs so that you can go and pee, and then you lock yourself back in again?"

Fuck, fuck, fuck. I was so sure that he had left. I saw him drive away, and I haven't heard anyone move at all. How the hell did he manage to sneak up on me without me hearing it? He must be much more skilled than I thought.

Rico comes to a halt in front of me, staring down at me like a god of death. "Now why would you do that, Isabella?"

My name rolls over his tongue like a promise, a threat, and a spine-tingling caress all in one.

I slowly climb to my feet, using the trunk behind me for support since my hands are now once again shackled behind it. "Look, I—"

"Did you or did you not pick the lock on the handcuffs, go and pee behind that bush, and then lock yourself back in?"

"You don't understand—"

"Don't tell me what I do or don't understand," he snaps, his voice cleaving the air like a blade. The sheer authority in it seems to vibrate against my very bones. "Just answer the fucking question."

My mind has finally settled on a very plausible explanation. One that, if I play this perfectly, should finally convince him completely.

I can't keep a gun next to my bed like I usually do, but that doesn't mean that I've forgone all my other habits. I always keep a pair of lockpicks sewn into the lining of the hot pants I sleep in. And in all my other pants too, for that matter. Sliding them out, I quickly pick the lock again and free my wrists. Then I let a mask of anger and desperation settle on my features as I take a step away from the tree and throw the handcuffs down on the ground before Rico's feet.

"Yes, I picked the lock on the handcuffs," I scream at him, my voice full of frustration. "And yes, I locked myself back in."

"Why?" he demands.

"Why the hell do you think?"

His brows furrow slightly.

"Gods," I curse, throwing my arms out before stabbing a hand in his direction. "You don't even know the effect you have on people, do you?"

Another flicker of confusion is briefly visible in his eyes.

"You walk into a room and just command the entire space." I'm not even lying about this part, because this is exactly how it feels. Holding his gaze, I shake my head. "Everything about you screams ruthless and overwhelming power. I swear, even the fucking wind would stop blowing if you ordered it to."

He blinks in what I think is surprise.

"So yes, I picked the lock." I shoot him a pointed look. "I'm not a complete idiot, you know." Letting a mask of embarrassment settle on my features, I glance away for a second. "And then I went to pee behind the bush because I didn't want to pee my fucking pants." I meet his gaze again. "And then, yes, I locked myself back in. Because three days ago, you put a boot to my throat and almost crushed my windpipe. All you have done since the day I met you is to hurt me and humiliate me. So what would you have done to me if you had come back tomorrow and found that I had escaped? I don't know. All I know is that it would've been something extremely painful and humiliating. So I locked myself back in to give you what you wanted."

His eyes are fixed on mine, but I can't read his expression at all. Hoping that I have him where I want him, I press on.

"Don't you understand?" I hold his gaze with desperate eyes. "I would give you anything you want. But I don't know *what* it is that you want from me."

He narrows his eyes slightly. Fuck, am I losing him? Or does this mean that I'm convincing him?

I take another step closer to him and then drop to my knees. Spreading my arms wide, I stare up at him with pleading eyes. "So go ahead. If you want to beat me, beat me. If you want to torture me, torture me. Do whatever you want to me until you're satisfied. But the answer will always be the same. I don't understand what you're asking me." I let my arms drop back down in a defeated way. "So do what you need to do and then tell me what you want me to say so that I can say it. Because I just want this to stop." I choke out a broken sob. "Please, just make it stop."

Damn, I really should win an acting award for that sob alone. So perfectly pleading and desperate. And the way my voice broke on that final word? Absolute perfection. There's no way he won't fall for this.

Only the soft rustle of leaves above us disturbs the stillness as Rico stares down at me in silence for another few seconds. I hold his gaze with eyes full of broken surrender. But on the inside, my heart is pounding, and I'm begging for an entirely different reason.

Come on, fall for it. Come on.

At last, Rico lets out a long breath. Then he jerks his chin. "Get up."

I pick up the handcuffs from the ground while getting to my feet. Once I'm standing again, I hold out the handcuffs to him. He plucks them from my open palms. I keep my hands out like that, silently offering him my wrists.

He shakes his hand, and hooks the handcuffs to his belt instead.

Smug victory sparkles inside me, and it takes great effort to keep it off my features.

"Let's go," Rico says, jerking his chin again.

We walk back to his car, which was apparently parked a short distance down the road, in complete silence. I steal glances at him from the corner of my eye, trying to read his mood. It's difficult in the dark. But he looks... thoughtful.

The lights flash as Rico unlocks the car. I move to the passenger side while he gets into the driver's seat. Two thuds sound as we close the doors behind us.

I reach for my seatbelt, and have to suppress a small smile while I buckle it.

This was how I knew that he wouldn't actually hurt me when he brought me to the woods. Yes, he broke into my apartment, kidnapped me, handcuffed me, and put a bag over my head. But when he got me into the car, he *put the seatbelt on me*.

It's such a small detail, but it makes a strange sense of sparkling amusement ripple through me. Like, *yes, I have no problems abducting you, but if we're in a car crash, I don't want you getting hurt*. The thought of it makes me feel unexpectedly warm inside.

I glance over at Rico as he starts the car and begins driving us back to Blackwater. There are so many contradictions to this man. And if I didn't desperately need to get his attention away from me, I think I would actually enjoy trying to figure them all out.

"What?" he asks.

Crap, he noticed me watching him. Scrambling for something to say, I settle on, "I was just wondering what it is that's so important about this."

He casts me a glance from the corner of his eye. "About what?"

"The questions you're asking me. Whatever it is that happened six years ago."

His jaw tightens for just a fraction of a second. But when he replies, his voice is neutral. Nonchalant. "I just need some answers to a few things. That's all."

My heart squeezes with a sudden surprising burst of pain. *Oh, I bet you do.* Answers to questions like, why did we murder your parents that night when you had done absolutely nothing to us?

Part of me wishes that I could tell him. It won't be a satisfying answer, but at least it will be an answer.

When I thought about Rico these past six years, I always imagined him living a great life. The life that I wish I could've had. But now that I'm here, now that I've studied the way his jaw clenches and his eyes flicker when he talks about that night, I realize what an absolute hell I must have left him in.

We swept in one night, murdered his family but left him alive, and then vanished like ghosts, leaving no trace and no explanation behind. And he has spent every day since then in hiding.

The tiny scrap that still remains of my long since butchered conscience throbs in pain. He really has every reason to hate me. To want me dead. And the only reason why I'm not dead yet is because he desperately wants those answers. Which means that I have to keep them from him at all costs.

He stops the car outside my apartment building but doesn't turn off the ignition.

To the east, the sun is just barely trying to climb over the horizon. The rest of the residential area around us is silent and still. I glance between Rico and the door.

"You're letting me go?" I ask hesitantly.

He keeps his eyes on the empty road ahead as he replies, "Yeah."

"Thank you."

His eyes remain on the road, and he says nothing.

I unbuckle my seatbelt and then slowly climb out of the car. He doesn't stop me. Once I have closed the door behind me, he drives away immediately. I release a long exhale.

For a while, I just stand there, even after his car has disappeared from view. Warm morning air smelling of stone and pine trees fill my lungs as I draw in a deep breath.

Because maybe, just maybe, I might have at last managed to fool that beautiful mafia prince for good.

14

RICO

The door to my bedroom is yanked open. It produces a bang that almost rattles the windows as it slams into the wall out in the hallway. I shoot upright, my hand already halfway to my gun before I realize that I know exactly who it is.

"Alright, get up," Jace orders as he saunters into my room with Kaden behind him.

"Fuck off," I reply, as I lie back down again.

The orange and red light from the setting sun shines in through the windows. Admittedly, it's far too early to go to bed. But I was up most of the night, kidnapping Isabella and then sitting in a forest watching her for hours, so I haven't exactly slept much since yesterday. And I also needed space to think.

Pain flares through my shoulder as something hard suddenly smacks into it. I sit up again, grabbing the object that slammed into me.

Raising my eyebrows, I lock incredulous eyes on Jace

while holding up the long hard item. "Did you just throw a bat at me?"

"Yes." He snatches it from my hand, spins it expertly, and then levels it at my chest. "That's what you get for moping around."

"I'm not moping."

Kaden shoots me a look while nonchalantly dropping into one of the armchairs by the wall. "You're moping."

"See?" Jace says, still pointing the bat at me.

"Get that bat out of my face," I mutter.

That damn troublemaker grin spreads across Jace's mouth as he keeps the bat right where it is.

I snatch up the gun from my nightstand and flick my wrist, motioning expectantly with the weapon. "I said, get that bat out of my face."

From his place in the armchair, Kaden snickers. Jace just rolls his eyes at me, but he does lower his damn bat.

My mattress bounces as he instead flops down at the foot of the bed, stretching his arms out above his head and letting the bat dangle off the side. His massive frame takes up nearly half of the fucking space, so I kick him in the side. He raises his head and narrows his eyes at me. With slow and menacing movements, he lifts his bat and points it at me in warning. I chuckle.

He grins at me and then lies back down on the bed.

I move so that I'm sitting with my back against the dark wooden headboard, and then look expectantly between the two of them. "So, did you want something or are you just here to annoy the crap out of me?"

"You've hit a wall with Isabella, haven't you?" Kaden says, not unkindly. But it's more of a statement than a question.

Damn those eyes of his that always see too much.

Drawing my legs up, I rest my elbows on my knees and heave a deep sigh. "Yeah."

Silence descends on the room. It keeps stretching. At one point, Jace looks like he's about to say something. But Kaden shoots him a sharp look, and he closes his mouth again. I don't know whether to laugh or curse.

Kaden has many ways of making people talk. This is one of them. He asks a question that someone doesn't really want to answer, and then just sits there quietly and watches them with those dark eyes of his until his victim can't take it anymore and starts filling the silence even though they didn't want to.

I know exactly what he's doing. But somehow it still works. Damn merciless bastard.

"Threatening her doesn't work," I say, drawing my fingers through my hair before raising my head again. "Humiliating her doesn't work. Surprising her doesn't work." I force out a harsh breath. "Nothing fucking works."

"You know that thing about the flies and the alcohol?" Jace says from where he's still sprawled along the foot of my bed.

I frown at him. "What?"

"You know, how you catch more flies with alcohol than vinegar, and all that?"

"Honey," Kaden says.

"Yes, darling?" Jace replies.

A laugh rips from my chest.

By the wall, Kaden shoots his little brother a dark look. Mischief glitters in Jace's eyes as he flashes him a grin.

Before Kaden can decide to stab him and get blood all over my cream-colored sheets, I intervene. "It's, *you catch more flies with honey than vinegar*. Not alcohol."

"You can catch plenty of flies with a half full can of beer

too," Jace says, returning his attention to me. He shrugs. "Just saying."

I massage my brows. "Alright fine. But what does this have to do with Isabella?"

"You've tried forcing her to tell you everything. I'm just saying that maybe it's time to try a different tactic."

"Such as?"

"Seducing her."

Kaden snorts. "Of course that would be your idea, you manwhore."

"Hey." Jace sits up straight, leveling the bat in his brother's direction while shooting him an angry glare. "Being experienced does not make me a whore."

"No. But sleeping with half of Blackwater does."

"Fuck you. It's not my fault that everyone here is so fucking boring." A vicious smile curls his lips. "And besides, at least I'm not obsessing over the enemy."

Kaden's expression darkens. "I'm not obsessing over the enemy."

"Alina is a Petrov. Have you forgotten that?"

"I'm not obsessed with her." Sliding a knife from his thigh holster, he starts spinning it threateningly in his hand. "I'm toying with her. Tormenting her. Using her as a tool to get back at Mikhail and to finally break that whole fucking family."

Jace snorts and rolls his eyes. "Sure. And—"

"Enough," I snap. Scrubbing a hand over my face, I heave a sigh and then rest the handle of the gun against my temple. The metal is cool, easing some of the throbbing headache that has started behind my eye. Looking from Kaden to Jace, I raise my eyebrows and give them a pointed look. "Either say something useful or get the fuck out before I shoot you both just to get some damn peace."

After one more dirty look in Kaden's direction, which Kaden answers with a true psychopath smile, Jace turns back to me. "I'm saying that maybe you should try to seduce her instead. You know, take her out to dinner and all that. Be nice to her. Get her to trust you. To like you. Then she might tell you what you want to know willingly."

"Or you could just torture it out of her," Kaden says, twirling the knife with expert movements while his customary sadistic smile settles on his lips. "Much faster."

Jace groans and rolls his eyes in annoyance. Then they launch into an argument about what the most effective way to get information actually is. I tune them out, because my mind is churning.

I already know that I won't torture Isabella. But Jace might actually be onto something. Fake dating her to get her to trust me?

It's worth a shot.

15

ISABELLA

When Friday evening rolls around, that tiny sprout of hope in my chest has finally started to take root. I haven't seen Rico in two whole days. Not since he dropped me off at my apartment after that little stunt in the woods. Could it be that he has finally fallen for my carefully crafted lies and my award-worthy performance as the mediocre student Isabella Johnson?

With that hope glittering in my chest, I stroll into my apartment and then lock the door behind me. Our afternoon class today involved getting through an obstacle course, which meant that some of that time was spent crawling through mud. It had mostly dried by the time class was finished, so I opted to drive home and shower here instead. Wouldn't want Rico to ambush me in the shower room again.

The memory of his dominant hands on my body flash unbidden through my mind, and a small voice deep inside whispers: *Or would I?*

I shake my head decisively. No. I would not want Rico to

ambush me in the shower. Or anywhere else. I need to stay as far away from him as possible.

Walking into my bathroom, I take a nice long shower in the privacy of my own apartment instead.

Once I'm done, I put on some fresh clothes and walk back into the living room.

And then I just... stand there.

The neutral white couch stares back at me expectantly. I look from it to the empty coffee table before it. And then to the pale wooden bookcase by the wall that I have filled with some random knickknacks in order to make it seem like I have a soul.

I drag my gaze back to the sofa.

Now what?

I've never really had free time before. All my life, I have spent every waking hour either training or executing a mission. I have never had an entire weekend to just do whatever I want. I haven't even had an entire day like that. What do people do in their free time?

My gaze drifts back to my bedroom where I have dumped the new course books that I was given. I could study. But I don't need to. The things that these people are learning right now are things that I learned years ago.

I glance at the black screen of the TV. Maybe I could watch something? But what? What do normal people watch? And can I even watch anything? Maybe I need some kind of subscription for that. Or to at least pay for the different channels or something.

On the wall next to the fridge, the clock ticks faintly into the oppressive silence.

For one single second, I get the overwhelming urge to both laugh and burst into tears at the same time.

I don't even know how to watch TV. What the fuck is wrong with me? I have infiltrated buildings with top level security. I have assassinated countless people from the most powerful parts of society. I can withstand hours of torture and pass every lie detector test available. I outclass every single student on this campus by miles. But I don't even know how to watch TV.

Steel bands tighten around my chest, and I suddenly feel like I'm choking.

I'm not even a real person, am I? I really am just a fucking ghost. I'm twenty-two years old and yet I feel like I'm still waiting for my life to even begin.

A firm knock comes from the front door.

The sound is so jarring in the suffocating silence that it actually startles me.

Snapping out of the soul-crushing thoughts I was drowning in, I give my head a couple of quick shakes to clear it as I stride towards the door and then glance out the peephole.

I bite back a curse.

Fucking hell. That's what I get for taking out victory prematurely.

Rico is standing on the other side.

I briefly consider not opening the door and just pretending that I'm not here. But if I do that, he will probably just break it down instead. And that would be annoying to fix.

So I draw in a bracing breath, let a mask of guarded wariness settle on my features, and then open the door. It swings open to reveal my tormentor standing there with a cardboard box in his hands.

For a few seconds, we just watch each other in silence.

Then he clears his throat. "Can I come in?"

"That depends on what's in the box."

His sudden presence here surprised me enough that it isn't until after I've already replied that I realize that he actually *asked* if he could come in this time.

A smile tugs at his lips, and mischief glitters in those warm brown eyes of his as he says, "Rope, duct tape, zip ties. Some knives and other torture instruments. A few explosives."

I'm pretty sure he's joking. Hesitation flickers through me. He *is* joking, isn't he?

Deciding that he must indeed be messing with me, I step aside and motion for him to come in. "Sounds like my kind of Friday night."

He chuckles and saunters across the threshold.

While I close the front door behind him again, he walks over to one of the counters in the kitchen side of my combined kitchen and living room. After placing the box on the wooden surface, he opens it and starts pulling out various kitchen items.

A rectangular food container made of glass, one bowl, two small plates, one large plate, and one mug.

Whatever I had been expecting him to have in that box, *that* had certainly not been it.

I stare at him. "Uhm..."

Not exactly my most eloquent response ever, but I'm so genuinely stunned by his actions that it's the only thing that makes it out of my mouth.

"To replace what Kaden broke when he searched through your kitchen the other week," Rico says as he turns back around to face me.

My gaze shifts from his sincere face to the kitchenware on the counter, and another wave of incredulous surprise pulses through me. Because he's right. Those six items are exactly the ones that Kaden broke. My brows furrow in confusion. Did Rico actually pay attention to that?

Rico apparently misinterprets my frown, because he draws a hand through his hair and blows out a long sigh while a deeply apologetic expression settles on his features. "Look, I'm sorry."

Now my eyebrows almost climb into my hairline instead.

A brief smile blows across his face at my shocked expression. Then the seriousness returns again as he holds my gaze with sincere eyes. "I really am sorry. I was so convinced, so sure, that you were… someone else. Someone from my past. But I realize now that you're not her." He grimaces apologetically. "Which means that I have put you through an absolute hell for no reason."

Both disbelief and victory clang inside my soul. I did it. I have finally convinced him that I'm just some random girl that he has never met before.

That hesitation from earlier snakes through my chest again.

I *have* convinced him, haven't I? Or is this just a trick? A lie to get me to lower my guard? I study his face. He looks so damn genuine. So sincere. But then again, he has been in hiding for the past six years, so he's probably an excellent liar.

Regardless, it doesn't really matter, because I still need to play along. So I shoot him a pointed look that is mixed with just a bit of grudging amusement in order to soften it. "Yeah, you did."

"And I'm really sorry about that."

I just nod, acknowledging the apology but not accepting it.

"Let me make it up to you," he says.

Amusement pulls at the corner of my lips as I arch an

eyebrow at him. "By letting me handcuff *you* to a tree in the middle of a dark forest?"

He laughs.

And gods damn it all, but I actually like that sound.

Blocking out the warmth that rippled through me at hearing that incredible laugh, I instead just continue watching him with one eyebrow raised.

"No," he replies, smiling at me. "I was actually thinking you might let me take you out to dinner."

Yet again, this dangerous man manages to shock me enough that I just stare at him in stunned silence. Take me out to dinner? No one has ever taken me out to dinner before.

Not that it matters. Because Rico is just a mark. One that I need to fool at all costs.

Since I don't want to risk spending more time with him than I absolutely have to, I wince and give him an apologetic smile. "No, that's alright. I accept your apology, but I don't think we should—"

"Please."

I blink.

"Please, let me take you out to dinner."

Remaining silent, I study his face for a few seconds. "You don't say *please* a lot, do you?"

"No," he admits.

His eyes remain locked on mine, his gaze steady. I resist the urge to grind my teeth. Fuck. I need to stay far away from this damn man, but if I refuse now when he is insisting, *pleading*, for me to let him take me to dinner, it might ruin everything. It might make him suspicious of me once more.

"Okay," I say.

His face lights up. "Okay?"

"Yeah. I'll let you take me to dinner."

A smile that makes my heart stutter spreads across his face. "Great."

I flick a glance down at myself. At my shorts made of soft blue fabric and my plain white t-shirt. At my still wet hair. Uncertainty swirls inside me as I meet Rico's gaze again and ask, "Right now?"

"No." He laughs again. An easy laugh. "Since it's already six o'clock, I'm guessing you already have plans for tonight. But what about tomorrow?"

Already have plans for tonight. Right. Like sitting on my couch alone, feeling like someone is strangling me because I don't know how to watch TV like a real person.

But I can't tell him any of that, of course, so I just shrug. "Sure."

He smiles again. "Good. I'll pick you up at seven."

Before I can reply, he starts towards the door.

"Wait," I call. "What's the dress code?"

Trailing to a halt, he turns back to me and raises an eyebrow. "Dress code?"

"Yeah. You know. What should I wear?"

Confusion pulls at his brows. "Whatever you like."

"Most restaurants have rules," I protest. "Even if only informal ones."

He flashes me a cocky smirk. "Like you said, no one refuses the Hunters. So the rules don't apply to me. Which means that when you're with me, they don't apply to you either." With another wicked grin, he turns back towards the door and saunters out while saying over his shoulder, "Wear whatever you feel comfortable in. I'll see you tomorrow."

And before I can decide if I want to punch that cocky smirk off his face or kiss him to see if his lips taste as arrogant as they look, he disappears out the door and closes it behind him.

For a long while, I just stand there, staring after him.

This evening did not go the way I thought it would. At all.

And now, I need to do something even more difficult than figuring out how to watch TV.

Survive a date with Rico.

16

RICO

What she decided on was something halfway between formal and casual. A dark blue dress that ends just above her knees and that is stylish enough to fit in at a fancy establishment, but not so extravagant that it would've made her stand out at a more common restaurant. I had been deliberately vague in my reply just to see what she would do. And God, this girl never does anything without properly thinking through each angle, does she?

Isabella sweeps her gaze around the candlelit restaurant while she slides into her seat. To anyone else, it would look as if she is just taking in the beautiful surroundings. But I can see her eyes moving over each potential entry and exit point. I see it because I do the exact same thing whenever I'm in a place I've never been before.

"What do you think?" I ask, keeping my voice casual as I sit down as well.

This time, her eyes focus more on the decorated wood

panels, the oil paintings of beautiful landscapes, and the glowing candles around the room.

She nods as she returns her gaze to me. "It's nice."

Nice. That's actually a very accurate assessment. This restaurant is *nice*. It's not super fancy and it's not shabby either. It has a cozy atmosphere with all the dark wood and the candles. The food is good. It's a perfectly nice place.

But it's not where I really wanted to go.

An unexpected pang hits my chest.

All of my favorite restaurants, the proper Italian restaurants that serve real Italian food and not the Americanized version of it, are within driving distance of both the Hunters' residence and Blackwater University. And yet, I haven't been to any of them in six years.

I haven't been to any of my favorite places, done any of the things I used to do all the time, since the night my parents were killed. Because Enrico Morelli died that night too. So I can't go anywhere where people might recognize me. I had to create a new life. A life for Rico Hunter. One that almost fits me but not entirely. Like a shoe that's just one size too small and in a design that I don't really like but one I can still survive being seen in.

It was just supposed to be for a short time. Until we caught the people who did it.

But it has been six years now.

Six years.

"I mean, it's great," Isabella says in an almost apologetic voice.

Snapping out of my gloomy thoughts, I realize that I've been silent too long and that she probably took that to mean that I was displeased with her answer.

I clear my throat. "Yeah."

Thankfully, a waiter arrives with a pair of menus before I can make a complete fool of myself. I use that time to push aside the uncomfortable feelings that had started to twist inside my chest like strangling vines. Giving myself a mental slap, I force my head back in the game.

I'm on a mission. I need to have my wits about me if I'm going to succeed in getting Isabella to trust me while I also sneakily interrogate her.

Once my mind is clear and back on track, I lower the menu and look over at Isabella. "What do you want?"

She glances up at me, looking oddly startled.

So I clarify, "To eat?"

A composed expression slides back onto her features, and she gives me a small smile. "What would you recommend?"

"Depends on what kind of food you like."

She just looks back at me for a few seconds, her mouth opening slightly but no sound making it out.

"Meat? Fish? Salad?" With a slight frown on my face, I shake my head in confusion. "Soup? Pasta? What kind of food do you prefer?"

She laughs. It sounds slightly forced. "Oh, I enjoy most kinds of food."

I almost narrow my eyes at her. Is she… nervous? I've had her pinned to a wall with a hand around her neck, multiple times, and yet she didn't look nearly as nervous then as she does now. Why would ordering food make her this disproportionately flustered? Or maybe it's just the situation in itself. Having dinner with me like this. It has to be.

"Would you like me to order for the both of us?" I ask.

"Yeah, sure," she replies casually, but I swear I can see a hint of relief flicker briefly in her eyes.

When the waiter comes back, I order the salmon and

white wine risotto for both of us, along with a glass of wine each. Isabella swirls the wine gently in her glass before taking a sip. I study her.

Candlelight glitters in her eyes, adding sparkles to those blue-gray depths. She's wearing a little make-up. Only enough to enhance her features but once again not enough to make her stand out too much. Her brown hair is smooth and straight, and it brushes her shoulders when she moves.

Appearance wise, there is nothing particularly remarkable about her. She's pretty in a normal kind of way, but nothing extraordinary.

And yet, to me, she's like a gravitational pull. The moment she walks into a room, she commands all of my attention. It's as if her entire being just calls to mine, her soul vibrating at a frequency that only the two of us can hear.

It has only been two weeks since she came to Blackwater, but I still somehow feel like I have known her for years. It's absolutely insane. And it scares the shit out of me.

"So, do you come here a lot?" she asks.

I take a sip from my wine as well, if only to give myself a few seconds to yet again get my head back on straight.

"Yes, it's one of my favorite restaurants," I lie smoothly. Then I chuckle. "I'm guessing you haven't really had time to explore the city much yet. Especially not since I've been... monopolizing your time quite a bit."

Her eyes glitter as she smiles back. "No, not really. You can be very persistent, you know."

"Oh, I'm aware. But so you never visited the city before you enrolled at Blackwater?"

"No," she lies. Leaning back in her chair, she releases a long exhale and then drags an embarrassed hand through her hair. "To be honest, I hadn't even left the state before I came here."

And it's so real, so genuine, that if I didn't know with every fiber of my being that it's a lie, I would have believed her. Fuck, she's skilled.

"But what I would really like to do is to go abroad one day." She rests her chin in her palm while a dreamy expression blows across her features for a second. Then her gaze returns to me. "Have you ever been?"

"No," I lie. "I've been out of state, of course, with my Dad and brothers. But never abroad." I cock my head. "Is that why you enrolled at Blackwater? Because you wanted to do the whole European spy thing that they do in the movies?"

She shoots me a look of mock affront. "Ouch. I could hear the judgement in your tone from all the way over here, you know."

I just chuckle.

"And when you put it like that, it does sound kind of silly," she continues. "But yeah, I guess that is part of why I enrolled." She rubs the back of her neck in a highly embarrassed way and then shrugs. "Mostly, I did it because… Well, because I've never really been excellent at anything. I've never found my thing. Math, science, sports… I did okay. But, I don't know, I guess I'm just getting tired of being mediocre. I just wanted to do something. To be something. For once."

Silence falls over the table.

For a moment it looks like she is about to say something else, but then she abruptly raises her hand and waves it in the air. "Actually, you know what? That sounded ridiculously pathetic now that I said it out loud. Please pretend I never said anything. Why did you enroll?"

Once again, it's so fucking genuine. The embarrassment. The breathless tone of her voice as she hurried on to ask *me* a question instead, as if she is mortified that she shared such private thoughts with me.

"Why did I enroll?" I chuckle. "I didn't really have much of a choice. I come from a very long line of hitmen. I'm kind of expected to continue the legacy."

She grimaces. "Oh. Right. Sorry. What a stupid question."

Before I can reply, the waiter returns with our food. Once he has placed the plates on the table and then retreated, I pick up my glass of wine and hold it out towards Isabella.

"Well, here's to doing something." I flash her a smirk. "For once."

While shaking her head at me in disgruntled amusement that I used her own phrase, she raises her own glass.

And as we clink our glasses together and look into each other's eyes, I know without a shred of doubt that every single word spoken at this table has been a lie. Both hers and mine.

I know it.

And she knows it.

After all, it takes one to know one.

I know that she is making all of it up. Her motivations, her dreams, her plans for the future. All of it. Because I have them too. Fake motivations, fake dreams, fake plans for the future.

I know that she is lying because I have been doing it for so long too. Living a life that isn't mine.

Sometimes, I just want to scream and scream until I shatter the glass walls that trap me in this fake life. The invisible barriers that no one else sees that keep me from living my life. My real life.

That pit opens up in my stomach again. And before I know

what I'm doing, I find myself asking, "Do you ever wish that you could just break everything so that you can finally stop it from spinning out of control and then just rearrange all those pieces to what you actually want them to be?"

"Yes."

The answer is immediate. No hesitation. No time to think.

It sends a pulse of shock through my soul. *She understands.*

Then, a second later, she blinks. As if catching herself. I swear that I can almost see her running through all the options in her head to check if that answer will somehow betray who she really is. Apparently satisfied that it won't, she sets down her glass while that composed mask returns to her face.

"Yes," she repeats, holding my gaze. "All the time."

I can't say anything else without revealing too much. And neither can she. So for a while, we just sit there, looking at each other from across the flickering candles on the wooden table.

All around us, other people are eating and drinking, their soft murmur drifting through the air along with the intoxicating scents of food.

Isabella breaks eye contact first. Picking up her fork and knife, she begins cutting into her salmon. I do the same.

As we eat, we go back to talking about more normal things. Our various classes at Blackwater. Failed hobbies we have tried when we were younger. Childhood memories.

And when our meal at last comes to an end, I know for a fact that those two sentences we spoke right before we started eating were the only true things either of us said during the entire evening.

Two honest sentences between us.

That was all we managed.

But that gaping abyss inside me somehow still shrank a little.

Because at least I now know that I'm not alone in feeling that way.

17

ISABELLA

It's strange to spend an entire evening talking to someone when you know that every word out of his mouth is a lie. Well, almost every word.

Do you ever wish that you could just break everything so that you can finally stop it from spinning out of control and then just rearrange all those pieces to what you actually want them to be?

I hadn't seen that coming. At all.

The raw honesty in those words, and in his tone when he said them, took me so off guard that I didn't even think my response through before I answered. I might have replied differently if I had taken a moment to consider before I spoke, but I don't think that answer ruined my carefully crafted persona either. Isabella Johnson would probably feel like that too sometimes.

But I have to admit, I am rattled. By this situation. And most of all by him.

Sitting in the passenger seat of the fancy Range Rover, I glance over at the incredibly dangerous man next to me. Rico is keeping his eyes on the road as he drives us back to

Blackwater. There is a neutral expression on his face, which bothers me more than I want to admit. Because I desperately want to know if he feels just as strangely off-kilter as I feel after this seemingly innocent dinner.

I didn't expect him to see through me like that. To feel the exact same things that I feel. As if the world just keeps on spinning, pushing you farther and farther down a road that you haven't even chosen, and all you want to do is to shatter everything just so that it will stop for one fucking second and give you a chance to take a breath.

A small voice at the back of my skull whispers that I did actually expect him to feel that. I block it out. It doesn't matter. What matters is that I fool Rico as quickly and as thoroughly as possible.

"Thank you," I say, adding a touch of shyness to my voice, as Rico parks the car right outside my apartment building. "For dinner."

Turning off the ignition, he twists towards me and gives me one of those smiles that I almost believe might be genuine. "Thanks for saying yes." His seatbelt clicks as he unbuckles it. "Come on, I'll walk you up."

I almost laugh. Walk me to my door. As if he is some kind of nineteenth-century gentleman and not a ruthless mafia heir who has spent the past two weeks tormenting the living hell out of me.

Ducking my head, I hide my amusement while I unbuckle my own seatbelt.

Warm night air washes over me as I step out of the car. From a house a little farther down, loud music thumps out of the open windows, echoing down the otherwise deserted street. I glance up at the building before me. Light pools out into the night from most windows. Not from mine. Only a dark empty apartment awaits me on the other side of them.

A jolt shoots through me as Rico places his palm on the small of my back, guiding me towards the door. I almost stumble as I take the first step.

He does it so casually. So effortlessly. As if that intimate touch is the most natural thing in the world.

And as I walk up the short path with him next to me like that, feeling his steady warm hand against the small of my back, I let myself imagine, just for a moment, that it's real. That I'm a real person who went on a date with a real guy who is now walking me up to my apartment. No hidden motives. No lies. Nothing. Just a real life.

Pain spreads through my heart, fracturing it like brittle glass.

Oh what I wouldn't give for it to be real. For *me* to be real. And not just this faceless ghost who moves through the world unseen, only doing things because someone else ordered it or because it is needed for my immediate survival.

But it's just a fantasy. A stupid dream. Always has been and always will be. Because instead of behaving like a real person on a real date with a real guy, I fucking panicked when he asked me what kind of food I like. My mind went completely blank. What kind of food do I like? What kind of question is that? I eat because my body needs fuel to function properly, which is vital for the success of my missions and for my continued survival. I hadn't even considered that I was supposed to have a preference. I eat whatever food keeps me alive.

What a sad fucking life, now that I think about it.

For what is certainly not the first time, I curse all the gods in all religions that I was born into that damn cult. That I never had a choice.

"You okay?"

The cracks spreading through my heart don't stop, but I block them out and shove all of those useless thoughts out of my mind as I turn to look up at Rico. "Yeah. Sorry. I was just… lost in thought."

He rubs a slow circle on my back with his thumb. And it's such a comforting gesture, something that no one has ever given me before, that I almost drown underneath that tide of emotions again. I just want to lean into that touch. Into him. But I can't. I really, *really*, can't.

When we at last reach my door, I'm grateful for the excuse to step away from him.

After unlocking the door, I open it before turning back around.

My heart stutters as I take in the sight of him.

Even in the unforgiving light of the fluorescents in the hallway, he still somehow manages to look like the devil's gift to mankind.

His dark brown hair that curls softly is perfectly styled, and there is a sinful glint in his eyes as he looks at me. He is wearing a black dress shirt with the sleeves rolled up, exposing his toned forearms. The muscles shift slightly as he flexes his hand. And those lips of his. Those damn lips that are lifted in a faint smirk, as if he knows exactly how fucking hot he looks, are just begging for permission to brush against my naked skin.

"Well, this is it," I say. But it doesn't come out sounding as breezy and final as I would've liked it to.

"Yes, it is," Rico replies.

But he doesn't move.

And I don't tell him to leave either.

He takes a step forward. I instinctively step back only to stop abruptly when my back hits the wall next to the now open door. Rico moves even closer.

My heart pounds in my chest as he reaches towards my face. But all he does is to brush his fingers over my forehead, pushing aside a lock of hair and hooking it behind my ear. It makes my skin tingle.

"We should do this again," Rico says in that dark alluring voice of his.

No, my instincts scream. But I hear myself saying, "Yes."

His lips curve in a smile.

I know that there is a very real risk that he is playing me. That he is just pretending to believe me and that this entire night, including what he is doing right now, is just a part of his plan to make me lower my guard around him.

But right now, I'm not sure if I care.

I just want to feel alive again. Like I did back in that shower room. I just want to do something because *I* want to do it, and not because my survival depends on it. I just want to make a fucking selfish choice for once.

Rico moves impossibly closer.

Bracing his forearm on the wall next to my head, he leans closer and places his lips next to my ear. "Good. Because I *really* want to do this again."

It's getting difficult to breathe. Decades of survival instincts, of professionalism drilled into me by painful lessons and harsh teachers, fight against that desperate need to feel alive for just one bloody second. The desperation that seems to grow stronger every time Rico is close.

He rests his knee against the wall between my legs. And it's such an effortlessly hot move that it sends a pulsing throb through my clit.

His lips skim across my jaw.

"Tell me to stop," he whispers.

A shudder rolls through my whole body as his warm breath caresses my skin.

My survival instincts are screaming at me to get the hell out. The desperation inside me is begging me to grab Rico by the collar and throw him into my apartment and then fuck his brains out right there on the floor.

With one forearm still braced against the wall, he reaches up with his other hand and places it on my throat. Not squeezing. Just holding my throat in that casually powerful way that drips of complete command.

Lightning flickers through my veins, and my pussy throbs. I rest the back of my head against the wall as that wicked mouth of his continues towards mine. My heart is slamming so hard against my ribs that I fear they might crack.

He slants his lips over mine, just shy of touching.

"Tell me to stop," he breathes against my mouth.

God, I want this. By all the gods and hell itself, I want this so fucking badly. I want to feel *alive*. I want to have a real life. I want—

"Stop," I gasp out breathlessly, forcing the word from the depths of my mind. "Stop."

Rico steps back immediately. His hand falls away from my throat as he takes two steps backwards, giving me space to breathe again without drowning in that intoxicating scent of him.

I drag in an unsteady breath, suddenly feeling both embarrassed and panicked. "I'm sorry. I—"

"Don't apologize. You have nothing to be sorry about. I

overstepped." He gives me a small smile while walking backwards down the hall. "Thank you for coming to dinner. I'll see you at Blackwater on Monday."

And with that, he turns around and strides down the hall before disappearing into the stairwell.

I slump back against the wall, feeling like I have just run a marathon. I can hear my own heart pounding in my chest.

Fuck, that was close. Too close.

Regardless of how sinfully hot he is, and regardless of how alive I felt when his dominating hands were on my naked skin, Rico Morelli is dangerous. I am his worst enemy. His most hated enemy. If he finds out who I really am, he will most likely kill me.

And if he finds out, and if I'm by some miracle still alive after that, it will only be a matter of time before the Hands of Peace find me. And then they will kill me as well as him.

I need to be careful. I need to keep my guard up at all times around Rico fucking Morelli. Because one slip-up, and we will both be dead.

So I push myself off the wall and drag in a deep breath to steady myself.

And then I walk alone into the dark empty apartment that belongs to the girl who doesn't exist.

18

RICO

If looks could kill, the entire metal table before me would be soaked in blood right now. Amusement plays over Jace's mouth as he glances between Kaden and the table a short distance from us in the university cafeteria.

"What did you do?" Jace asks, that wicked amusement leaking into his voice as well.

Kaden just continues eating his lunch. "I have no idea what you're talking about."

"The Petrovs are staring at us like they want to bathe in our blood."

"The Petrovs are *always* staring at us like they want to bathe in our blood."

"Yeah, but they're not staring at us this time. They're staring at *you*."

At last, Kaden looks up from his plate of cod and potatoes. After setting down his knife and fork, he twists in his seat so that he is looking directly at the table where all five Petrovs are sitting. His gaze settles on Alina, and that psychopath smile of his slowly spreads across his lips.

Alina quickly drops her gaze to the table.

Her brothers and cousins instinctively shift closer to her. Mikhail grips his utensils so hard that his knuckles turn white, and he raises the knife in Kaden's direction in a clear threat. Kaden just chuckles and then turns back to us.

With that sadistic gleam in his eyes, he gives us a lazy shrug. "They shouldn't have brought such a pretty little toy to campus if they didn't want me to play with it."

Jesus Christ, we're going to find ourselves in an outright war with the entire Petrov clan if this keeps up. I wish Eli was here. Actually, no I don't. Because then I would just have one more psycho to keep in line.

Amusement ripples through me.

It would be rather fun to watch Eli beat the crap out of Mikhail, though. He did it last year. And it ended with his little brother Anton having to beg for mercy on his behalf. Good times.

My gaze slides to Kaden, who is smirking faintly as he picks up his knife and fork again.

Yes, Eli is good. But I know that Kaden can more than hold his own too. Eli is unhinged and Jace is unpredictable. Both of them are forces of chaos. Kaden is the complete opposite. He is cold. Methodical. And the most vicious one of us all.

And that really is saying something.

He will be able to fight his own battles.

"Just let us know if you need backup for anything," I say, keeping my tone casual. Because Kaden is also proud. And territorial.

Kaden meets my gaze and holds it for a few seconds. Then he nods. Relief flickers through me. He interpreted that comment the way it was meant. As a genuine offer, not as a challenge to his own skills. Because if he ever does end up getting in over his head with the Petrovs, I want him to be able to tell us without feeling like his ego takes a huge hit. He and Jace and Eli are my brothers in every way that counts, and we will always have each other's backs.

That unmistakable gravitational pull suddenly yanks at me.

My gaze snaps to the door.

A second later, Isabella walks across the threshold. Her gaze sweeps across the room in that calculated casual way, which I know means that she is scanning for threats. I know that she sees me, but she pretends not to as she walks up to one of the counters and gets some food. When she's done, she immediately starts heading for one of the empty tables at the back.

Oh no, she's not getting away that easily.

"Isabella," I call.

Half of the canteen goes silent.

Clothes rustle and chairs scrape against the floor as the people at the tables around us turn to stare between me and Isabella, who is now standing frozen on the floor. Her shoulders are tense. Her posture rigid. Even from across the room, I can almost feel the panic radiating from her. She really doesn't like being the center of everyone's attention, does she?

Then she recovers.

With that shy and slightly embarrassed mask she often hides behind on her face, she turns towards our table and gives me an uncertain smile as if wordlessly asking me what I want. I twitch two fingers at her. She flicks her gaze from side to side before starting towards us. The rest of the students track her every move.

Anticipation hangs like mist inside the now silent room.

Everyone is probably expecting me to humiliate her or punish her in some way.

But when she reaches our table, I just motion at the empty chair next to Jace. "Sit."

Some of the people at the tables closest to us raise their eyebrows in surprise. A soft murmur of confusion ripples through the room. As if waiting to see if it's just a trick, they all watch as Isabella sets down her tray and then pulls out the chair opposite me and sits down.

When nothing else happens, everyone grudgingly goes back to eating their lunch.

"Thanks," Isabella says, and then casts an uncertain glance between the three of us.

"Of course," I reply with a nonchalant shrug. "Why sit alone when you have friends now?"

"Friends." The word sounds strangely awkward on her tongue. As if she has never said it before. "Right. Sure."

I arch an eyebrow at her. "Are we not friends?"

"Of course," she hurriedly presses out. That shy apologetic mask settles on her features again. "I'm sorry, I—"

"Alright," Kaden interrupts. "Since you're now *friends,* let me lay down the ground rules."

Setting his utensils down, he locks cold eyes on Isabella. She blinks in what seems like genuine surprise as she twists slightly to meet his gaze. A knife, a proper knife, appears in Kaden's hand as he raises it.

Using the blade, he motions towards me while holding Isabella's gaze with hard eyes. "If you hurt him..." He shifts the blade and points it at her instead. "I will kill you."

"Kaden," I groan.

I know exactly what he's doing. He is using the fact that Isabella and I are supposedly dating as an excuse to deliver a threat to the real assassin behind Isabella's fake persona. If she decides to stop pretending and instead come after me for real, Kaden is going to make it his mission in life to kill her as painfully as possible. And all of that is delivered between the lines and under the pretense of 'if you hurt his feelings now that you're dating, I will metaphorically end you'.

Clever.

And highly unnecessary.

Though I suppose I can't really complain, seeing as we did the exact same thing to Raina last year when she and Eli got together.

"If *I* hurt *him*," Isabella replies, her voice incredulous.

It surprises me enough that I forget the next protest I was about to direct at Kaden. Closing my mouth, I slide my gaze back to Isabella.

She stares at Kaden with a look of utter bafflement on her face. "Did you miss the part where *he* has spent the past three weeks ambushing me and attacking me and abusing the crap out of me?" Crossing her arms, she flicks a pointed look up and down Kaden's body. "Highly doubtful, given that you were present for parts of it."

It takes everything I have to stop a smirk from spreading across my lips.

When I first met Isabella, that shy and weak and apologetic fake version of her was all she ever showed. But the more time I've spent with her, the more she has started to show this version. The mouthy sarcastic version that I'm pretty sure is the real her.

I wonder if she even realizes that she's doing it.

At first, everything out of her mouth stayed true to that fake character. *Please. I'm sorry. Don't hurt me. You're a Hunter, so I'll let you do what you want to me.*

But then those snarky comments started slipping out. One after the other.

How very mafia of you.

Sounds like my kind of Friday night.

And now, the real her is escaping from underneath that iron-clad mask more and more frequently.

I hope she doesn't realize it. Because I like this version of her.

"No, I didn't miss that part," Kaden replies, flashing her one of those psychopath smiles. "I'm saying that *that* will feel like a leisurely beach vacation compared to what I will do if you hurt my brother."

Jace shrugs and hikes a thumb in Kaden's direction, the picture of lazy arrogance, but his eyes are hard as he stares Isabella down while adding, "What he said."

"Wow. Okay. Message received." She holds up her hands in a show of mock surrender before giving both of them an expectant look. "Anything else?"

"Yes," Kaden replies.

And then he launches into a very thorough, but still seemingly innocent, interrogation. As if only wanting to make sure that the girl his brother is dating is a good person. But there are hidden layers behind every seemingly inconsequential question.

I watch her as she answers each one. Studying her face, her tone, her words, I try to catch her in a lie. But everything lines up exactly with what she told me at the restaurant and also with everything that she hasn't told me but that I have read in the background information I requested on her earlier.

Not one single inconsistency.

It's incredible.

I wonder where she comes from and how she became this

way. How she turned into someone who can change her identity and personality as easily as everyone else changes clothes.

A cold slimy feeling spreads through my chest as those thoughts cross my mind.

Because, when it all comes down to it, aren't I exactly the same?

19

ISABELLA

The moment I step out of my car, I know that something is wrong. There is a charge in the air. Like the world is holding its breath before a violent storm.

It makes ice spread through my veins like poison.

Have they finally found me? Have the Hands of Peace at last manage to track me down despite all of my precautions?

They couldn't have. I went into town just yesterday to check my communications, and my contacts have found no indications that my former colleagues have even entered the state.

I flick my gaze around the parking lot. To get to my apartment, I first need to make it around the building. I glance back towards my car. Maybe I should just get into the car and make a run for it. Retrieve my go-bag and then drive and drive and drive until Blackwater University and Rico fucking Morelli are no more than specks of dust in my rearview mirror.

Would I make it?

Is there any other place where the Hands of Peace would never think to look? When I plotted out my escape plan, Blackwater University was the only place that fit all of my criteria. Why did Rico have to be here too? Why did he have to ruin my perfect escape plan?

Panic pulses through my heart.

Rico.

If I run, he will chase me too. Could I really survive being hunted by both the Hands of Peace and Rico Morelli when I have no other safe place to hide?

Fuck, I should—

A figure moves at the corner of my eye. I whip around, falling into a fight stance while my heart pounds like a battle drum in my chest.

Only to be faced with Mikhail Petrov.

The relief that crashes through me is so intense that I almost can't stop the laugh that threatens to rip from my throat.

It's not the Hands of Peace.

It's the disgruntled Russians. Normal people with normal petty vendettas. Not an authoritarian cult of assassins.

I must have shown some of that relief on my face, because Mikhail's expression darkens.

"You think you're untouchable because you run with the Hunters now, huh?" he says, menace lacing his voice. "Guess what? It's the other way around. You're one of them now, which means that you have just inherited all of their enemies."

While stifling the urge to heave an exasperated sigh, I make a mental note to beat the crap out of Rico the next time I see him. Why the fuck did he have to call me over in front of the entire cafeteria like that? Not only did it put me on everyone's radar, it apparently also landed me a whole new set of enemies. Just because I sat at the Hunters' table, the Petrovs now think they can use me to get revenge in their little internal war.

I was trying to stay invisible, for fuck's sake! That is getting increasingly difficult when the psycho kings of Blackwater decide to show the whole bloody university that I'm with them now. Gods fucking damn it.

"Kaden thinks he can mess with Alina," Mikhail growls. "Let's see how they like it when we return the favor."

We.

Yes, one glance over my shoulder confirms that his little brother Anton is closing in behind me as well. I scan the rest of the parking lot too, searching for their cousins. But apart from the mass of silent cars, the three of us are alone.

Two opponents. Both of them probably decently skilled. No long-range weapons as far as I can see. No close-range weapons either. Just two guys and their fists.

If I could go all out, this fight would be over within a couple of minutes.

But I can't go all out. Not without revealing my true skills.

Fuck, this is going to be annoying.

"Please," I say, raising my hands and adding a tremor to my voice. "It's not what you think. I'm not—"

Mikhail lunges for me.

I leap away on instinct, evading both his hands and Anton's as he tries to grab me from behind. Both of them whip around to face me again, looking slightly surprised. Crap. I need to slow my reflexes.

"Please," I repeat while edging backwards. "Don't—"

Mikhail swings at me.

This time, I force myself to remain in place and instead yank up an arm to block the strike. His fist connects with my forearm, sending a pulse of pain through it. Damn, he's strong.

From my left, Anton draws back for a punch as well. I see it coming but let it go through anyway.

I let out a huff as it hits me in the side of the ribs. He's not as strong as his brother, but still a bloody inconvenience.

While I stagger sideways from Anton's punch, Mikhail slams his fist into my jaw. My head snaps to the side.

Oh come on, not the face. That's just mean.

Since it's better to get this beating over with quickly, I let Anton's kick to my knee go through. My leg buckles and I crash down on the ground on one knee. Then I block Mikhail's boot to my chest just enough to make sure that he won't bruise any of my ribs. The force of it still sends me toppling backwards.

My back hits the ground, and I let out an audible huff to make it more convincing.

"Please," I beg, very convincingly, as I crawl backwards into an empty parking space between two cars.

The Petrov brothers follow, towering over me.

Then Mikhail reaches behind his back and withdraws something.

Steel glints in the afternoon sunlight.

Coldness spreads through my veins as my gaze lands on the knife in his hand.

Fuck. A knife changes things. I can't let myself get seriously hurt. While continuing to crawl backwards, I flick my gaze from left to right. But because I'm on the ground, all I can see are the two cars beside me.

Can I get away with using a little bit more skill without drawing attention? Just enough to make sure that the bastard doesn't cut me too badly with that damn knife of his.

Before I can make a decision, Mikhail swipes at me. I roll sideways to protect my throat and chest, and the knife slices across my shoulder blade instead. A short burst of pain sears through my skin, but it's very mild so it can't have been more than a scratch.

Mikhail lets out a snarl of frustration above me, and then his boot slams into my chest, flipping me over on my back again. Flashing down, he grabs me by the collar of my shirt and yanks my face closer to his. The knife glints in his other hand.

"This is going to hurt," he promises. "So I would suggest you—"

One second, he's spitting threats in my face. The next, he's hauled backwards and thrown several feet back. Anton whirls towards his brother, but before he can so much as open his mouth, Jace comes leaping over the hood of the car to my left and slams into him. Both of them go crashing into the car on the other side.

I snap my gaze back to Mikhail, and find Rico standing above him looking like the devil himself.

"Don't touch her," he growls.

Mikhail leaps to his feet right as Kaden appears from behind the car on his right. The blond Russian grips his weapon hard. Sunlight glints in the knife that Kaden is twirling in his own hand.

Then violence erupts around me.

I push myself up into a sitting position but remain seated on the rough asphalt, out of shock rather than any overwhelming pain, as I watch Rico, Kaden, and Jace fight the two Petrov brothers.

And what a fight it is. They're good. All three of them are incredibly skilled, moving with the lethal grace of born predators. In the back of my mind, I catalogue their fighting styles in case I need to fight them myself at one point.

But most of my brain capacity is taken up by trying to figure out what the hell they're doing here. How did they know where I was? And most importantly, why did they intervene?

If Rico is in any way uncertain of whether I am who I say I am, wouldn't it be in his best interest to just watch the fight? To see how I react. How well I fight. And then confront me about it later. Why would he intervene? It makes no sense.

Air explodes from Anton's lungs as Jace slams his boot into his stomach. He doubles over, which gives Rico a clear shot. Driving his elbow into the back of Anton's neck, he sends the Russian collapsing to the ground.

A short distance away, Kaden and Mikhail are swiping at each other with their knives.

The fight has barely gone on for a minute. But with three against two, and the sheer skill level that Rico and the Hunters possess, the battle was over almost before it started.

While Anton groans and tries to groggily push himself up from the ground, Rico jerks his chin at Jace, who immediately bends down and grabs Anton by the throat. Hauling him to his knees, Jace forces Anton to keep his back pressed against Jace's legs. The youngest Hunter keeps his hand locked around the Russian's throat.

Merciless rage drips from Rico's entire being as he positions himself slightly behind and to the right of Anton. Reaching down, he grabs the young man's wrist and then raises his arm so that it is stretched out straight to the side. With his grip still around Anton's wrist, he places his boot on the back of the guy's elbow. And then he pushes forward with his leg.

A cry of pain splits the air.

Mikhail immediately stops and whirls towards the sound. All color drains from his face when he sees his little brother.

Rico stares back at him with ruthless eyes.

If he puts more pressure on Anton's elbow, he's going to snap his arm in two.

"You really, *really*, shouldn't have come after Isabella," Rico declares.

A ripple goes through my soul at the way he says my name.

"If you hurt him—" Mikhail begins through a snarl.

"Does it look like you're in any position to make demands?" Rico cuts him off.

And as if to really drive the point home, he pushes his boot down a little farther.

Anton cries out again and tries to bend over to ease the pressure. But Jace keeps him trapped upright with that hand around his neck. Another whimper spills from Anton's lips as Rico pushes down slightly again.

Power pulses from every inch of Rico's muscular body as he stares Mikhail down. "Last year, little Anton begged for mercy on your behalf. Now, it's your turn."

"No," Anton calls. "Don't—"

Jace abruptly tightens his grip on the guy's throat, cutting off his air and the rest of his sentence.

Rage and desperation flash across Mikhail's face.

"Unless you want me to shatter his elbow and break his arm, that is," Rico continues. Cocking his head, he looks every bit the ruthless mafia heir that he really is. "Do you think his career would ever recover from that?"

On the ground, Anton gasps in a breath as Jace loosens his grip on his throat slightly.

Mikhail flicks a quick look down at his brother before

meeting Rico's eyes again and then spitting out a long and vicious curse in Russian.

A cruel smile spreads across Kaden's lips as he watches Rico push down his boot until Anton screams loud enough to pierce my eardrums.

"No!" Mikhail yells.

Rico stops moving his boot, but his eyes remain merciless. "What's it gonna be, Petrov? Because something is going to break here today, and it's either going to be his arm or your pride."

The very air seems to tremble from the power dripping from his every word.

"Kneel," Rico orders.

Mikhail's blue eyes dart down to his little brother again. Then he slowly lowers himself to his knees. Next to him, Kaden pulls out his cellphone and starts filming him. Cold amusement dances in his eyes.

"Beg," Rico commands.

Shame shines on Mikhail's features as he swallows and presses out, "Please."

"Better."

"Please, Hunter. I'm begging you."

"For what?"

"Mercy."

Rico only stares him down in silence.

"Please. I'm begging for mercy for my brother."

Behind the camera, Kaden's smile widens.

After another few seconds of silence, Rico turns to me. "Did he cut you? With the knife? Did he hurt you?"

Across the warm asphalt, Mikhail's blue eyes shift to me. We both know that he did. But I can feel him silently imploring me not to say anything. I hold his gaze for a second before looking up at Rico again.

"No," I lie.

"Good." He turns back to Mikhail. "Lucky you. I was just about to ask Kaden to carve a pound of flesh from your body in retribution, but it seems you'll be spared that now."

Mikhail's eyes flick to me for just a fraction of a second. And I know that I have just bought myself a truce with the Petrovs. Regardless of what happens in their war with the Hunters, they won't come after me again. Because Mikhail owes me now.

And thank fuck for that. I have enough enemies as it is.

"But know this," Rico continues. "If you ever come after Isabella again, I will fucking kill you."

He puts a little more pressure on Anton's elbow, making him cry out in pain, as if to really drive the point home.

Despite the raw violence of it all, it makes warmth spread through my stomach.

Part of it is purely sexual heat because of how fucking hot Rico is when he goes all mafia prince and makes his enemies kneel and beg for mercy.

But the rest of it is another kind of warmth. Something unfamiliar. And it comes from realizing that someone just had my back.

I've taken part in multiple group assassinations, of course. Like the one we did the night I should have killed Rico. But if shit hits the fan, it's every man for himself. No one in the Hands of Peace would even consider staying and helping someone else if they were surrounded and outnumbered. Either you're competent enough to survive on your own, or you die. There is no backup. No comrades-in-arms. Only a mission that needs to be executed at all costs.

But here, Rico and Jace and Kaden came to help me. To back me up. They didn't need to. It certainly didn't serve their interests to save me before I could incriminate myself by beating up the Petrovs with skills I'm not supposed to possess. But they did it anyway.

They had my back anyway.

And I'm not sure what to do with that information.

20

RICO

Once the two Petrov brothers have at last gotten the hell out of my sight, I turn to Kaden and Jace. "I'll meet you back at the house."

They cast a glance towards Isabella before giving me a nod. Then they start back around the building towards where we left our cars. I don't watch them leave. Instead, my eyes go straight to Isabella.

She is still sitting on the ground in the empty parking space between two cars. There's a red mark on her jaw where I assume someone hit her, but apart from that, she appears to be unharmed.

The expression on her face says differently, though. She looks… shocked.

Or that's the best description I can come up with, at least. She's just sitting there, staring at the spots where Mikhail and Anton Petrov were kneeling before we allowed them to leave. And there is this strange, stunned expression on her face.

For a moment, that kernel of doubt about her flickers to

life again. If she truly was the assassin from that night, she wouldn't get shellshocked by an ambush like this.

I stamp out that flicker of doubt again. It must be due to something else.

While she's still staring at nothing, I close the distance between us and then crouch down next to her.

Her gaze finally snaps back to me when I slide my arms underneath her back and legs, and lift her into my arms. That stunned shock on her face grows impossibly larger.

"Wait, what are you…?" She trails off as if she doesn't know how to finish the sentence.

She looks from me, to the ground, to the parking lot, and then back to me again while I start carrying her around the house and towards the front door of her apartment building. I can almost hear the gears turning in her head as she processes what is going on. Then, at last, the confusion clears from her eyes and she looks up at me. And this time, I can't read the expression in those storm-swept eyes of hers at all.

"It's okay," she says. "You can put me down. I'm not hurt. I can walk on my own."

Meeting her eyes, I flash her a teasing grin. "Oh, come on. After I performed such a heroic rescue, you're really going to deprive me of the chance to finish my dream role as Prince Charming and carry the damsel to safety in my big strong arms?"

A laugh rips from her chest. A real, genuine, laugh. She seems even more shocked by it than I am. For a moment, she just blinks down at her own chest, staring at the offending body part as if she doesn't understand how it manage to produce such a sound without her permission.

Then she gives her head a short shake as if to clear it.

My heart stutters as she shifts slightly, settling herself more firmly in my arms.

When she looks up at me, there's a small smile playing over her lips. And I swear to God, this one is real too.

"So, you've dreamt of being Prince Charming, huh?" she says, a gentle teasing note to her voice.

"Nah." I flash her a smirk. "Honestly, I think I'd prefer to be the Evil Queen. Wearing black, handing out poisoned apples, and then cackling while disappearing with a dramatic sweep of my cloak seems a lot more fun."

She laughs again. And then flicks another glance down at her chest.

"Who would you be?" I ask as I walk us into the building and start us towards the stairwell.

Her brows knit slightly as she looks up at me.

"From Snow White?" I clarify as I start us up the stairs.

"Oh, uhm, I don't know." She frowns again and then clears her throat. "I've never watched it."

"Seriously?"

"Yeah."

From everything she has told me about her fake childhood, that doesn't sound very likely at all. But I don't press the matter.

However, she seems to realize it too because she quickly changes the subject. "How did you even know that they were attacking me? You can't see the parking lot from the street."

"The Petrov twins. They were lurking outside school when we walked out, trying to keep us occupied. They wouldn't do that without reason, so we cornered them. It didn't take long to… *convince* them to tell us what the hell they were doing." My gaze drifts down to the red mark on her jaw, and a hint of regret flickers through me. "Though I guess it still took too long. I'm sorry we didn't make it here in time to stop it before it even started."

She studies my face, as if checking whether I'm sincere. I am. And she seems to understand that too, because she gives me a small smile. "It's alright. It's not your fault."

Oh, but it is. Because I'm the one who told her to sit with us at lunch today, which is why those damn Petrov brothers decided to come after her. I swallow down a mix of guilt and anger, and instead change the topic as we draw closer to her door.

"Can you reach your keys?" I ask.

She fishes them out of her pocket. Shifting my arm slightly, I take them from her hand. She raises her eyebrows at me.

"I really can walk on my own, you know," she says.

"I know," I reply.

But I don't set her down. Instead, I unlock the door and carry her into her apartment.

Golden afternoon sunlight streams in through the windows and illuminates the living room as I walk across it and then set her down on the white couch. Then I at last pull my arms back.

I freeze as my forearm, the one that was bracing her shoulder blades, comes back red. Staring down at that crimson smear, I know exactly what it is. Blood.

My gaze snaps back to her. "You lied to me."

She winces while an apologetic expression blows across her face. "Yeah."

"Fucking hell. The next time I see Mikhail, I'm going to—"

"Don't," she interrupts, shooting me a pleading look. "He will only take it out on me."

"No, he won't. Because I will fucking kill him."

"Please. Just... let it go."

I flex my hand, itching to hunt down Mikhail and carve him up until he's begging for death. But the pleading look on Isabella's face stops me. She really doesn't want to get involved in our war with the Petrovs. And I don't want to drag her into it either and make her a target.

"Fine," I force out. "I'll let it slide. *If...*" I begin, stressing the very conditional nature of this bargain, "you at least let me patch up the wound."

She rolls her eyes in what seems like half exasperation, half amusement. "Fine." Then she jerks her chin towards the kitchen side of the room. "The first aid kit is in the cupboard under the sink."

After giving her a nod, I head back and close the front door before going to the cabinet she specified. I don't even need to search for the first aid kit. It's right there on the side. One of those normal home kits people have. Not the extensive first aid kit fit for a secret assassin that I'm sure she has stashed somewhere else. I pull it out and then close the cabinet door while I straighten again.

When I turn back to face Isabella, she is just sitting there on the couch, watching me. My gaze drifts down to the tight black t-shirt she's wearing.

"You'll need to take your shirt off," I say, the words coming out a bit more hesitant than I had planned.

She looks down at her body before meeting my gaze again, and I swear some heat creeps into her cheeks. "Oh. Right."

Grabbing the hem of her shirt, she pulls it over her head. Then she folds it up and places it on the pale wooden table in front of the couch. I know that I shouldn't, that it will only bring trouble, but I slide my gaze over her body again.

She's now sitting there wearing only a black lace bra and a

pair of jeans shorts that barely cover the top half of her thighs. Blood rushes to my cock. The curve of her breasts in that bra combined with her toned shoulders and legs makes her body a perfect mix of soft and hard.

I give myself a mental slap. Focus, God damn it.

This time, I know that I see some red flush her cheeks.

Fuck, did I show any of that on my face?

However, before I can figure that out, Isabella shifts her position on the couch so that she's twisting away and has her back to me. I sit down on the white cushion next to her. After putting the first aid kit on the low table before me, I turn back and study the cut on her shoulder blade.

It is a very shallow cut, and it has almost stopped bleeding already, but rage still sears through me at the sight of it. All I want to do is to hunt down Mikhail and make him pay tenfold for every drop of blood he spilled. But I can't. Not without putting Isabella in the line of fire again.

Something inside my chest deflates.

This is why I can never let anyone get close to me. Why I'm terrified of it.

Because everyone who is close to me always ends up getting hurt.

First it was Eli.

My heart almost cracks at just the thought of that.

Eli. My brother in everything except blood. The one I grew up getting into all kinds of shit together with. And getting out of shit together with too.

It was just like any other weekend. He was sleeping over at our place, in my room, because I had already passed out on the bed he usually sleeps in. And then they came. Kidnappers who were there for me but who took him instead. They held him captive and tortured him and humiliated him until his mind snapped. And it should have been me. It fucking should have been me!

Then a few years after that, the assassins came. They killed my parents but let me live.

And now, the Petrovs went after Isabella just because I invited her to sit at our table while we had lunch.

Everyone around me gets hurt. Because of who I am, people close to me will always be in danger. Which is why I can never drag someone else, someone normal, into this bloody world of mine.

"That bad, huh?" Isabella says. "Damn, if I had known I would be dying today, I would've written up a will. But alas, too late now, I suppose."

Her joking words pull me out of my bleak thoughts, and I chuckle. "Alright, calm down there, smartass."

She doesn't say anything, but even with her back to me, I swear I can feel her smile.

The supplies in the first aid kit rustle and clink as I pull out a small bottle of antiseptic and some wads of cotton. After pouring some liquid onto it, I dab it against the top of her wound.

This kind of substance stings when it's applied to a wound, and yet Isabella doesn't even flinch. Doesn't react one bit.

As if she also realizes that, she sucks in a sharp breath between her teeth even though it's two seconds too late. I don't comment on it.

Instead, pain and anger flashes through me as I glance down at the old scars and burn marks on her body. If I ever get my hands on the one who did this to her…

"There should be some Band-Aids or something in there," Isabella says.

I finish wiping away the dried blood before searching through the kit until I find a large enough Band-Aid.

Even though her hair only reaches her shoulders, I find myself drawing my fingers at the edge of it to push it out of the way. A shudder ripples through her body as my fingers gently brush against her skin. I know that it's stupid, and dangerous, but I still take my time moving her hair aside. Then I draw my fingers down her shoulder blade and towards her wound.

After I put the Band-Aid on, I trace the edges of it. To make sure that it will stay in place. And because I can't make myself pull my hands back just yet. Completely transfixed, I trace the edge of her shoulder blade with my fingers before trailing them down her spine.

Her skin prickles at my touch.

I swallow. Hard.

Fucking hell, what is it about this damn assassin that makes me want to throw all sense of caution and logic to the wind.

She's an enemy. A mark that I'm trying to con into telling me what I want to know. Nothing more.

She's dangerous.

She's so fucking dangerous.

And yet, all I want to do is to run my hands over her body, taste those lying lips of hers, and hear her moan my name as I draw pleasure from her lethal body.

Why does she have to affect me like this?

Why does she have to make me feel less empty? Why does she have to make me feel more real? Why does she have to make me *feel*?

I can't do this. *We* can't do this. This is too dangerous. She is too dangerous. I need to put some distance between us. I need to remind myself that she is my enemy. She is a part of the group that killed my parents. This would be crossing a line that cannot be uncrossed. I cannot sleep with my parents' murderer.

She didn't murder your parents, my mind whispers to me. *She is the one who saved your life.*

I block it out. No. Too dangerous. Far too dangerous.

Pulling back abruptly, I let my hands fall away from her back.

I'm just about to stand up and leave when she turns around.

And those blue-gray eyes trap me in place.

Because in them, I see the exact same desperation that is shredding my own soul apart. That desperate need to feel alive, to feel real, for one fucking minute instead of just playing a scripted part in the fake lives we both lead.

Sliding my hands into her hair, I crush my lips against hers.

She stiffens like a board.

I jerk back, breaking the kiss.

"I'm sorry," I blurt out.

Shaking my head at my own stupidity, I quickly get to my feet and turn to leave.

But before I can, her hand shoots out and wraps around my wrist, stopping my retreat and turning me back to face her.

I can almost see the war raging behind her eyes. As if she is fighting the same battle with her own emotions as I am. Her fingers remain locked firmly around my wrist. I just look back at her, my heart beating erratically in my chest.

She draws in a shuddering breath while those conflicting emotions continue warring behind her eyes. Reaching her other hand hesitantly towards her face, she draws her fingers over her own lips. Where mine were pressed just a few moments ago.

Then complete determination flares up like burning flames in her eyes, and she yanks me back to her.

21

ISABELLA

Maybe it's because I'm annoyed that I had to lose an ambush on purpose. Or because I'm rattled by the realization that I liked having someone in my corner. Someone who has my back. Or maybe it's simply because both of us are living fake lives and, for once, we need something that is real.

Because I know now, without a doubt, that Rico hasn't bought my act for a second. He knows exactly who I am. That internal battle he just went through was clear as day on his face. Which means that he didn't kiss me as some kind of twisted way to get me to let my guard down. He did it because he wanted to, even though he knows that he shouldn't.

He knows that I am an assassin who was a part of the group that killed his parents. And he still wants to do this. He *still* wants me.

Probably for the same reason that I desperately want this too with every shred of my soul even though I know that it's stupid and dangerous as hell.

He knows who I really am. And I know who he really is. He knows that I know. And I know that he knows.

Even though almost every single word out of our mouths when we speak to each other is a lie, we are the only two people on this entire campus, apart from Kaden and Jace, who know the truth about us. We can never admit it to each other. But it doesn't matter. All that matters right now is that this is real. *We* are real.

His lips crash against mine as I yank him back to me.

Releasing his wrist, I lock my hands around the back of his neck, holding him firmly to me as I return that kiss he started that shocked me so much that my heart stopped for a second.

He braces his knee on the edge of the couch between my legs and slides his hands through my hair while kissing me back deeply. Violently. As if he has waited years for this.

I draw my hands down from his neck and over his chest. A low rumble comes from his throat as I trace my fingers over the sharp edges of his abs before brushing them along the top of his pants. Slipping my hands underneath the dark fabric of his shirt, I start pushing it up his stomach. His skin is soft and warm against my palms.

When I reach his chest, I swear I can feel his heart pounding underneath my hand. It makes my own heart skip a beat.

Rico breaks the kiss.

I blink, disoriented, only to realize that he did it so that he could pull his shirt up the rest of the way and yank it over his head. The shirt flutters through the air as he tosses it aside.

Heat pools at my core as I stare at his half-naked body. At his firm chest. At the way the muscles in his arms shift when he flexes his hand. At those defined abs that I just want to trace with my tongue. At his tan skin that betrays his Italian roots and his dark hair that I just want to run my hands through and his warm brown eyes that burn with need as he looks down at me.

Fuck, it should be illegal to be this fucking hot.

His gaze sears into mine as he locks his eyes on me. "Take your pants off."

The words pulse through the air like a shockwave. It's not a request. It's an order. And it makes my pussy throb and my breathing hitch.

Reaching behind me, I unclasp my bra and toss it to the white cushions next to me before I start unbuttoning my jeans shorts. Once I've slid the zipper down, I lie back on the sofa and lift my hips so that I can push both my shorts and my panties down.

I only make it halfway down my thighs before Rico grabs the garments and all but yanks them the final bit off me. He tosses them to the smooth wooden floorboards next to where his shirt is. Pushing myself up on an elbow, I move to get myself back into a sitting position.

Rico just plants a hand against my chest and shoves me back down on the couch.

A yelp slips past my lips as he grabs the back of my knees and yanks my body closer. Once my hips are right at the edge of the sofa, his strong hands slide upwards. With a firm grip on my thighs, he spreads my legs wide.

My heart pounds in my chest. I have never felt more exposed in my entire life, being so completely laid bare before this beautiful mafia prince.

He lets out a low and dark sound, a sound of approval, that makes my cheeks flush.

I'm just about to raise my head to see what he is doing when he suddenly draws his tongue along my pussy.

I arch up from the couch as lightning crackles through my veins.

Gasping in a breath, I tilt my head down and find Rico kneeling on the floor between my legs. There is a wicked smirk on his lips, and his eyes dance with mischief, as he watches me for a second. Then he draws his tongue along my pussy again, swirling it around my clit.

Something between a whimper and a moan escapes my throat. Throwing my head back down on the sofa cushions, I squirm against the soft fabric as Rico works his tongue around my clit with expert precision.

Pleasure builds inside me like a thrumming storm.

He nips at my clit with his teeth.

My hands shoot down, sliding through his hair and gripping the silken curls hard. Oh fuck, it feels just as soft as I imagined it.

A dark laugh rumbles from his chest. It makes his warm breath caress my sensitive skin, and I let out another pitiful whimper.

He takes my clit into his mouth, rolling it between his lips. I tighten my grip on his hair. The tension inside me grows.

"Rico," I gasp out.

But he shows me no mercy. He just continues working his mouth, pushing me closer and closer towards that sweet release.

My heart is beating so hard that I can hear the blood pound in my ears. I squirm on the cushions again, wiggling my hips in an effort to relieve some of the terrible tension trapped inside me.

Rico grabs my hip, forcing me to stop moving.

I let out a small whine. It feels like I'm going to shatter.

"Rico," I moan. "Please."

He executes a combined move with his lips and tongue.

Pleasure shoots through my body.

I arch up from the couch again as release sweeps through my limbs. A breathless cry rips from my throat. Gripping his hair hard, I collapse back onto the cushions as Rico continues working his mouth, prolonging my orgasm. My legs tremble and every nerve inside me feels like it's pulsing with electricity.

When the last waves of it have faded out, I just lie there, staring up into my white ceiling while my chest heaves.

"Fuck, you really are gorgeous when you come," Rico says, his voice coming out low and rough.

Dragging in a deep breath, I push myself up to my elbows to find Rico staring at me the same way he did in that shower room. As if I'm the most glorious thing he has ever seen.

"I would say the same." I shoot a pointed look down at the bulge in his pants. "But I still haven't seen you come."

A grin spreads across his mouth as he gets to his feet. "Wanna go again, huh?"

"Do I look satisfied to you?"

His eyes glint. "Is that a challenge?"

"Yes."

"Good. Because I'm not done with you yet."

Bending down, he slides his arms underneath me. I wrap my legs around his waist and lock my fingers behind his neck as he lifts me off the couch and then starts walking us towards my bedroom.

Halfway there, I shift my weight so that I grind myself against his hard cock.

A low moan rips from his chest. His eyes promise delicious vengeance as he locks them on me.

"Oh, you'll pay for that, you little menace," he warns.

I do it again. His eyes shutter and he clenches his jaw while tightening his grip on my ass.

"The things I will do to you," he growls.

Before I can do it a third time, we reach my bed. The mattress bounces underneath me as Rico tosses me down on it. I scoot back and shift into a better position while Rico strips out of the rest of his clothes.

My gaze drops down to his cock, and my eyes widen slightly at the size of it. Fire sears through my veins, making my core pulse with need.

When I return my gaze to his face, I find him smirking at me as he prowls up to the bed, as if he knows exactly the effect he has on me.

The mattress dips as he climbs onto the bed. With commanding hands, he grips my thighs and spreads my legs wide before settling himself between them. I rake my gaze over him, drinking him in.

Afternoon sunlight falls in through my bedroom window, illuminating parts of his criminally handsome face and making his brown eyes glitter like gold. I reach up, drawing my hands down his hard chest.

He leans down over me. The move makes his cock brush against my entrance, sending a pulse through my spine. I slide my hands over his abs. But before I can get any lower, he suddenly grips my wrists and moves my hands away.

Shifting my arms, he positions them so that he is holding both of my wrists in one hand. Then he forces my arms up over my head and pins my hands to the mattress there. I narrow my eyes at him. There is a wicked smirk on his face as he uses his other hand to trace teasing shapes around the curve of my breast.

Pleasure flickers through me.

His fingers circle around my tit, drawing closer to my nipple with each lazy arc.

My heart patters in my chest.

He shifts his hips.

A jolt shoots through me as his cock brushes against my throbbing pussy again.

I yank against his grip on my wrists, but he keeps them mercilessly trapped.

With that sly smile on his lips, he draws his cock over my pussy again while his fingers tease closer to my nipple. I let out a whimper.

He smirks. "Told you that you would pay for that."

Before I can retort, his fingers at last reach my nipple. A moan drips from my lips instead as Rico rolls my hard nipple between his thumb and forefinger. Then he pinches. Hard. It makes me arch up, which only makes my pussy brush against his cock again. I let out something between a plea and a curse as Rico rubs his thumb over my nipple while drawing his cock along my entrance again.

My whole soul thrums with pent-up need.

Dragging in a steadying breath, I lock eyes with Rico and flash him a smirk to rival his own. "You really are an expert."

"Oh, I know—"

"At leaving women unsatisfied."

His eyes flash, and a grin dripping with challenge spreads across his mouth as he slides his hand from my tit and up towards my throat. It settles there, right underneath my jaw for maximum control. "Careful now."

I just match his challenging grin.

He shifts his hips, positioning his cock right at my entrance. With his eyes locked on me, he slowly pushes forward.

A breath escapes my throat as I feel the crown of his cock enter me.

Moving slowly, he keeps pushing forward. His eyes study every inch of my face as he goes deeper.

My heart slams against my ribs. Fuck, he really is big.

But he gives me time to adjust to his size, so there is no pain as he sheaths himself fully inside me. Once he is settled all the way to the hilt, he pauses for a moment.

Then he draws out.

And slams into me again.

A groan rips from my chest.

He releases my wrists and throat, and instead braces one hand on the mattress next to my head. The slight shift in angle makes his cock grind against my clit with every movement.

Pleasure pulses through me as he starts up a steady rhythm of powerful thrusts.

I slide my fingers through his hair and then down over his neck before raking them along his back. A moan slips from his mouth. I move one hand back to his neck, yanking his face down and stealing that incredible sound from his lips with a violent kiss. He kisses me back while slamming his cock into me again. I gasp into his mouth.

He pulls back, studying my face as if searing every flicker of emotion into his mind forever, while he pounds into me. His thick cock creates mind-numbing friction with each thrust. I drag my fingers down Rico's muscular chest as the storm of pleasure inside me grows. He pushes me mercilessly towards another orgasm while keeping those commanding eyes firmly locked on me.

Every inch of his chiseled body thrums with power.

Fire sears my veins.

Rico Morelli fucks the way he does everything else. Dominantly. With complete and utter control. As if he expects the whole world to submit to his will and bow before him in unconditional surrender.

And by all the gods in all religions, when he has me pinned to the bed and fucks me like this, like he owns every part of my body, mind, and soul, I am about ready to do just that.

I suck in a shuddering breath, tilting my head back as the pent-up pleasure inside me reaches unbearable levels.

His strong fingers wrap around my jaw immediately, forcing my head back down again.

"Eyes on me," he commands, his voice pulsing with that ruthless authority. "I want you to look at me when I make you come."

A dark thrill races down my spine. I draw my fingers down his sides, but obey his order and keep my eyes locked on his.

The bed thuds against the wall as Rico continues railing me.

Lightning flickers through my body with each dominant thrust. I grip his biceps hard, digging my fingers into his muscles.

My mind is fraying, and it feels as if my body is coming apart at the seams.

I need release.

I need it now.

His cock hits the perfect spot inside me.

And light bursts before my eyes.

I gasp as a second orgasm crashes through my body.

My pussy tightens and my inner walls flutter as waves of pleasure sweep through me.

Rico keeps fucking me through it all while his eyes drink in the sight of me coming undone beneath him.

Then a deep groan tears from his chest as release explodes through him as well.

I stare up at him through the haze of sparkling pleasure, studying his features as he climaxes with his cock buried deep inside me.

And gods above, *he* also looks gorgeous when he comes.

22

RICO

We fuck each other's brains out four more times after that. After a short burst of panic when I ask her if she's on birth control, which she thankfully is, I fuck her once against the wall, then bent over the dresser, and then one more time on the bed, and then once in the shower too.

When we at last collapse on her couch, after taking a second shower that actually involved washing off instead of me railing her against the shower wall, my body is utterly spent. And yet, in the past six years, I have never felt more alive than I do right now.

"That was…" Isabella begins, lying slumped on the couch beside me. "Some seriously impressive stamina."

I let out a surprised laugh. Tipping my head to the side, I look over at her. "Likewise."

A decidedly smug and proud smile plays across those soft lips of hers. And suddenly, all I want to do is to roll over and straddle her body again so that I can kiss her breathless once more.

Pain stabs through my heart.

God, I just want to stay in this moment for a little while longer. This moment suspended in time where she knows who I really am and I know who she really is, and we're both aware that the other knows, but neither of us acknowledges it. This stolen moment where we're real for just a little while before we go back to our fake lives and continue lying through our teeth with every word we speak.

Isabella is still staring up at the ceiling, her chest rising and falling with even breaths.

It's dark outside the windows now, but light from the lamp above glitters in her eyes.

I stare at those eyes. Those eyes that both ended me and brought me back to life all at the same time.

Confusion flickers over her face, as if she can feel me staring at her, and she turns her head to meet my gaze. "What?"

And because I can't bring myself to lie, not in this moment of honesty that we have stolen for ourselves, I reply, "You have beautiful eyes. I've always thought so. From the moment I first saw you."

Surprise pulses across her features, and I can't tell if it's because of my words themselves or the fact that I was being completely honest when I said it.

"Oh." Her cheeks flush slightly, and she glances away, as if she's uncertain how to respond to that. "I, uhm… I've always considered them too noticeable for…"

She trails off, leaving the rest of her sentence unspoken. Reaching over, I place gentle fingers on her chin and turn her face back to me.

"I've always thought your eyes look like storm-swept seas." I smile softly. "Wild and fierce. It suits you."

Her mouth drops open ever so slightly while a whole host of emotions blows across her beautiful face.

And I suddenly realize that I've gone too far. I've said too much. Shown her too much. Given her too much honesty.

Letting my hand drop from her chin, I clear my throat and return my gaze to the ceiling instead. Next to me, I can feel Isabella scrambling for control as well. To get back to where we should be. Enemies who lie to each other with every word. It appears to go as poorly for her as it does for me.

Thankfully, before either of us can say something that we can't take back, her stomach rumbles. Loudly.

She laughs. The sound is more relieved than embarrassed.

"Sorry," she says, that casual note back in her voice again. "I guess I'm just hungry after all the… physical activity."

I chuckle. "Yeah, me too."

Abruptly sitting up straight, I rise from the couch and give the side of her knee a soft slap. "Alright, let's go."

She sits up too. Her brows pull together in confusion as she stares back at me. "Go? Go where?"

"You'll see."

"Or you could just tell me."

"Hmm." A sly smile tugs at my lips as I hold her gaze. "Or I could just handcuff you and put a bag over your head."

She gives me a flat look.

I laugh and raise my eyebrows. "Too soon?"

Rolling her eyes, she clicks her tongue in a show of exasperation. But I can see the amusement dancing in her eyes too. While shaking her head at me, she gets to her feet as well.

"I'm still waiting for an apology for that, you know," she says, giving me an expectant look.

The wicked smile on my lips grows as I nod towards the

white sofa behind her. "I just got down on my knees and worshipped your cunt on that very sofa. That not enough groveling for you, Isabella?"

Heat floods her cheeks. I grin at the embarrassed look on her face as she flicks a glance towards the couch before returning her attention to me. While muttering something under her breath, she stalks over and gives my shoulder a shove that actually does put me a little off balance, betraying that she's much stronger than she normally pretends to be.

"Shut up," she huffs, that flush still on her cheeks, as she starts towards the door. "Or I might decide not to come after all."

"Oh I can make you come whether you want to or not." I smirk at her. "As I've demonstrated several times in the past few hours."

The red flush in her cheeks deepens even more as she snaps her astonished gaze to me. I let out a dark laugh.

Fuck, I love making her flustered like this. She's always so calm and composed behind the perfect mask of her fake life. So it brings me incredible delight to shatter that composure and watch her flounder like a clueless teenager.

She narrows her eyes at me and then pointedly turns away from the door. "That's it. I've changed my mind."

"Isabella."

I don't miss the way a small shiver ripples through her body when I say her name. Fuck, I love making her shudder like *that* too.

Turning back to me, she arches an arrogant eyebrow in silent question.

My smile turns even more devilish as I give her a warning look. "Don't make me get the handcuffs."

Even though she tries to hide it behind another eye roll, I can see the flicker of lust in her gaze too.

"Fine," she sighs dramatically as she once more starts towards the door. "You win. Let's go then."

I follow her, but my mind is still churning from that flicker of lust in her eyes. Did she want me to handcuff her in bed earlier? I'll have to try that next time.

Shock pulses through me, and I give my head a quick shake. Next time? There will be no next time. This was just a one-time lapse in judgement.

And now, I'm only taking her out to eat because I need to continue to stealthily interrogate her. Nothing else.

But as I walk Isabella down to my car outside, even I know that that last part is nothing more than yet another lie.

23

ISABELLA

When Rico said that he was taking me somewhere, I'm not sure what I was expecting. But I do know that it wasn't this.

Stopping in front of the door, I tilt my head back and stare up at the colorful sign above.

Waffle Kingdom, it reads. There is even a little illustration next to it depicting a waffle with whipped cream and strawberries on top.

I still haven't really wrapped my mind around this, but Rico is already standing by the door, holding it up for me while giving me an expectant look, so I just quickly shake my head and hurry to catch up with him.

An absolutely intoxicating scent hits me the moment I step across the threshold. My stomach growls in responds. Gods above, does it always smell this delicious when someone is making waffles or is it just this place in particular?

Trailing to a halt, I briefly close my eyes and draw in a deep breath.

When I open them again, I find Rico watching me with a

faint smile on his lips, so I wipe the astonished look off my face and then quickly stride over to once again catch up with him.

He leads me to a table in the corner. The best table in the entire restaurant because it gives us an unobstructed view of the entire place, along with the door and any other points of entry, while also allowing us to have a wall at our backs. It's the best possible location to be in if we were to suddenly be attacked. I let out a soft huff of amusement. He really is as paranoid as I am, isn't he?

I slide onto the padded seat on my side of the booth. The fabric is soft and in a deep red color, contrasting against the pale wood that the rest of it is made of. There is a pink and white striped tablecloth covering the table. In fact, red, pink, and white seems to be the theme of the restaurant because almost all decorations along the walls are in those colors as well.

"So," I begin as Rico settles himself opposite me. "Waffles, huh?"

"Of course." He lifts his broad shoulders in a shrug. "Post-sex waffles are the best kind of waffles."

"Come here a lot then, do you?"

He raises his eyebrows and gives me a pointed look. "Did you just call me a whore?"

"Uhm…"

Something between a laugh and a huff of mock affront escapes his chest. Then he narrows his eyes slightly as a knowing expression settles on his features. "Given how fucking incredible you are in bed, I'm betting you're not exactly a virgin either."

The first half of that sentence sends a surge through me and makes the world tilt momentarily, so it takes an extra second to process the rest of it. *Given how fucking incredible you are in bed.* Gods, the way he said that. Apparently, he enjoyed our activities this afternoon just as much as I did.

Memories of it immediately flash through my mind again, which really isn't helping me keep my wits about me. Blocking it all out, I clear my throat.

"No," I admit. "I'm not a virgin either."

The Hands of Peace believe in a thorough education, so all members also train in the art of sex. In case a mission requires that sort of assassination plan. When I was eighteen and nineteen, I regularly fucked some members who were my own age in order to practice how it's done. I've slept with some marks too. But all of it was for a purpose. To train. Or to kill. Never because it was simply something I wanted to do for my own enjoyment.

"I would like a list."

I blink, yanked back to the present by Rico's nonchalant demand. Frowning, I stare at him from across the table. "A what?"

"A list of names." He holds my gaze. Dead serious. "Of the people you have slept with."

Suspicion blows through me as I narrow my eyes at him. "Why?"

"I just want to know which names to put at the top of my hit list once I graduate."

I laugh. A sly smile plays over his lips, but he keeps his eyes locked on mine. He must just be joking. He *should* be joking. And yet…

"Hi and welcome to Waffle Kingdom," a young man suddenly says from right next to us. "I'm…" He trails off. "Oh. Mr. Hunter. I, uhm…"

Rico keeps his eyes on me, that odd look still on his face,

so I break eye contact and turn towards the waiter who has now trailed off. Just like his voice indicated, he is indeed a young man. Can't be more than nineteen. With blond hair and blue eyes that look slightly too big for his face.

"Welcome back. It's so nice to see you here again." He casts a nervous glance between me and Rico, who is still only staring at me. "And your lady friend too."

At last, Rico drags his gaze to the young man. "You can just give us the menus and then leave. I'll summon you when we're ready to order."

"Yes, sir. Of course. Sorry."

He quickly places two menus on the table in front of us and then hurries away. There was nothing threatening or rude about the way Rico spoke to him. And yet, the guy leaped to obey and even apologized when he hadn't actually done anything wrong. As always, the world and the people in it bend to Rico's will as if it's the natural order.

Mr. Hunter, he had said. I almost scoff. If he only knew who Rico really is, then he would probably have been on his knees begging forgiveness for the imagined slights too.

"What?" Rico asks.

Tearing my gaze from the retreating waiter, I shift my attention back to the mafia prince before me. "You can't tell me you don't see it."

"See what?"

I motion towards where the waiter was standing a few seconds ago. "This. The way people act around you."

"I have no idea what you're talking about."

But there is a sly smile tugging at his lips and a glint in his eyes as he nonchalantly looks down at the menu instead. Letting out a grudgingly amused huff, I glance down at the menu as well.

Panic immediately surges up inside me. I flick a quick look up and down the page, but I don't understand what I'm supposed to order because there are no dishes that actually say 'waffles' on the menu.

As if he can feel my panic, Rico looks up from his own menu and points towards mine. "Here's how it works. You get a stack of waffles. Just tell him if you want a large or a small stack. And then you order some toppings for it." His finger moves down the rows on my menu. "From here. You'll get them in a bunch of small bowls on the side, so you can mix and match the toppings differently on each waffle when you eat them."

Relief washes through me. Okay, that explains the strange menu.

But the relief is short-lived as I stare at the sheer number of toppings. How am I supposed to pick something that would make sense? How many should I even get? What would be a normal thing to put on waffles? Is all of this normal or are some things more normal than others?

I think I must have frowned or something because Rico chuckles.

"Yeah, I know," he says. "There are a lot of options. But just… What do you normally put on your waffles?"

"I don't know. I've never eaten waffles before."

The words are out of my mouth before I can stop them. I snap my gaze up from the menu to find Rico staring at me in surprise.

"Seriously?" he asks.

Since I can't take it back, I just shrug as if it's no big deal. "Yeah."

"Alright. Uhm…" He runs a hand over his jaw while casting a look down at my menu. "We'll get you some whipped cream then. It's a good neutral one. And…" He squints down at the mass of choices. "Some ice cream too." His gaze flicks back up to me. "What kind of ice cream do you like?"

Cold panic crackles through my veins as I quickly glance down at the list of ice cream flavors. There are like ten of those alone. "Uhm…"

"Don't tell me you've never eaten ice cream either."

My gaze slowly returns to Rico's face. And this time, I can almost feel the incredulity radiating off him as he stares at me in complete bafflement. I get ready to lie. To evade. To laugh and then joke my way out of it.

But I just… can't.

I don't know if it's because he offered me that tiny bit of truth earlier, the comment about my eyes that made my stomach flip and my heart ache, but I just can't bring myself to lie about this.

So I hold his gaze, my pulse pounding in my ears, and admit, "No."

Deafening silence falls over our table as Rico just stares at me. Somewhere on our left, the sound of clanking pots drifts through the air and joins the murmur coming from the other guests.

Then the spell breaks and Rico abruptly flips his menu closed. Reaching over the table, he grabs mine and closes it as well.

My heart sinks like a stone into my stomach as he stacks them and places them at the edge of the table while signaling to the waiter.

Fuck, I shouldn't have said anything. He tried to do something nice for me and take me out for waffles, and I'm such a fucking shell of a human that I can't even tell him what kind of ice cream I like. And now, he's frustrated with me instead. Pain stabs through my chest. Gods above, why can't I just be normal? Or at least be better at pretending to be. I'm usually excellent at passing for a normal human being. But there is just something about Rico that throws me off. That makes the real me slip through the cracks in my carefully constructed mask.

"Yes, sir?" the waiter replies, looking to Rico, as he comes to a halt next to our table.

"A large stack of waffles for both of us," he begins. "I'll have whipped cream, mango sorbet, raspberries, and chocolate."

The waiter scribbles furiously in his notepad. I just sit there, feeling completely deflated, because I have no idea what I'm going to order when the waiter turns around and asks me.

Once he's done, he looks up at Rico for a second before his gaze starts sliding to me. I open my mouth, but Rico cuts me off.

"And she'll have one of everything."

The waiter blinks. I do too.

Turning back to Rico, he flicks a confused glance between the menu and Rico's face, "I'm sorry?"

Rico just looks back at him with a steady gaze. "One of each."

"I, uhm…"

Pulling out a sleek black credit card, Rico puts it down on the table in front of the waiter. His gaze hardens as he repeats, "One. Of. Each."

"Y-yes, of course. Sir." His gaze darts to me. "Ma'am. One of each. Coming right up."

Once he has scrambled away, Rico leans back against the padded backrest and gives me a smile that knocks the breath right out of my lungs. After sliding his hands casually into his pockets, he shrugs.

"Since you don't know what you like, I figured it's best to just try everything." He smiles again. That real, genuine smile that makes his eyes glitter like golden sparkles. "Until you find your favorites."

I almost burst into tears.

I have never thought about what I like or dislike before. Everything I have ever done has been in the service of a mission someone else has decided for me. I don't know what kind of food I like, because what I personally prefer to put in my mouth has always been irrelevant. I don't have a favorite style of clothes, because I wear whatever the mission requires me to wear. Hell, I don't even have a favorite color.

Because it doesn't matter.

I'm a ghost.

A collection of fake people who don't exist.

No one has ever bothered to ask me what I like or dislike. Because I'm not a real person.

And yet, here is Rico, a ruthless mafia prince and the man who should hate me more than anything, ordering everything off the menu just so that I can try it all and figure out what kind of toppings I like on my waffles.

No one has ever done something like that for me before.

"Thank you," I press out. It comes out sounding thick and choked.

Rico looks startled by that. Sliding his hands out of his pockets again, he sits forward and opens his mouth, and I can feel him getting ready to ask me questions that I don't want to answer. But then he pauses, as if changing his mind.

Leaning back against the backrest once more, he instead gives me an easy smile and replies, "Anytime. After all, knowing your preferred waffle toppings is crucial to surviving three years at Blackwater. I know you won't believe me, but Professor Lawson always puts that as the hundred-point question on her final exams."

A relieved laugh rips from my throat. The tension eases out of my shoulders as I slouch back in my seat as well and flash him a smirk. "Well then, I will make sure to repay you, with interest, when I ace her test."

"You'd better. I don't share my waffles secrets with just anyone."

I laugh again, though I can't help but feel like there was some truth to that last part.

However, I don't acknowledge it. And neither does he. Right now, we seem to be in this strange place where we don't outright lie to each other anymore. But we don't tell the whole truth either. And because of who we are, I suppose that is as good as we will ever get.

When the waiter, or rather *waiters*, arrive with our food, they end up having to drag over another table in order to fit all of my toppings on it.

I try it all. Every single flavor of ice cream and every type of topping. I try it all in different combinations. And it's so damn good.

When I combine some strawberries and chocolate along with a bit of pear-flavored ice cream, it tastes so good that I just close my eyes and moan. It feels as if my soul floated away from my body for a moment.

Then I mix another few toppings and try that too.

Rico watches me from across the table while he eats his own, much more organized, waffles. A smile plays over his mouth the whole time, but he says nothing. I don't either.

Except to tell him what I think about different topping combinations.

We can't be honest with each other anyway. And neither of us seems to want to spoil the wonderful mood by spouting meaningless lies just for the sake of talking.

So we sit there and eat our waffles.

And during the entire meal, I feel like my whole soul is thrumming with energy.

I thought having sex with Rico, just because I wanted to and not because it was required of me, made me feel alive. And it does.

But this, right here, just sitting here and eating waffles with him, might be the most real I have ever felt.

24

RICO

Every time I try to focus on something else, my mind just keeps drifting back to that waffle dinner. To the way Isabella's eyes lit up each time she tried a different topping on her waffles. Lit up like brilliant sunlight through clear water. It was the most beautiful thing I have ever seen, and it took my breath away each and every time.

It also baffled me. *Still* baffles me. How can she never have eaten ice cream before? Waffles, fine. But ice cream? Every kid has eaten ice cream at some point.

Not for the first time, I wonder who she really is. What kind of person was she before she became an assassin? And what made her become one?

It's a strange feeling. In some ways, I feel like I know her so intimately, so completely, that I can see right through her soul. Like I know her and understand her in a way the rest of the world does not. Because I also feel those exact same emotions that she hides deep within her heart.

But at the same time, I know absolutely nothing about her. I don't know where she came from or what her family was like. I don't know where she went to school or why she decided to become an assassin while she was still in high school. Hell, I don't even know her real name.

How is it possible to know someone so deeply while at the same time not knowing them at all?

"Ha! Loser."

I blink, realizing that I spaced out, *again*, and turn my head to find Jace grinning at me with a smug look of victory on his face. I flick a glance back at the TV. Yes, my video game character is indeed lying there on the ground, dead.

From the other side of the couch, Kaden scoffs. "That wasn't a real victory, Golden."

"Uhm, hello." Jace stabs a hand towards the TV. "Did you not just see me shoot him in the head?"

"You didn't win because you were better than him. You won because he was daydreaming."

"I was not *daydreaming*," I protest, shooting him a dirty look.

"Uh-huh." He smirks at me. "So you weren't thinking about Isabella?"

"Oh, he totally was," Jace says before I can reply.

Turning around, I narrow my eyes at him. "And how would *you* know? I thought you were focused on our game."

"I can sense these things." With a grin on his face, he taps his fingers against both temples. "Mind tricks, baby."

I snort and roll my eyes before hurling a pillow at him.

He catches it deftly and then arranges it behind his head before letting out a contented sigh. Mischief dances on his face as he looks back at me with a victorious smile. "See? You even gave me the pillow I wanted without me having to ask for it." He winks. "Told you. Mind tricks."

On my other side, Kaden snickers. I let out a chuckle as well, because that was indeed well played.

Jace picks up his controller from his lap and flashes me a grin full of cocky challenge. "Alright, ready to get your ass kicked again?"

"No," Kaden replies before I can even open my mouth. "Give me that." Leaning over, he snatches the controller out of my hands. "You're too distracted, and I refuse to allow his ego to grow any larger. I will personally escort Jace back down to the bottom of the food chain."

Jace snorts. "Come try it."

"So go handle the source of your incessant daydreaming instead," Kaden finishes, his gaze on me, as if Jace hadn't said anything.

Narrowing my eyes, I give him a sharp look, which he answers with an even sharper psychopath smile. I huff out a laugh.

"Fine." After heaving a sigh, I push myself up from the couch and start towards the doorway while speaking over my shoulder. "The loser is responsible for dinner."

"You're only saying that because you're not even in the game anymore," Jace calls after me.

"Scared, little brother?" Kaden mocks, and even though my back is to them now, I can hear the smirk in his voice.

"You wish," Jace retorts. "When I win, I'm going to make you wear an apron as you cook us dinner."

"Not unless you prefer your eyeballs still attached to your face. And where would you even get an apron?"

"Don't you have a French maid costume or something in that massive fucking stash of yours?"

Their bickering voices fade out as I leave the living room

behind and instead walk into the study across the hall. It's probably the neatest room in the entire house, since no one ever really comes here. I close the door behind me before sliding my phone out of my pocket. Only rows of silent bookcases watch me as I stroll over to the desk and flop down on the chair. Then I pull up Isabella's number.

For a few seconds, I just stare at it on the screen while my heart does strange things in my chest. Then I give my head an annoyed shake and hit *call*.

Leaning back in the chair, I throw my feet up on the corner of the dark wooden desk and cross my ankles.

The line keeps ringing. And ringing. And ringing.

Eventually, the call is cut off.

I scowl down at my phone before hitting *call* again.

It rings. And rings. And rings.

The scowl on my face deepens.

Then, at last, Isabella picks up.

"Yes?" she says, her voice slightly hostile.

"Is that really the way to greet your knight in shining armor?" I reply, grinning even though she can't see it.

She laughs. The sound is somewhere between relief and exasperation. "Knight in shining armor? I think you mean eternal tormentor."

"Have you forgotten my gallant rescue just a few days ago?"

"Have you forgotten that you kidnapped me just a week ago?" Her tone is full of both mock outrage and amusement. "How did you even get my number?"

"You gave it to the admin office when you enrolled."

"That's supposed to be confidential."

"Yeah, well, as you said, no one refuses the Hunters."

"So you've leveled up from bully to stalker. Congratulations. I knew all your hard work would pay off eventually."

I laugh. "Careful now. Or I might level up to something even worse."

"Was there a point to this call?" I can hear the teasing smirk in her voice. "Apart from delivering vague threats and sucking your own cock, I mean."

Another astonished laugh threatens to escape my throat. She certainly has started letting her real personality come out to play more often now. And I fucking love it.

"Oh, Isabella." I grin up at the ceiling as I imagine her own smirking face before me. "The things I will do to you." Sitting upright, I add in a more serious tone, "Speaking of, are you free tonight?"

Suspicion creeps into her voice. "Why?"

"That was a yes or no question, Isabella."

"And my answer depends entirely on what you're about to say next."

I just laugh and shake my head.

"Does it involve handcuffs?" she asks when it becomes apparent that I'm not going to answer.

A sly smile pulls at my lips. "My, my. Am I imagining things or did you actually sound excited about that prospect?"

Something between a flustered huff and a scoff makes it out of her mouth. "You're definitely imagining things."

"Hmm. If you say so."

"I do."

Silence falls for a few seconds. Afternoon sunlight streams in through the windows, hitting the spines of the books on the shelves and making the ones that have metallic foil on the titles glitter.

"Well?" I prompt.

"Well what?"

"Are you free tonight?"

"I'm about to head into town for an errand."

"Good. I'll come with you."

"No."

"I'll meet you afterwards then."

She is silent for a while. I can almost picture her scrunching up her brows as she tries to figure out how she can talk her way out of this. Then she heaves a deep sigh, as if she realizes how futile that is.

"Fine." That tone of mock outrage mixed with amusement returns to her voice as she adds, "But if I see even a hint of handcuffs, I'm leaving."

I chuckle. "Deal."

After we arrange a meeting time and location, we hang up. I let my head fall back over the backrest. Staring up at the ceiling, I blow out a long breath.

I don't even know what I'm doing anymore.

My plan was to get Isabella to like me and to trust me enough to tell me the truth. But I know, and I always have known, that she never will. No matter what I do, she will never willingly tell me the truth about her. About us. Our past together. I knew it from the moment Jace suggested that I try to seduce her instead of bullying her into doing what I want.

So why did I still go along with the plan?

Why am I still spending time with Isabella like this?

My grandfather is searching day and night for the people who killed my parents. And here I am, eating waffles and going on dates with one of them. I should just hand her over to Federico. Or I should at least do something drastic to force her to spill the truth to *me*.

I should...

But first, I just want to carve out one more real night in my otherwise fake life. One more night with someone who understands everything I'm feeling. Someone who feels it too.

25

ISABELLA

I half expected him to have me followed. But to my surprise, there were no mafia men tailing me as I drove into town and walked to my secret stash of supplies. However, I still cast another quick look up and down the alley as I at last reach the door.

When I'm sure that no one has magically appeared out of thin air in the last twenty seconds or so, I pick the lock on the door and then slip inside.

The abandoned building looks exactly the same as it does every time I come here to check my encrypted phone. Broken planks and discarded tools are strewn across the dirty floor. I step over them as I make my way towards the metal box by the wall. Crouching down, I unlock it and then lift the lid.

My black duffel bag is still in there. Undisturbed. Just the way I left it. I unzip it. Several guns, a half dozen passports, and multiple stacks of cash remain neatly piled next to my clothes and the rest of my supplies. But I only reach for the cellphone that I now keep at the top of the bag.

I turn it on and then unlock it with my fingerprint and password.

There is a notification on our dedicated messenger app. While praying to gods I don't believe in that it's the same 'no signs yet' message I have been receiving all other times I've come here, I tap to open the app.

My blood freezes solid in my veins.

They have entered the state.

For a while, all I can do is to stare at that first sentence. My heart hammers in my chest. They have crossed the state line, which means that they're closing in on me.

Fuck, fuck, fuck.

I flick a glance down at my go-bag.

I should make a run for it. I should just grab this right now, get to my car, and disappear. I should—

No. Closing my eyes, I drag in deep breaths and force myself to calm down. There is nothing to suggest that they're coming here because they think I'm here. They're probably coming here to find Rico. Because he actually used to live here in this state as Enrico Morelli too. That's why they're here. To find him. Not me.

Once I have forced my heart to stop trying to crack my ribs, I read the next sentence.

Two people.

That makes sense. They have sent the two people who were with me the night we were supposed to have wiped out most of the Morelli family. They have been sent both as a punishment and a reward. They were supposed to make sure that Rico died that night, and they are in part responsible for the fact that he didn't. So they have been ordered to find him so that they can drag him back and then finish the job. With interest. And to do the same with me. To drag me back to face torture and then death. To exact vengeance for the fact that I dared to disobey.

I read the final part of the message.

Will update as soon as I can pin down a more exact location. Stay alert.

Heaving another deep sigh, I send back 'Received' before turning off the phone again. After I swap out the powerbank for a freshly charged one, I zip up the bag and then close the lid on the box again. The padlock clicks as I snap it into place.

My mind churns as I head back to my car and then drive to another parking lot closer to the city center. As I walk to where I'm supposed to meet Rico, I run through the options in my head.

The Hands of Peace are coming.

There is no mistake about that.

I could run. But there is nowhere for me to run to. They will never think to look for me at Blackwater University. And besides, they're not even here for me. They're here for Rico.

The thought sends a stab of panic through my spine.

Should I warn him? But there is no way to do that without revealing who I really am. And if I tell him the truth about that, things will only get worse. Either he will kill me himself, or he will make such a ruckus about everything that the Hands of Peace will find us both. Which will just end with both of us dead anyway.

Something cold and sharp and slimy twists in my stomach.

So I… what? Just let them waltz right in and kill him?

I shake my head. No. That won't happen. Rico is the sole surviving Morelli heir. His grandfather must have people out looking for them too. They will see my former colleagues coming and protect Rico before anything happens.

Straightening my spine, I nod to myself. Rico is not my problem. My own survival is all that matters.

The words taste sour even in my own mouth.

But I stubbornly block it out as I at last reach the meeting spot. Rico isn't there yet, so I take up position by the glass windows that belong to the closest shop. And then I wait.

I'm half an hour early, but I didn't want to give Rico a chance to somehow track where my car came from.

While I wait, I watch the people stroll along the street. Talking. Laughing. Window shopping. It makes me unreasonably sad. Because I know, in the depths of my nonexistent heart, that I will never be able to do that. Even if I survive the next week, the next year, or the next three years at Blackwater, I will be on the run from the Hands of Peace my entire life.

They will never stop wanting me dead. The best that I can hope for is that the worst intensity of their hunt will gradually fade during the three years I will spend hiding at Blackwater, so that I at least have a shot at making it out of the country afterwards without them finding out. But even then, even if I somehow manage to make it to another country unnoticed, I will still have to live the rest of my life looking over my shoulder. In case they find me.

Bitterness crawls up my throat.

I fucking hate them all and I wish I could just slaughter them all so that I can finally start living. A real life. I would wade through rivers of blood and crawl over corpses for a chance to have a real fucking life.

But it's just a dream. A bloody fairytale. Because I could never go up against the entirety of the Hands of Peace alone and hope to win.

So I tear my gaze from the people strolling along the street and instead glare into the shop window so that I won't have to see their stupid smiling faces.

That is a mistake, because the window belongs to a jewelry shop. Earrings and bracelets and necklaces glitter from swirling silver stands. And there, displayed right in the middle, is a beautiful necklace that makes pain slice through my insides like burning knives.

It's made of silver. A delicate chain leads down to the pendant. In truth, there is nothing particularly remarkable about the pendant. It's just shaped like a ring made of flattened silver. But it still makes me want to shatter the whole glass window just so that I can hear something break. Something other than my heart. Because on that thin flat ring, a name has been engraved.

Isabella.

I feel like the universe itself is mocking me. Tormenting me with what I can't have. What I can't *be*. A real person with a real name.

Heartache and longing tear through my chest as I stare at that necklace. Because by all the gods, I want it. I want that necklace so fucking badly. I want that *life* so fucking badly. A life where I can own things that are mine and mine alone. A life where I don't have to constantly wear someone else's clothes and decorate my home in someone else's style. A real life. My life.

And if I could have that desperate dream, I would begin it by buying *that* necklace. I would change my last name, because I don't like Johnson. I only picked it because it's the second most common last name in the US. But I would keep Isabella. I like the sound of it. And it's the first and only name that I have ever chosen for myself. So I would buy that necklace. And then I would live.

But I can't. Because the Hands of Peace are coming. Two truly vicious hitmen out for blood are now in the same state as me. And if I make one careless mistake, I'm dead.

So after whatever it is that Rico has planned for us tonight, I need to break things off with him.

Apart from my brief visits to check my phone, I can't keep coming into town like this. I can't go out to waffle restaurants. It's too dangerous. Too great a risk of being spotted. I need to stay hidden behind the walls of Blackwater as much as possible.

So this is it. One more date. Then he will either have to let me go completely or go back to trying to drag the truth out of me by force. No in between.

After this, our stolen moments of a shared life, a *real* life, are done.

Enemies once more.

26

RICO

My intention was to get there first so that I could see which direction she came from, but even though I arrive twenty-five minutes early, Isabella is already there. It sends a ripple of amusement, rather than annoyance, through me.

She is staring into a shop window as I approach, and she doesn't turn around when I close the final distance. It feels very unlike her. I frown as I sweep my gaze over the window. But right as I'm about to announce myself, she speaks up.

"You're early," she says, her back still to me.

I give her a knowing look as she at last turns around. "So are you."

"Yes."

For a few seconds, we just stand like that. Holding each other's gaze in silence as if we're confirming to each other that tonight is going to be one of those nights where we don't outright lie to each other, but we don't tell the whole truth either.

All around us, the streetlamps cast pools of glimmering

golden light on the dark cobblestones while people stroll up and down the street. A pleasant murmur hangs in the warm evening air.

"Come on," I say, jerking my chin. "There's something I want to show you."

She falls in beside me as we start down the street. There is little we can say without lying, and we have decided not to lie tonight, so we just walk in silence. But I steal glances at her, watching the way she studies the area and the people around her. Watching the way her hair ripples when she moves. The way her eyes glitter every time we pass under a streetlight.

I lead her away from the busy city center and in the direction of one of the more rundown parts. Her shoulders tense slightly when she realizes that, and she flicks a quick glance at me. I suppress a laugh. What does she think I'm going to do? Lead her down a back alley and jump her with a broken bottle?

I wait for her to ask me about it.

She doesn't.

So we walk in silence until we've crossed the edge between the rundown part and the much nicer one that we have passed through now. I take a left between two tall buildings. And then we're there.

Isabella raises her eyebrows in surprise as we walk right into a park. Slowing her pace, she looks from side to side. And I know what she sees. Because I thought the same thing the first time I came here.

It's not a well-manicured lawn with park benches and wide paths for strolling. Quite the opposite. It's packed with trees and bushes that rise like a wall of leaves, obscuring the rest of the park. It's wild. Overgrown. And very out of place here.

The tall buildings press right up against the edges of the park. As if the original plan was to raze the park to the ground so that the houses could be built instead, only for someone to change their mind at the last minute and decide to keep both the buildings and the park.

"I never knew that there was something like this here," Isabella says at last, sounding genuinely surprised.

I give her a smile. "Most people don't."

She follows me as I start into the vegetation. There are no streetlamps to light the path inside the park, so we have to move carefully as we walk farther in. Thick, gnarly roots grow across the narrow paths that were frequently used once upon a time but which have now been left for nature to reclaim. I push aside a low-hanging branch as I lead Isabella deeper into the dark trees.

Even though I can almost feel the questions brewing on her tongue, she says nothing. Only follows me in silence. It's not lost on me that she is putting quite a lot of trust in me right now. But I don't point that out. And neither does she.

At last, we reach the spot I was aiming for. Ducking down under a tangled web of branches, I motion for Isabella to do the same. She moves effortlessly underneath it and then straightens beside me on the other side.

She sucks in a breath. It's not a gasp. It's barely more than a rapid intake of breath. But it's more surprise than I have ever heard from her.

"This is… beautiful," she says, breathless, as she stares out at the view before her.

My heart aches as I let my gaze sweep across it as well.

We're standing in front of a large pond. Thick trees and bushes stretch out on all sides, framing it with rustling leaves and blooming night flowers. And because it's so far from any light source, the stars in the dark sky above are reflected in the water like silver stardust.

"Yes, it is," I reply. That ache in my heart intensifies. But it's a good ache. One that is filled with warm memories. "I have always loved coming here. Because it looks like a piece of the night sky has been placed here. Hidden by the trees in the middle of the city. Like a secret treasure."

Tearing her gaze from the pond, she turns to look at me instead. Her eyes are wide and her mouth slightly open as she stares at me, looking lost for words.

A soft smile drifts over my lips. "I've always liked the stars. And that special scent that nature gets during the night." I look out at the pond again. "What do you like?"

"I don't know." Her gaze doesn't travel back to the pond. Instead, she continues watching the side of my face. "I've never thought about it."

And the raw honesty in those words makes a piece of my heart crack. She doesn't even know what she likes. How can she not know? How can she never even have considered what she does and doesn't like?

I turn back to Isabella, meeting her gaze head on again.

Who is this girl? And what kind of life has she led up until now?

"I used to come here with my parents," I find myself saying.

She flinches. It's a barely perceptible stiffening of her posture. And if I hadn't been watching her so closely, I wouldn't have seen it.

"It used to be their secret spot," I continue. "When they first started dating. And then when I was born, they shared it with me too."

Pain bleeds from my heart at the memory. I haven't been

back here since the night they were killed. Just like everything I used to do before that night, I was never allowed to go back again. In case the assassins were watching it. Lying in wait to finish the job.

This place, this pond in the middle of an overgrown park, used to be such an important part of my life. And yet, this is the first time I have seen it in six years. Six years of stripping away everything that used to be a part of me. Six years of living a fake life. Six years…

"And now," Isabella begins with a strange strain in her voice, "you've shared it with me."

I hold her gaze. Starlight glitters in her eyes, adding a silver shimmer to that stunning color.

"Yes," I reply simply.

She draws in a ragged breath. But she doesn't ask me why. And I don't tell her.

Instead, I turn back to the pond. "Did you ever do something like this with your parents?"

For a few seconds, she just continues staring at the side of my face. Then she turns and gazes out at the pond as well. "No."

Silence falls over us like a silk sheet. In the bushes around us, insects perform their nightly serenades and a few birds flutter between the trees. Leaves rustle as a warm wind caresses the branches. But the surface of the pond remains still as a mirror, reflecting those glittering stars back at us.

"Thank you," Isabella says. She swallows thickly. "For sharing this place with me."

I can't make my tongue work, so I just nod in acknowledgement.

For a long while, we just stand there side by side. Watching the starlight above and below. Listening to the humming insects and the rustling leaves. Breathing in the scent of blooming night flowers.

I know that I have already said too much. Shown her too much. Given her too much honesty. *Again*. But I still can't stop myself as I ask one more question.

Keeping my eyes on the pond, I draw in an unsteady breath. "Do you ever feel like everyone who looks at you knows exactly who you are, but when you're all alone, all you can do is to just stare at your own reflection in the mirror and wonder how the hell you've managed to fool everyone?"

"Because they only ever see the carefully constructed façade you're showing them, but in reality, you have no idea who you are anymore," she finishes, her eyes also on the dark water before us.

A shudder ripples through my soul at how dead-on her words are. "Yeah."

"Yeah," she echoes.

I don't say anything else. Because I can't. And I know she can't either.

So we just stand there.

And watch the stars.

27

ISABELLA

Since the Hands of Peace are in the state, I have to check my communications every day now instead of a couple of times a week. Yesterday, there was no news. Hopefully, today will be the same.

I glance towards the tall building that runs along the left side of the street as I walk through this rundown part of town. On the other side of it is an overgrown park. And until two days ago, I had no idea. It's not on any of the maps, and the opening between this building and the other one is so narrow that it can't even be classified as a path.

My gaze drifts towards the road coming up on my right. This is only two streets away from where I keep my go-bag.

At first, I thought that that was why Rico was taking me here. Because he had somehow figured out where my secret hiding place is, and was going to confront me about it. I had been plotting ways to neutralize him and escape when he instead led me into that park.

Pain pulses through my chest in a short sharp burst.

Why did he have to show me that park? Why did he have

to share that place and those heartbreakingly honest words with me? It made me feel like a real person for a moment. And for that one moment, I didn't feel lonely anymore. I felt like I had found someone who truly saw me for who I really am.

But then that moment ended. And now I feel even more empty than before.

With great effort, I block out the cracks spidering through my heart and instead focus on my task. I need to know if the Hands of Peace have reached the city.

After picking the lock on the door, I slink inside and pull it shut behind me again. A rusted hammer lets out a metallic grinding sound as I push it aside with my boot while striding across the room. I quickly unlock the padlock on the box and then open it.

My heart is pattering in my chest as I turn on my phone.

One new notification.

Dread seeps through my bones like cold water.

Fuck.

No news is good news. So if there is news, it means that it's bad news.

While bracing myself, I open the messenger app.

They have been spotted. Here.

I click the embedded link, which brings up a map with a red pin in it. I stare at that red dot. It's a small town just a few miles away from here.

Exiting the map, I go back to the message.

Today (Friday) at 07.34.

Which means that they were spotted in that small town this morning. It has been more than twelve ours since then.

The message ends with another one-word embedded link.

Photo.

I click on it.

A slightly grainy photo that looks to be from an ATM pops up on my screen. It shows a woman in her sixties. But behind her shoulder, across the street from the ATM, two people are walking down the road.

My mouth goes dry.

Fuck.

It really is them.

I hurriedly send back 'Received' and then toss the phone back into my bag. I won't need to check that anymore now. If they were in that small town early this morning, it's only a matter of time before they show up in this city.

From now on, I will need to stay at Blackwater the entire time. No more trips into the city. No more visits to restaurants outside. All of my time will now be spent either on campus for class, or in my apartment in the residential area. Nowhere else.

Rising to my feet, I'm just about to flip the lid shut again when I hesitate.

For a few seconds, I only stare down at the pile of guns inside the duffel bag.

Bringing one to campus will draw attention. Especially if the university staff, or Rico, finds out. But on the other hand, it might be crucial to my survival.

And survival trumps everything.

So I bend down and snatch up a gun along with two extra magazines before closing and locking the box again. Then I hurry back to my car.

But as I start it, another wave of hesitation washes over me. And this time, for an absolutely ridiculous, illogical reason.

The necklace. This is the last time I will go into the city for weeks. Months, probably. And I just… I just need to see that necklace one more time. To really commit it to memory. Of what could have been if things were different.

Driving over to the other parking lot, I quickly park my car and then walk to that store at the fastest pace I can without drawing attention. I know that I'm being stupid. That I'm taking an unnecessary risk by lingering in town longer than I absolutely have to. But I just… I just need to see it.

It's Friday evening, so the streets are filled with people in fancy clothes heading out to different bars and nightclubs. I weave through them, my pulse thrumming in my ears, until I at last reach that large glass window.

The whole world seems to stop for a second as I stare at that display in the middle. The chattering and music go silent. The moving people freeze mid-step. The very air comes to a halt.

Because the necklace has already been sold.

Those cracks in my heart spread.

Of course it has. Of course it has already been sold. Because yet again, the universe is mocking me, *tormenting* me, with everything I can't have.

Bitterness and heartache clog my throat as I stare at the empty jewelry display for another second. Then I forcefully swallow all of those emotions and stalk away.

It doesn't matter. It was just a necklace. And coming here was stupid anyway.

I have to remind myself not to stomp as I walk back towards my car. I'm so bitter and annoyed at myself that I almost miss it. Miss that faint feeling. But an entire life spent as an assassin thankfully leads to senses that can't be overshadowed by temporary anger.

Halfway to my car, the back of my neck prickles.

My heart leaps into my throat, but I force myself to keep walking normally.

I'm being followed.

I pull up my mental map of these streets, searching for a place that will work. If I remember correctly, there is a narrow alley between the back of two restaurants two streets to my left. It's secluded enough to afford some privacy, but not so far off that it's completely empty.

Taking the next left, I set course towards it.

Those eyes that I can feel boring into my back follow me.

The moment I round the corner, I sprint down the street in order to increase the distance between us. Once I estimate that my pursuers should be reaching the corner as well, I slow to a walk again.

Because of my head start, I now reach the next corner almost before they have rounded the first one.

Just as I had guessed, it takes me into a narrow alley between the back of two restaurants. It's dark and deserted, and the smell of food drifts out of a metallic vent set into the brick wall. I sprint towards it.

With a quick jump, I grab that vent and pull myself up on the roof. Using the raised edge for cover, I crawl along the flat stone roof and back towards the mouth of the alley that I came in through.

Faint footsteps sound from below.

They stop as they reach the opening where I was earlier as well. Then one pair starts down the alley. A few seconds later, the second pair of footsteps do the same.

I quickly swing myself over the edge of the roof and drop down.

The moment my feet land, the man halfway down the alley whips around and aims a gun in my direction.

But the second man is too late, because my gun is already pressing against the back of his neck before he can turn towards me as well.

"Don't," I warn when his hand drifts down to where I know he keeps his own gun concealed.

He stops moving, keeping his arms slightly out from his body and his hands spread. He knows that I can and will shoot him if he tries anything.

"Hello, Anna," the man halfway down the alley says, his sharp brown eyes locked on me as he continues staring me down from behind the barrel of his gun.

Anna was the name I went by at the time the Hands of Peace found out that Rico was still alive.

"Derek," I reply.

It was the name that he went by before I had to flee. I have no idea if he has changed it since then. But it doesn't matter. None of the names are real anyway.

"I suggest you put down your gun and come with us willingly," Derek says, his voice hard.

He had wavy brown hair last time I saw him. Now, his hair is cropped close to his scalp in a military style cut. It's still dark, though, so I assume he hasn't dyed it as well. He is in his forties, and I've been on several missions with him throughout the years. He's good. But most of all, he's ruthless. If I were to do as he says and come willingly, he would still torture me.

"I suggest you lower your gun before I shoot Sebastian in the head," I retort.

Sebastian, or whatever name he goes by right now, doesn't even flinch. He is taller than me and in his thirties. He isn't as overtly cruel as Derek can be, but he's vicious enough that I never want him anywhere near me with a set of tools. So I keep my gun firmly pressed against the straight blond hair the falls down his head and covers his neck.

"If you shoot him, you lose your human shield," Derek says. "Which means that I can then shoot you."

He is right, of course. So I don't reply.

For a few seconds, silence falls over the alley like a death shroud. Only the humming of the air vent breaks it.

"Where is he?" Derek demands eventually.

"Where is who?" I reply.

"Don't play stupid, Anna. It's beneath you."

I just stare back at him in silence.

"Where is Enrico Morelli?" he growls at last.

"I don't know."

"Of course you do. It's why you're here, isn't it? You've come to rectify your mistake in the hopes that we might let you live if you finish the job now."

I neither confirm nor deny anything.

Impatience flickers in Derek's eyes. "Where is he?"

I just continue watching him in silence.

"Tell you what," he begins. "If you give me Enrico Morelli's location, I will put in a good word with the Master. I'll even try to convince him to skip the hundred days of torture before your execution."

"That's a generous offer."

"It is."

"But I still can't take you up on it. Because I don't know where he is."

"Liar."

Voices come from down the street behind my back.

Relief washes through me. *At last.*

"FIRE!" I scream at the top of my lungs. "Help! There's a fire!"

Cries of alarm erupt from the people down the street. A second later, pounding footsteps sound as they race towards me.

A snarl rips from Derek's throat as he starts backing away down the alley. "There will be a reckoning for this, Anna. For your betrayal and for the six years you spent covering it up."

I don't bother replying. Instead, I shove Sebastian forward and sprint out of the alley one second before a mass of people come skidding into it with the intention of helping put out my fake fire.

While hiding my gun, I race through the streets and back to my car before Derek and Sebastian can pick up my trail.

My heart pounds in my chest the entire way back to Blackwater.

It's only when I have locked my apartment door behind me again that I'm able to force my thundering pulse to slow down a fraction. If I stay at Blackwater, I should be fine. Now that they have found me, they will assume that I will get the hell out of this city and this state as fast as possible. They would never even consider that I would risk remaining here now that they know where I am.

So I will stay at Blackwater. And everything will be fine.

I repeat those two sentences to myself over and over again while I stand there in the dark, leaning my forehead against the now locked door.

Once I at least half believe it, I drag in a deep breath and turn around. I flip the light switch by the door. Warm light floods my apartment.

I suck in a sharp breath and yank out my gun as I notice a small package on my kitchen table. Thinking that it might be a bomb, I slowly edge forward. But I know that I'm being too paranoid, that I'm too tense after the run-in with the

Hands of Peace, because the package is far too small to be a bomb.

Placing my gun on the table, I lean forward slightly and study the tiny box. It's dark blue, no bigger than my palm, and has a white ribbon tied around it.

Very carefully, I pull open the ribbon and lift the lid.

There is a note on top.

I saw you looking at it, and I agree. It really would look great on you. Rico.

A strained laugh full of both exasperation and relief rips from my chest. Of course this is Rico's doing. Who else would break into my apartment like this and leave a strange box on my table?

Dragging a hand through my hair, I blow out a long breath before reaching for the note so that I can move it aside and see what's in the box and find out what kind of wicked game Rico is playing now. Given our conversation on the phone the other day, it's probably a pair of miniature handcuffs.

The note slips from my fingers the moment I have moved it aside.

It flutters down to land on the table while I just stand there, staring into the box.

A silver necklace sits there on a small blue cushion.

The necklace.

I draw in an unsteady breath as I reach in and trace my fingers along the delicate chain and then over the small silver circle where *Isabella* has been engraved.

A sob tears from my throat.

Gently gripping the necklace, I hold it up. It glints in the warm light from the lamp above.

I stagger over to the counter, throwing out a hand to brace myself. But it's not enough.

My knees buckle and I slide down the front of the counter until I hit the floor. With my back pressed against the cabinet door behind me, I draw my knees up to my chest as another violent sob escapes my chest.

Clutching the necklace in my hand, I press that closed fist hard against my chest. Cracks are forming all over my heart now. Like brittle glass underneath a sledgehammer.

I tighten my grip on the necklace as I hold it over my heart. As if that can somehow stop if from shattering behind my ribs.

Another broken sob rips from me.

I slap my other hand over my mouth.

My shoulders shake. My whole body shakes.

I can't even remember the last time I cried like this.

But I cry now.

I cry so hard that my chest aches and my hands go numb. I cry until I fear that I will never be able to pick up all the broken pieces of myself. I cry until I can't feel anything at all anymore.

Because Rico gave me the necklace.

He gave me the beginning of the dream that can never be mine.

28

RICO

When I walk into my grandfather's mansion, the tension is so thick that I could've cut it with a knife. Andrea didn't even let me walk in alone this time. Instead, he left the car at the curb and escorted me all the way to the upstairs study. Only when he had knocked on the door and announced us did he finally leave.

I watch him retreat down the hall while Federico calls through the door for me to come inside. Narrowing my eyes, I turn back to the door and push down the handle. I have a bad feeling about this, but I still walk inside with a confident posture.

"Enrico," my grandfather says. He is not smiling this time. "Have a seat."

God, I have a really, *really*, bad feeling about this.

Federico is sitting behind his grand mahogany desk, his back straight and his hands steepled before him. I cross the room and then lower myself into the chair opposite him.

"You're moving back here today," he announces without preamble. "As soon as we're finished here, Andrea will return to the house you share with the Hunters and retrieve all your belongings."

I jerk back in my seat. "No."

"It's not a discussion, Enrico."

"No, it's not. Because we've already had this discussion weeks ago. And we agreed that it was better if I stayed at Blackwater, because this house is the first place they will look if they come back—"

"It's not an *if* anymore," he interrupts, his voice still hard but now also laced with an undercurrent of panic. "They're back."

Blinking, I sit back in my chair again.

"They were spotted in a small town a few miles from here yesterday morning." He holds my gaze. "Two of them. The two men. There are still no signs of the girl your age who you said got cold feet that night."

Got cold feet. That was what I told them. That was how I explained what Isabella did that night. Because how else was I supposed to explain it? *I* don't even fully understand what happened back then.

"But we will find her too," Federico finishes.

Guilt twists my insides. I have already found her. And I've been keeping it a secret for weeks now. I'm *still* keeping it a secret.

"Are you sure it's them?" I ask. "The two men. We only caught them partially on one camera in the dark. How can you be sure it's them?"

"It's them."

"How can you be certain—"

He slams his palm down on the desk, making the pens clatter in alarm. "Because I've been searching for the bastards who killed *my son* for six years. I know that it's them. And you are coming home to live here now." Desperation leaks into his voice. "Because I cannot lose you too. Do you hear me?"

My heart aches at the pain written all over his usually so composed and stern face.

Heaving a long sigh, I meet his gaze with soft eyes. "If you truly want to keep me safe, you need to let me return to Blackwater. I know that you're scared…"

He huffs and flicks his gaze to the side, as if the great patriarch of the feared Morelli family could never even consider admitting that he was scared.

"But it is the best place, the safest place, for me to be right now," I finish.

"I want you here. With me."

"And here is exactly where they will look for me. They will never think to search for me at Blackwater."

He clenches his jaw. I just keep holding his gaze with soft eyes, silently praying that he will see reason. If he decides to keep me here, there is nothing I can do about it. Because no one disobeys the head of the Morelli family. Not even me.

"Then I want you surrounded by guards," he says at last.

Relief flickers through me, but I keep it firmly off my face as I reply, "I can't have guards following me around campus. It would be like erecting a giant flashing sign pointing straight at me."

"Around the house then at least."

"In civilian clothes and undercover, in that case."

"Yes."

I nod. "Deal."

He smiles faintly then.

Raising my eyebrows, I ask, "What?"

"This was not a negotiation, and yet you managed to turn

it into one." He gives me an approving look. "You will make a great king when I'm gone."

My heart twists. "Don't say that. You're not dying yet."

"No. But with my illness—"

"You will beat that. You will be fine. It will all be fine."

Another smile drifts over his lips. "Now who is doing the excessive worrying?"

I huff out a short laugh.

"I will see you soon, my boy," he says, and then nods towards the door, giving me permission to leave.

I incline my head before getting to my feet and leaving the study.

Uneasiness slithers through my stomach as I descend the stairs towards where Andrea is waiting.

The people who killed my parents are here. Just a few miles away. I can't draw this out any longer.

No more dancing around each other. I need the truth. It's time to confront Isabella once and for all. I have waited six long years to ask these questions.

I will have my answers.

And I will have them now.

29

ISABELLA

Dread pools in my stomach before I even open the door. Rico is standing there in the corridor outside when I do, his face serious.

"We need to talk," he says.

"Yes, we do," I reply.

Stepping aside, I motion for him to come in. He keeps that serious expression on his features as he walks into my living room while I close the door behind him. Then I move until I'm standing in front of him.

For a few seconds, no one speaks. Outside my windows, a car blares past on the street below.

"It's time to stop," Rico announces at last.

"I agree."

"You need to stop pretending and tell me the truth," he says at the same time as I say, "You need to stop coming here and leave me alone."

He draws back in surprise. I do too.

"What?" we say in unison.

Shaking my head, I recover first. "Enough of this. I know

that you're only pretending to like me because you're trying to get me to tell you something that I don't know. But it's time to stop now. The waffle dinner, the park, the necklace. Playing with my heart like this is cruel. And you need to stop."

He flinches. Actually *flinches*. His mouth drops open as he just stares at me for a moment.

"You think *I'm* playing with you?" he blurts out eventually. "You're the one who is playing with me!"

"I'm not playing with you! I'm not that girl from your past. No matter how much you try to force me to be, I'm not her. And you need to accept that and leave me alone now."

"Six years!" The words rip out of his throat as he stabs a hand towards the windows. "I have waited six years for these answers."

"And I'm sorry for that. I'm sorry for whatever happened to you and that girl. But I don't *have* the answers that you're looking for." I point at the door. "Now, get out."

Without waiting for an answer, I turn on my heel and stalk towards the kitchen. I only make it a few steps before Rico's hand wraps around my wrist, spinning me back around.

"Don't you walk away from me," he growls. "We're not done—"

"Yes, we are," I snap back at him, yanking my wrist out of his grip. "Because we didn't even start. You and me, we were never real. Everything you did was done solely to fool me into thinking you care about me. And I went along with it because I needed to survive your damn attempts to force me to tell you something that I don't know. None of it was real and we both know it."

His dark eyes sharpen. "None of it was real, huh? You know that's a lie."

"Get out."

"Look me in the eye, Isabella, and tell me that it was all fake. Every single thing between us."

An involuntary shudder rolls down my spine at the way he says my name. Gritting my teeth, I block it out and instead stab a hand towards the door. "Get. Out."

"Tell me it was fake."

Closing the distance between us, I try to physically push him towards the door while all of the emotions that I'm trying so desperately to keep buried are surging up inside me like an unstoppable flood.

"Isabella," he says, and my name is a plea on his tongue.

For a moment, the entire world stops while that desperate battle wages inside me.

Then I shove him up against the wall and crush my lips against his.

He grabs the back of my neck, holding me pressed hard against him while I steal that dangerous name that I can never let him speak again from his troublesome damn mouth.

Burying my fists in the collar of his shirt, I kiss him with such furious anger that I can feel fire licking through my veins. He kisses me back with equal frustration.

I slide my hands down his chest, crumpling his shirt in my hands as I grip the dark fabric and yank it upwards. He tears his lips from mine while reaching down to the shirt that is now bunched halfway up his stomach. His chest heaves as he yanks the shirt over his head and throws it aside.

Then he grabs the collar of my shirt.

And rips it open.

Heat sears through me, and I suck in a gasp as I stare back at him. He pushes the ruined garment off my shoulders, letting it flutter to the ground, but then freezes in place.

The silver necklace gleams on my naked chest now that the shirt is no longer covering it.

A storm of emotions whirl through Rico's eyes as he stares down at it.

My heart pounds wildly in my chest, and I can't handle the emotions I see in his eyes, so I quickly unbutton my shorts and shove them down instead.

That snaps Rico out of his stupor. Shaking his head, he lets his hands drift down to his pants instead.

His belt clinks as he unbuckles it while I strip out of my underwear.

The moment I'm naked, I grab the back of Rico's neck and yank him towards me even though he hasn't even pulled his pants down yet. Sliding my hand down, I wrap my fingers around his hard cock.

A dark moan escapes his chest as I free his cock and run my hand up and down the thick shaft.

I flash him a look brimming with challenge.

His eyes darken. Then he flips us around so that I'm standing with my back to the wall instead. Taking my thigh in a punishing grip, he hoists my leg up and then presses closer. His other hand wraps around my wrist.

With his eyes locked on mine, he forces my hand away from his cock and up over my shoulder. He pins it against the wall next to my head. Keeping me like that with one leg up and my hand trapped to the wall, he holds my gaze.

His cock brushes my entrance.

A question and a challenge dance in those dark eyes of his.

I just stare right back at him.

He slams into me.

This time, it's me who lets out a deep moan.

After pulling out slightly, he thrusts his cock in deeper. I moan again as he sheaths himself fully inside me, filling me completely.

His fingers dig into my thigh as he holds my leg up while starting up a hard pace. I slide my free hand around the back of his neck and yank his mouth back to mine. Our lips meet in a violent clash. I kiss him hard, angrily, biting his lip and trying to force his tongue into submission while he rams his cock into me with dominant thrusts.

We fuck like we're fighting a war.

He rails me as if he's trying to fuck the defiance right out of me.

And I slam my hips right back against his and dominate his mouth as if I can fuck the stubbornness right out of him too.

Pleasure builds inside me. But it's not sweet or gentle. It's a thrumming lightning storm filled with anger and frustration and lies and truths that we can never share and terrible, terrible, desperation.

My back hits the wall as Rico pounds into me.

I gasp into his mouth as his cock hits the perfect spot over and over again.

The swirling storm of release pulses inside me, threatening to rip my body apart if it stays trapped any longer.

I bite his bottom lip.

It draws a desperate moan from deep within his chest.

Release explodes through me.

I throw my head back, gasping in air as lightning bolts crackle through my every limb. Rico keeps fucking me through it, making the pleasure soar even higher. I can feel him about to come as well.

But then he stops.

A growl rips from me.

Oh, I don't fucking think so. He is not going to walk away the only victor in this war.

The moment that the final remnants of the orgasm have finished sweeping through me, I yank my wrist out of his grip and slam my leg back down. Rico takes a step back, and I use that moment to give him a shove. He stumbles backwards a few steps, bumping into the kitchen table. I stalk after him.

Or I try to, at least. My legs are still a bit unsteady, so it looks a lot less powerful than I would've liked. As if Rico can see right through me, he smiles.

I flash him a sharp smile as I reach him and wrap my hand around his still hard cock. Then I start lowering myself to my knees. Let's see how long he can hold out with my lips around his cock.

But before I can even get halfway down, Rico's hand shoots out and locks around my throat. With a firm grip, he pulls me back to my feet.

"Oh, I don't think so," he says, smirking at me. "You're the one insisting that everything between us is fake, which means that you're the one who gets fucked until you admit that this part, if nothing else, is at least real."

While still keeping his hand around my throat, he sweeps his other arm under my ass and lifts me up on to the kitchen table. Then he spreads my thighs and steps in between them. His still hard cock brushes over my pussy. I sit there, my legs spread wide, and stare back at him.

"It's not real," I declare, my voice coming out more stubborn and petty than I meant it to.

He slides his other hand up my thigh and towards my hip. Taking my it in a firm grip, he moves even closer, slowly pushing his cock inside me.

"It's not real," I repeat.

Keeping one hand on my hip and the other around my throat, he slowly slides all the way inside. Because of the angle it creates when I'm sitting on the table, his cock rubs against my sensitive clit with every excruciatingly slow inch. A shudder of pleasure ripples through me at the sensation.

With his commanding eyes locked on me, he pulls back out.

And then slams in again.

A groan rips from my throat.

Reaching up, I wrap both hands around his forearm. The muscles shift and the veins become more prominent as he flexes his fingers around my throat.

"It *is* real," he says.

I open my mouth to retort. But before I can, he thrusts into me again. I let out something between a moan and a whimper as he starts up a brutal pace.

The table rocks underneath me as Rico fucks me with merciless dominance.

Pleasure surges up inside me again.

Clenching my jaw, I dig my fingers into his forearm as I try to hold back the tide of pleasure now mounting inside me. Rico just stares me down with hard eyes as he continues fucking me into oblivion. Power and utter command pulse from his muscular body with each thrust.

Heat pools inside me at the sight.

Fucking hell, he is a damn work of art. And he's even more glorious those times when his face is flooded with pleasure as release crashes through him. As *I* make release crash through him.

The table scrapes against the floor as Rico slams into me, but his hand on my hip keeps me steady.

My heart thuds in my chest. Wild. Out of control.

I gasp in deep breaths as the mounting tension reaches even greater heights. I'm tumbling headfirst towards another orgasm. And Rico is just staring down at me with demanding eyes, knowing damn well that there is nothing I can do to stop it.

His movements become a little harder. A little faster. Making his shaft rub against my clit with every thrust, adding to the already mind-numbing friction that his cock creates inside me.

Violent thrumming tension ripples through my whole soul.

My chest heaves.

A breathless scream tears from my chest as release crashes over me. My legs tremble on the tabletop, and I dig my fingers even harder into Rico's forearm. He doesn't even react.

He just keeps fucking me through the orgasm, making spears of pleasure shoot up and down my spine with each thrust, until he is close to his own release.

And then he starts slowing down again.

"No," I gasp, suddenly desperate to see that incredible look of pleasure on his face. "I want to watch you come."

"Then tell me that it's real," he demands.

I clench my jaw.

He slows his pace even more.

Frustration rips through me.

"Alright!" I scream into his face. "It's real. The sex is real." The moment the words are out of my mouth, emotions start flooding my chest again. And even I can hear the terrible desperation in my voice as I repeat, "It's real. The sex is so fucking real that I can barely breathe."

Even though I didn't mean that he was physically cutting

off my air with his hand, he releases his grip on my throat and instead slides it around the back of my neck. His pace picks up again.

While pounding into me and finally chasing his own release, he pulls my face to his and kisses me with such heartbreaking gentleness that I almost start sobbing again.

"I know," he breathes against my lips as he breaks the kiss.

It's barely more than a whisper, but it still makes those damn cracks in my heart start spreading again. But before the ache can take over too much, Rico reaches the edge of his own release.

I study every inch of his face, drinking in every flicker of emotion on his lethally handsome features, as pleasure washes over him. I commit it to memory and bury it deep inside my fracturing heart. Because *I* did that. I put those emotions in his eyes. I made him feel all of that.

When at last that wonderous look on his face fades and he gasps in a deep breath, I feel a pang of sadness in my chest.

Because I know that it was the last time that I will ever see him like that.

Instead of pulling out straight away, Rico leans forward and rests his forehead against mine. My throat thickens. Closing my eyes, I let him rest his forehead against mine like that while I allow myself one moment to just feel everything.

Then I draw back and drag in a breath to steady myself.

Rico straightens. His eyes remain on mine for a long second before he slowly pulls out and takes a step back. The belt clinks faintly into the dead silence as he pulls his pants back up fully and buckles his belt again.

"This changes nothing," I say. "We're still done."

"Oh, you and I are far from done, Isabella."

Another shudder ripples down my spine when he says my name. I ignore it.

Making a split-second decision, I reach up and pull the necklace off. My throat closes up and my hand shakes a little, but I have already made this choice so it's too late to change my mind now.

"Here," I say, holding out the necklace to him. "Take this and then leave."

His features soften a fraction.

I steel myself as he reaches towards my open palm. It's better this way anyway. The necklace would only be a reminder of the life I can never have.

But even though I try to convince myself of that, I know that it's going to hurt like hell to watch him take that necklace from me.

Because that necklace is the only thing that has ever truly been mine.

All my life, I have never owned anything. My clothes, my weapons, everything, has come from a shared pool of resources that anyone can use. Because owning something is the first step to creating an identity. A real identity. And ghosts do not have those.

So to give away the only thing that has truly been mine and mine alone will break me more than I want to admit.

But it's not just that.

It's what the necklace symbolizes. A dream, a hope, that this fragile thing between us could somehow be real.

Panic crackles through my soul because *he* almost made me believe that it could be real. He made me feel things. Made me think, for just one second, that maybe I could have a life. A real life. And it scares the hell out of me because I know that I can't.

So to have this reminder that Rico knows me well enough to notice me looking at the necklace, and to then buy it for me as a gift, will only be a painful reminder of the delusions that I almost started to believe.

And yet, that sharp ache still slices through my chest as Rico reaches for the necklace.

But he doesn't take it.

Instead, he places his hand over mine, curling my fingers back around the silver necklace. There is a sad smile on his lips as he pulls his hand back.

"It was a gift. Keep it."

Then he turns around, picks up his shirt from the floor, and walks out the door.

30

RICO

A storm of emotions swirls behind my ribs as I stalk through the residential area at the crack of dawn. I can be such a fucking coward sometimes. I went to Isabella's apartment last night determined to confront her once and for all. But then she tried to break up with me, as if we were some kind of normal couple. And worse, she tried to tell me that none of those stolen moments we have shared these past few weeks have been real.

And I just… lost it.

How could she even suggest that all of it was fake? That it was all pretend? When those moments with her were the most real I have ever felt.

But then I saw that she was wearing the necklace that I gave her, and I *knew* that she was yet again lying to me. So I threw aside my plan to confront her about her real identity and instead focused it all on getting her to admit that at least one part of what we'd had was real.

I went there to confront her about the night my parents

were murdered, but instead, I fucked her and then left. Like a bloody coward. Because there were just too many conflicting emotions whirling through me.

There are *still* too many conflicting emotions whirling through me.

But I can't afford to feel any of that anymore, so I force myself to block it all out.

I know what I need to do in order to get my answers.

In truth, I have *always* known what I need to do. But I just haven't been able to bring myself to do it.

Isabella will never willingly tell me what I want to know. She will never trust me. And I will never be able to trick her into telling me either. I could also torment and torture her endlessly, but I know that she would never break. None of those methods would work.

There is only one way to make her answer my questions truthfully. One way to break that iron will of hers. And it's time to do it.

It's time to stop behaving like Rico Hunter and to become Enrico Morelli for a day.

Raising my fist, I pound on the door of a house three streets away from ours.

Nothing happens.

I bang my fist against the door again.

A light comes on in one of the upstairs windows. It's not even six o'clock yet on a Sunday morning, so the guy who lives here was no doubt asleep.

Pounding on the door again, I tell him to hurry the fuck up.

At last, lights are turned on in the hallway inside as well. Then the lock clicks and the door is shoved open to reveal a blond man wearing only a white t-shirt and a pair of blue boxers.

"What the fuck do you think you're..." he begins before trailing off. His eyes go wide when he realizes who I am, and he curses himself under his breath. Then he clears his throat before speaking in a much more respectful voice. "Hunter."

"Jacques Lefevere," I say.

It's a statement, not a question, because he's a senior like me so I already know who he is. But he answers anyway.

"Yes," he replies, somehow making that sound more like a question.

"The upcoming annual tournament," I begin, keeping my voice hard and emotionless. "You have a first-year called Isabella Johnson on your team, correct?"

His face scrunches up and he looks to the side for a moment, as if he is running through the names and faces of his team members. Then he meets my gaze again and raises his eyebrows. "The brown-haired chick who doesn't really have any noteworthy skills?"

"Yes."

He nods. "Yeah, she's on my team."

"Team training starts tomorrow."

When I don't immediately elaborate, Jacques flicks a hesitant glance from side to side and then replies, "Yes."

"Where are you taking your team?"

"Gun range. The small one close to the lake."

"Good. Tell everyone else on your team that that's where you're meeting. Everyone except Isabella Johnson."

He frowns. "Why?"

I arch a pointed brow.

Clearing his throat, he hurriedly amends it to, "What should I tell her instead?"

"Take her to the forest. You know that small clearing by the rock wall?"

"Yeah?"

"You will personally make sure that she gets there. Make up whatever story you like about why you're there. But you get her to that location. And then you leave and go back to your team at the gun range."

Uncertainty swirls in his gray eyes, and it looks like he wants to ask more questions, but all he says is, "Okay."

"And Jacques?"

I pause, making the silence stretch until he is shifting his weight uncomfortably. Letting a bit more of Enrico Morelli shine through, I stare him down with commanding eyes.

"Yes?" he asks nervously.

"If you linger instead of going straight back to the gun range, I will shoot you in the head." It's not even a threat. Just a simple statement of facts. "Understood?"

He must realize how dead serious I am about that, because his face pales slightly. "I understand."

"Good. Make sure she's there tomorrow afternoon, or I will come after you instead."

"She'll be there. I swear."

"Excellent." A smile that is more threat than anything else slides across my mouth. "Have a good Sunday."

Before he can reply, I turn around and stalk back to the street. Rolling my shoulders, I straighten my spine as I start back towards our house.

I draw in a deep breath to block out the last remnants of those inconvenient feelings that I have for Isabella. The time for half-measures and talk is over. It's time for answers. It's time to do what I should have done the moment I saw her.

Releasing a long exhale, I watch the first faint light of dawn push the darkness away from the horizon.

The decision is made and now the plan is in motion.

Tomorrow, I will show Isabella why she really should have killed me that night six years ago.

31

ISABELLA

Even though I'm fairly confident that Derek and Sebastian are in fact not lurking in these woods, I still remain alert and discreetly sweep my gaze back and forth as I follow Jacques, the third-year who is the informal leader of our team, deeper into the forest outside Blackwater.

"We'll be doing several short tests in here today," he says.

I quickly shift my attention to him instead. "Okay."

"I need to get a sense of where everyone's skill level is at before we can start training for real, so I need to see how well you all can actually handle yourselves in the woods."

Which means that I need to quickly figure out the rules and scope of these tests so that I can make a plan for how to complete them in the most average way possible.

"That makes sense," I reply before adding casually, "What will the tests be like?"

"I'll fill you in before each one."

Damn it. Then I will need to improvise before each one. But since I can't show any irritation, I just shrug. "Alright."

We continue in silence.

Thick gray clouds cover the sky today, painting the forest in bleak hues. But it thankfully doesn't look like it's going to rain. Or at least, it didn't when we went into the forest. In here, the canopy is so thick that I can barely see the sky through the mass of leaves.

I flick another glance towards Jacques, debating whether to press for more specific details of the first test at least. When he contacted me last night, he told me to wear clothes fit for the woods, so I put on my boots, a pair of long pants, and a thin long-sleeved shirt. All in colors that would help me blend in between the trees. And he told me to not bring any equipment or weapons. Which means that this will most likely be a test that involves staying hidden or finding someone else who is hiding.

After a while, a small clearing becomes visible. I raise my eyebrows as we walk into it. There is a tall rock wall on the other side of the open stretch of grass. It blocks the way forward.

Fucking hell, don't tell me that we're climbing that. It's one thing to fake being mediocre at hiding. But if I have to pretend to be bad at climbing a sheer rock wall, I might get myself seriously injured.

"Alright, we're here," Jacques says, and stops about halfway between the tree line and the rock wall.

I make a show of looking around me. "Okay. And what are we doing here?"

"For this first test, *you* will not really be doing anything. You will just be the end point. The bait."

Great. I can certainly be mediocre bait without issue.

"I've told the others to wait for me on the others side of the forest," he continues. "So that they won't know your exact location. Once I get back to them, the hunt will start. Each of them will try to find you as quickly as possible. So your job for this test is to just stand here until one of them finds you."

The way he slightly stresses the words 'just stand here' makes me frown, but I quickly smoothen my features before he can notice.

"Any questions?" he asks.

I shake my head. "No."

"Alright then, I'll see you later."

Before I can say anything else, he turns around and walks back the way we came.

Narrowing my eyes, I study his retreating back. His shoulders are suddenly a little tense, and he turns his head several times as if nervously checking for something. And he's walking just a bit too fast.

Uneasiness curls around my spine.

It could just be that he is eager to get back to the rest of our team before they do something stupid on the other side of the forest. But my instincts are telling me something different. Telling me that he is trying to get the hell out of here as fast as he can without alerting me.

And my instincts are very rarely wrong.

I edge two steps back, whipping my head from side to side in order to try to spot whatever it is that's about to happen here. But there is nothing out of the ordinary. Only grass covered with some twigs and fallen leaves around me, gray clouds in the sky above, a tall rock wall behind, and trees starting in a half circle at the end of the clearing.

But something is wrong. I know it is.

To my left, Jacques clears the tree line and disappears into the forest.

The moment he's gone, someone else steps out of the woods straight ahead of me.

Rico.

At first, I feel only relief. Because for half a second there, I was worried that Derek and Sebastian had somehow gotten to Jacques and threatened him into leading me here.

But as Rico closes the distance between us, that relief withers and dies like a fragile flower.

Something is different now.

I can feel it in the way he walks. In the way he carries himself. In the way he is looking at me.

A flash of alarm shoots through me, and I instinctively reach for weapons that I don't even have, because with sudden clarity, I realize that *something* is not different now. No. *Everything* is different now.

Rico comes to a halt three strides away, his face a cold mask as he looks at me. Merciless power radiates from his muscular body. It's so intense that I'm half convinced that the fucking grass itself is bending away from him.

I flick a quick assessing glance over his body.

Based on the way the fabric of his t-shirt moves, he has a gun tucked into the back of his belt.

I resist the urge to swallow as I meet his hard stare again.

There is no mistake about it. Rico means business this time. He has thrown aside all sense of restraint and scrapped all other schemes.

He knows who I am, and he knows that I know it.

I know who he is, and he knows that I know that too.

And now, he is done pretending.

Flexing my fingers, I call up what I learned about his fighting style that day when the Petrovs ambushed me in the parking lot. Because this time, I need to fight to win.

No more pretending to be mediocre.

If I let Rico win, he is going to kill me.

Blackwater is no longer a safe place for me to stay, because there will be no coming back after what will happen between me and Rico here today.

Our painful and confusing and wonderful time together ends here.

I need to kill him. And then I need to escape.

32

RICO

From the moment I walk into the clearing, I can see that she understands. Understands that there is no middle ground anymore. I will either have my answers. Or she will die.

Convincing myself to do this, to fully commit to this, was more difficult than anything I have ever done. But this is what needs to be done. The only thing that will work. Bullying, humiliation, fear, torture, even kindness and joy... None of that will ever sway Isabella. The only thing that she will never give up, and the entire reason why she is holding on to her secrets so fiercely in the first place, is her life. She does not want to die. So that is what I will use as a bargaining chip. Her life in exchange for the answers I so desperately need.

For a few moments, the forest is dead silent around us. No leaves rustle. No birds chirp. The gray clouds don't even seem to be moving across the heavens anymore.

The world is entirely still and silent as Isabella and I watch each other from across the grass.

Then I yank out the gun from behind my back.

Pain pulses through my wrist as Isabella's boot slams into my hand right as I get the gun out. The sheer force of her sweeping kick makes the weapon fly from my fingers. I start in shock at the sheer precision of that move. But I don't have time to get distracted by it, because Isabella is already going for the gun that is now hitting the ground a few steps away.

I lurch into motion.

Leaping forward, I aim to get my arms around her.

She sees the move coming and abruptly throws herself sideways, abandoning her attempt to reach the gun. My fingers just barely brush her side, but it's not enough to grab her.

Whirling around, she uses her momentum to swing her fist at my jaw. I yank up my forearm to block it.

Pain vibrates through my bones, traveling up my arm like shockwaves as her strike connects.

Jesus fucking Christ, the woman knows how to throw a punch.

While shaking out my arm to stop the rippling sensation, I twist to the side and slam my boot towards her hip. She knows better than to try to block it and instead leaps back to avoid it.

The moment my leg passes through the air, she lunges at me.

I barely manage to get my balance back before her fist crashes into my side. Since I saw it coming, I had time to brace myself for it, but it still sends a jolt through my body. I swing back at her, but she ducks and then throws a punch towards my throat. Yanking my arm back down, I slam my fist into her wrist, forcing her strike down before it can hit. She doesn't even grimace at the pain. Instead, she just lunges at me again.

And my God, she's fucking fast.

Alternating between kicks and punches, she comes at me so relentlessly that I'm forced to back up several steps.

She's fucking perfect for me.

The thought flashes through my mind so suddenly, and so unexpectedly, that I miss the chance to block her next kick. Her boot smacks into my thigh, making me stagger a step to the side. I leap into the air as she sweeps her foot along the ground, trying to take my legs out from underneath me.

But the more I think about it, the more I know that it's true.

She *is* fucking perfect for me.

Not only does she understand me in ways that no one else does, she's also absolutely *lethal.*

As the heir to the Morelli family, anyone I bring into my life will always be in danger. Any woman I married would always be at risk of getting kidnapped as a way for my enemies to put pressure on me. But Isabella... If I were to marry Isabella, she wouldn't live her life in fear of our enemies. No. Our enemies would live in fear of *her*.

I leap backwards as Isabella yet again presses the advantage. Her hand shoots towards my solar plexus, and I only barely manage to shove her fist sideways so that it strikes me in the side instead. Once more, pain pulses through my bones.

With every passing moment, it becomes increasingly clear that I'm outmatched.

I am outmatched against Isabella.

Yes, I'm bigger than her. And yes, I'm stronger than her. But her technique is so flawless, so effortless, that she somehow still has me on the defensive.

When I was younger, my parents and grandfather

naturally made sure I had a solid training in both hand-to-hand combat and in handling weapons. And I've gone through over two years of training at Blackwater.

But Isabella… She fights as if she was born doing it. As if she knew how to move in battle before she even knew how to walk. It's effortless. Graceful. And so fucking hot that I almost forget what we're doing here.

Watching her skills, her *true* skills, makes my soul sing and my blood heat so much that I almost want to lose just so that she can put me on my back on the ground and then ride my cock while that fierce wildness burns in her eyes.

It takes all of my willpower to force that image out of my mind and instead concentrate fully on the fight.

Yes, Isabella would be perfect for me in every way.

Too bad we're enemies.

She feints a strike to my face while twisting sideways to deliver a savage kick towards my knee. I jump backwards before she can shatter my kneecap. Landing on the ground, I yank my arms up in preparation for her to push the advantage. But she doesn't.

Instead, she dives forwards and a little to the side.

And that's when I realize what she has been forcing me to move back towards these past couple of minutes.

The gun.

I lunge forward, but it's already too late.

Isabella grabs the gun while still diving forward. And in one fluid motion, she rolls into a crouch, leaps to her feet, and spins around.

I freeze as she levels the gun at my head.

33

ISABELLA

Shoot him, my brain screams at me. *Do it. Shoot him.*

My chest heaves as I stare at Rico from two steps away. His chest is heaving even worse than mine.

Damn, he's good. Much better than I had expected, even after watching that brief fight against the Petrovs. Against just him alone, I expected to be able to finish this fight much, *much* faster than I did. He might not have the almost two decades of harsh battle training that I have, but gods above, the man knows how to fight.

If I ever were to settle down with someone, it would be a man like him. Not only because he sees the parts of me that no one else does, but also because he can hold his own. With the Hands of Peace out for my head, anyone I dare to get close to will always be in danger. But with Rico, I wouldn't have to worry. He is just as paranoid as me, and one hell of a fighter.

It takes everything I have to force those images, those dreams of a real life, out of my mind.

He came here to kill me. So now I need to kill him and

then get the hell out of this city before both the Hands of Peace and the entire Morelli empire descend on me.

Shoot him, my logical brain snaps at me again. *Shoot him now and rectify your mistake from six years ago.*

Barely a second has passed since I aimed the gun at his head, but I feel like time has stopped moving.

I know what I should do. What I need to do. Just one squeeze of my finger and this will all be over. Rico was supposed to have died that night six years ago anyway. He has already had six extra years to live because of me. Because I let him live that night. So I'm not taking anything from him. I have already given him too much.

Pull the trigger, my brain screams at me again.

My heart balks at the idea.

However, before I can come to a decision, another second ticks by.

And three red dots appear on my chest.

I stiffen.

Keeping the gun steady, I flick a glance down at my chest just long enough to confirm that all of the dots are aimed straight at my heart. Then I sweep my gaze across the trees around the clearing, trying to spot where the fucking Hunter brothers must be hiding with their sniper rifles.

There is no sign of them.

"If you shoot me, I will shoot him," I yell at the silent trees.

"No, you won't," Rico replies.

I snap my gaze back to him, keeping the gun leveled firmly on his forehead. "If you think I have any sort of conscience or any feelings for you whatsoever, you are entirely mistaken. If they make a move on me, I *will* fucking shoot you in the head."

"No, you won't," he repeats. While holding my gaze, he

slowly reaches into his pocket and slides out a loaded magazine. "Because there are no bullets in that gun."

Cold dread explodes inside me.

I suck in a few shallow breaths, trying to keep my suddenly mounting panic under control.

"Do not move," I warn.

He just spreads his hands in a nonchalant gesture.

While still keeping the gun aimed at him, I quickly eject the magazine.

One look confirms that he was telling the truth. It's not loaded. He must have known that he might be outmatched against me and taken precautions. Must have used the empty gun as bait so that I would focus on getting it instead of trying to knock him out. And it worked.

Fuck.

With panic clanging inside my skull, I carefully lower the gun and spread my arms while keeping one eye on the three red dots still aimed at my heart.

Rico starts towards me. I half hope that he will walk right up to me so that he will be blocking the sniper rifles for a few seconds, but of course he's too smart for that. He approaches at an angle and then plucks the gun from my hand.

With expert movements, he quickly swaps the empty magazine for the full one he had in his pocket.

Two of the three red dots start moving to each side.

Remaining perfectly still, I watch the dots move upwards and to the sides until I can no longer see them. It's impossible to tell, but I assume that they are now either trained on my temples or the back of my head.

That distinct clicking sound drifts through the warm afternoon air as Rico finishes loading his gun. The ominous sound seems to echo across the forest.

His eyes are the hardest and most merciless I have ever seen as he raises the gun and levels it at my head.

"On your knees," he commands.

I remain where I am, staring back at him.

He takes a step forward and presses the cold barrel directly against my forehead. And when he speaks, when he presses out a single word between clenched teeth, the sheer power in that word vibrates through my bones.

"Kneel."

This man before me is no longer Rico the unexpectedly kind guy who bought me waffles. This isn't even Rico the bully. No. The man standing before me now is Enrico Morelli, the heir to the most dangerous mafia family in the state.

And suddenly, I know without a doubt that any further resistance is futile. I grew up in a cult where the law was obedience or death. That same feeling is present here now. I am entirely at Rico's mercy, and he will kill me if I refuse to follow his orders.

While keeping my eyes on his, I slowly lower myself to my knees before him.

The gun moves with me, staying pressed against my forehead.

"I am going to ask you some questions," he declares. "And you are going to answer them. If you refuse to answer even one question, I will shoot you in the head. If you lie, I will shoot you in the head. But if you answer all of my questions truthfully, I *might* let you live. If you don't, I *will* kill you. Do you understand?"

Looking up into his merciless face, I can tell that he means every word. If I don't cooperate, he will put a bullet in my brain and then wash his hands of me and be done with it.

"Yes," I reply.

"Good. Let's start with an easy one. What's your name?"

"Isabella Johnson."

An exasperated sigh rips from his chest, and I swear I can almost see regret flash across his face as his finger starts squeezing the trigger.

"Wait!" I yell, yanking up my hands and holding them up in an appeasing gesture. "I'm not lying. I—"

"Not the name you're using right now," he growls, pushing the barrel a little harder against my forehead but thankfully easing his finger back from the trigger. "Your real name."

"I don't know." I stare up at him while a suddenly overwhelming feeling of desperation pulses inside my chest. Because I want to live. By all the gods in all religions, I desperately want to live. So this time, I answer with the full truth. "I don't have one."

His dark brows furrow. "What do you mean you don't have one?"

"It's... complicated. And kind of a long story."

"We have nothing but time."

"I was born into a cult called the Hands of Peace."

He scoffs, because he knows just as well as I do that they bring anything but peace.

"Every member of the cult is raised and trained to be a ghost. A nameless, faceless assassin who changes identity depending on what each mission requires. So I've had hundreds of names over the years. When I was young, they changed my name very frequently so that I wouldn't grow too attached to one. When we're older, we can keep one for about a year at most."

"What about your parents? Didn't they at least call you something?"

"I don't know who they are. They're members of the cult,

that much I know. But every child is raised by a whole bunch of people, so I don't know which two members it is. Again, so that we won't form any attachment to anyone."

For a fraction of a second, some kind of emotion flickers in his eyes. But it's gone so fast that I can't even begin to interpret it before that merciless expression is back again.

"And *Isabella* is...?" he demands.

"It's the name I chose for myself after I escaped from the cult," I reply.

He is silent for a while, as if processing the information.

Across the clearing, some branches rustle and a bird flaps away as a strong wind sweeps through the forest. There is a small twig digging into my shin where I'm kneeling. But I can't even feel it. All I can feel is the cold metal barrel of Rico's gun against my forehead, and all I can see is those hard brown eyes staring me down.

"Why did you come to our house to kill us that night?" he asks eventually.

I'm not sure if he means *you* as in the Hands of Peace or as in me specifically, so I answer, "I, along with two other members, were there because we had been given a mission by the Master. That's what the leader of the cult is called," I add. "A mission to wipe out your entire family."

His jaw clenches. "Why?"

"Because that's what the Hands of Peace do. They travel the country and eliminate families who have grown too powerful. It's their whole mission statement. To bring peace to the country by making sure that no single family grows so powerful that it would jeopardize democratic rule. And your family, the Morelli family, is incredibly powerful. So we were given a mission to kill you and your parents so that Federico Morelli wouldn't have any direct heirs to his empire."

Rage burns in his eyes now. "That's it? You killed my parents for... for *that*? To end our bloodline in order to *preserve democracy*." He practically spits the words.

I just hold his furious stare. Because there is nothing else to say. No excuses to make. That *is* the reason why his parents are now dead and why he has spent the past six years of his life in hiding.

He lets out a truly vicious string of curses in Italian, a lot of it directed at me and my former colleagues. Then he drags in a breath, as if with great effort, and forces it out again. The searing rage in his eyes fades as he composes himself.

"When you speak of the Hands of Peace, you keep saying *they*," he remarks. "And you said that you chose the name Isabella when you *escaped* from them. Is that why you're here at Blackwater, pretending to be a random mediocre student? Because you left the cult and are hiding from them?"

"Yes."

"Why?"

"Because they found out that you're still alive."

"Which is a problem for me. But it doesn't explain why you are in hiding too."

"Because I betrayed them. Six years ago, I was given the mission to kill you. I didn't. I disobeyed their orders and let you live. Which means that I forfeited my own life. In the Hands of Peace, you only have two options. Blind obedience. Or death."

A considering look blows across his features, and he is silent for a while. Then he asks, "Why didn't you leave? Why did you wait until they found out that I was still alive? Why not leave before they found out, if you knew that it was a death sentence?"

"Because it's not a fucking football team," I snap,

frustration bubbling up inside me. "You can't just *leave* the Hands of Peace. Once you're in, you're in it for life. And if you're *born* into it… Well, guess what? You will never know one single moment of free will in your entire life because every choice has already been made for you."

The moment I finish speaking, I realize that I probably shouldn't take that tone with the guy holding a gun to my head. But I can't bring myself to apologize. I'm too angry for that. So I just glare up at him, waiting to see if he will punish me for my outburst.

He doesn't. Instead, those emotions flicker briefly in his eyes again. Then he draws in a deep breath, as if he is bracing himself for something. It sends a spike of alarm through my spine.

But when he at last speaks again, I understand exactly why he needed to brace himself. Because he finally gets to ask me the question that must have been whirling inside his head for six years now.

"Why did you spare my life that night?"

Dread and panic mix inside me like foul-tasting poison. Because I don't want to answer this. It's too personal. Too tightly connected to the fear and the useless bloody dreams I keep buried inside me. Too tightly woven into that gaping wound in my heart that is torn open every time I delude myself into thinking that maybe, just maybe, I could be a real person with a real life.

"Answer me," Rico growls, pressing the gun harder against my forehead.

But I can hear the desperation in his voice too. He needs this answer. He needs it more than any of the other answers I have given him.

He gives me a warning look and tightens his finger on the

trigger.

"Because you sighed!" The words rip out of me so forcefully that I swear I can taste blood on my tongue.

Rico jerks back a little and blinks, completely stunned.

"Because you fucking sighed," I repeat, my voice breaking. All the fight bleeds out of me, and I slump down so that I'm kneeling while sitting on my heels instead. A broken sob threatens to spill from my lips as I look up at Rico with desperate eyes. "I didn't kill you because when you woke up, you didn't react the way any of my other targets ever had. You didn't look scared. You didn't plead with your eyes for me to spare you. You didn't even look angry."

The pain in my chest just keeps spreading with every word, and I have to fight down the urge to press a hand over my heart to stop it from breaking. Instead, I drag in an unsteady breath.

"You didn't do any of that," I continue, holding his now thoroughly confused gaze. "Instead, you only looked disappointed and resigned. And then you fucking sighed!" This time, I do yank my hand up and stab it against my chest. "And I felt that fucking sigh all the way into the heart that I didn't even know I had. Because I knew that sigh. I knew exactly what it meant. What the entire expression on your face meant."

He stares down at me, eyes wide and confusion still evident on his features.

I drag in another shuddering breath, and then force myself to finish. To finally speak the words that I promised myself that I would never utter aloud.

"I let you live because I saw in your eyes what *I* have always felt too. That I don't want to die without even having lived."

34

RICO

Her words send a chill down my spine because of how dead right she is. That was exactly what I was thinking when she held a gun to my head that night. I knew that I was going to die and that there was nothing I could do about it. And I was so fucking disappointed that I would never get to start living for real, like I had promised myself that I would.

After that kidnapping when Eli was thirteen and I was twelve, where a rival family abducted him and tortured him for a week while thinking it was me, my family tightened security around me. I was pulled out of school and instead continued my education with private tutors inside the safety of our compound. I had to drop out of all the sports and activities I had liked as a child. My entire world was cut down until it basically only contained the Morelli compound and a few visits to town and to the Hunters' mansion every now and then. But only when my family deemed it safe.

Eli and Kaden and Jace were still allowed to come over and spend time with me, but apart from that, I was practically isolated from the world. It's the reason why I was able to set up a new identity as Rico Hunter just on the other side of the city. Because almost no one outside knew me well enough to recognize me.

I had no life, no real life whatsoever, from when I was twelve and all the way until that night my parents were killed when I was sixteen. And every one of those days, I swore to myself that when I was eighteen, I would finally be allowed to properly live again. Because by then, my family would be confident that I could take care of myself. That I didn't need to be surrounded by guards. And then they would let me live. Or I would force them to let me live, because by then, I would be powerful too.

But then my parents were murdered, and I was forced into hiding. And now I'm twenty-two, and I *still* haven't even started living that life that I promised myself I would have.

Isabella is right. I don't want to die without even having lived. I feel it now. And I felt it that night she stood next to my bed holding a gun to my head.

What shocks me, and honestly terrifies me, is that she didn't even know me back then and she still managed to understand exactly how I felt. It terrifies me because it confirms what I have always suspected. Isabella can see right through me. Can see all the emotions I try to hide. See all the dreams I secretly have.

We met for less than a minute in a dark room six years ago, but every day since then, I've had the strangest feeling that I know her. That I know her soul.

And now, I understand why.

Because when it all comes down to it, we're the same. We share the same fear, the same frustrations, and the same dreams.

Another burst of pain spears through my heart when I think about what she told me. About her past. How she grew up.

I thought I grew up being forced to obey the rules set forth by my grandfather, but Isabella had even less free will than I did. Less of a *life* than I did. She doesn't even know who her parents are. She doesn't even have a real name, for fuck's sake.

My heart aches for her when I think about what growing up like that must have been like.

It also explains why she acts in such a strange way sometimes. Why she panics when someone asks her what kind of food she prefers. Why she has never eaten waffles or ice cream. Why she doesn't even know what she likes.

She has lived her whole life in an authoritarian cult of assassins who forced her to become a ghost. A person without an actual identity. It's so fucking sad and heartbreaking that I can barely stop myself from showing just how angry it makes me.

But I can't falter now. So I block out any empathy I have for Isabella and instead keep the cold mask on my face as I continue to interrogate her.

"The other two people, the two men who killed my parents, where are they?"

She almost looks a bit hurt that I didn't comment on, or even acknowledge, her explanation of why she let me live that night. But she's not in a position to push the matter, so she just swallows down her disappointment and replies, "I don't know their exact location. But they're here. In the city."

"How certain are you of that?"

A brief hint of annoyance flickers in her eyes. "They ambushed me when I was there on Friday, so… very."

Surprise shoots through me. She was ambushed by them?

Narrowing my eyes, I study her. But she doesn't appear hurt, which means that she walked away from that encounter unharmed.

When I ask her about it, she explains that she noticed them following her and ambushed them instead before yelling that there was a fire and escaping. I almost smile. *Smart.*

"Tell me everything you know about them," I demand.

"When I left, they went by the names Derek and Sebastian. Derek is in his forties, and he has dark hair cropped close to his scalp and brown eyes. Sebastian is in his thirties, and he has blond hair down to his shoulders. I was standing behind him holding a gun to his neck, so I don't know for sure, but since he has the same hairstyle as he did when I left, I assume that he is still wearing gray contacts too."

"Did you do that as well?" I nod at her face. "Change your appearance."

"Yes. I was wearing brown contacts when I arrived on campus. They washed out during the test in the pool that day I ran into you."

A huff of amusement escapes me.

Her lips curve in a faint smile too.

"After that, I had to stop wearing them because it would have made you even more suspicious."

"It would." I can't stop another short breath of amusement. "And your hair?"

"My natural hair color is auburn. More dark red in tone than orange."

In my mind's eye, I try to picture what that would look like on her. And fucking hell, it would be a gorgeous contrast against those stormy blue-gray eyes of hers.

Forcing that image out of my head, I slam the emotionless

mask back onto my features and instead demand, "Tell me more about Derek and Sebastian."

She shares her own assessment of their skills in different areas, but apart from that, there isn't much more that she can tell me. They're ghosts. Just like her. So they have no family or friends or anything that can be used against them. And since the Hands of Peace moved and changed their protocols after she left, she doesn't know their location either.

When she's done, she just sits there on her knees, looking up at me.

It makes dread curl around my spine. Because this is it. Isabella and I are officially done. I have asked all my questions now. And she has given me all the answers that I have been waiting six years for.

I almost want to ask another question, something entirely meaningless, just so that I can drag this out a little longer. Because this is the last time that I will ever look into those beautiful eyes. The last time that I will ever talk to this dangerous and incredible and complicated woman whose loneliness and determination calls to mine.

"I should kill you for the part you played in my parents' death," I say, my voice coming out so flat and emotionless that it shocks even me.

Isabella just kneels there before me, holding my gaze. She doesn't say anything. Doesn't try to protest that she isn't the one who killed my parents. Doesn't try to remind me that she was the one who let me live. Doesn't beg. All she does is to just meet my eyes with a steady gaze. A resigned gaze. The same one I must have given her six years ago.

Something fractures in my heart when I look at her like that. Something big. And it takes all of my willpower to keep myself from flinching at the pain that floods my chest after that massive break.

"But you also spared my life." I lower the gun from her head. "So, a life for a life."

She blinks, looking genuinely stunned.

I don't know whether I want to laugh or shake her in frustration. Did she actually believe that I was going to kill her?

It took everything I had, every ounce of skill that I have with lies and deception, to convince myself that I would kill her if she refused to answer my questions. Because she would be able to tell if I wasn't serious. So I had to make myself believe the lie. It was one of the most difficult things I have ever accomplished, because I knew deep in my heart, that I would never follow through on it. I would never have killed her. But I had to make her believe that I would, which means that I had to make myself believe it too.

Apparently, she's not the only master liar here.

"You're letting me live?" she asks, her tone guarded.

"Yes." Still keeping my eyes locked on hers, I signal to Eli, Kaden, and Jace to stand down. "Grab your stuff and get as far away from here as possible. We're even now."

She glances at the trees around us, as if checking whether she's about to be shot by a sniper rifle regardless of what I just said. Then she slowly climbs to her feet. Her gaze darts down to her chest, but no red dots appear. After that, she shifts her attention to the gun that I still hold in my hand. I keep it pointed down at the ground beside me.

At last, her eyes meet mine again.

For a few seconds, everything is completely silent and still.

Isabella opens her mouth.

My heart jerks as I wait to hear what she's going to say.

Hesitation blows across her face. Giving her head a quick shake, she snaps her mouth shut again.

Disappointment floods my chest. But I say nothing as she slowly starts backing away in the direction that she came from. I simply watch her.

When she reaches the tree line, she pauses. And yet again, I get the feeling that she's about to say something. But then she just turns around and sprints away.

I stand there in the middle of the clearing, staring at the spot where she was last visible, and feeling completely drained. If someone were to poke at me with a stick right now, I'm pretty sure I would just crumple to the ground.

Figures move at the corner of my eye.

I just keep my eyes on the spot where Isabella disappeared while Eli, Kaden, and Jace approach me from all three sides. Once they reach me, I at last force myself to tear my gaze from the tree line and focus on them.

All three of them still keep a sniper rifle in their hands, courtesy of Eli, but the weapons are now angled down towards the ground. I sweep my gaze over them, feeling like I should thank them for helping me do this. But I can't seem to find the words.

As if he can read all of that on my face, Eli just reaches out and places one hand on my shoulder, giving it a comforting squeeze. On his other side, Jace and Kaden give me a nod as well, acknowledging the words I can't speak right now.

My throat closes up. Because I fucking love these three unhinged psychos who will always be my brothers in every way that matters.

"You let her go," Eli says at last.

Dragging in a shuddering breath, I turn to meet his gaze.

His eyes, more gold than brown, hold no judgement whatsoever.

"Yeah," I reply. It sounds more like a gasp.

The scar that runs through Eli's eyebrow and down to his cheek shifts as he gives me a small smile, as if he always knew that I would let her go, even though I didn't tell them that when I asked them to come.

"What will you tell your grandfather?" Jace asks. And there is no judgement in his tone either. Only curiosity.

"That I have information about the two men who killed my parents."

"And Isabella?"

I just shake my head.

Kaden watches me with those dark, perceptive eyes. I can feel him thinking it. And I know that he knows. He always does, somehow. But he thankfully doesn't say it out loud.

Someone else does, though.

Eli gives me another smile. And it's one of those smiles that practically never appeared on his mouth before he met Raina.

"You love her, don't you?" he says.

My heart spasms at hearing those words spoken out loud.

Isabella is… an absolute enigma. She's fierce and lethal and kind and skilled and inexperienced all at once. She's gorgeous and powerful. She understands me in a way that no one else does. And she completes me in ways that I never thought possible.

All of that is right there on my tongue.

But what I say is, "No."

35

ISABELLA

Shock still clangs through my soul as I park my car and hurry towards the abandoned building where I keep my go-bag. I can't believe that he let me live. That he just let me walk out of there. After I told him exactly who and what I am. After everything, all the unspoken secrets about himself, that he has shared with me these past weeks. All of that makes me a massive security risk. A massive threat to him. And still, he let me go.

As I hurry through the streets, I focus on that shock. Because at least it covers up the ache in my heart that seems to be getting worse with every step away from Blackwater.

We're even now.

Yes, we sure are.

He owes me nothing. I owe him nothing.

We're done now.

Over.

So why do I feel like my heart is fracturing into irreparable pieces in my chest?

I'm so distracted by the pain pulsing through my ribcage,

that I almost miss the signs completely. And when I finally notice them, it's almost too late.

Two streets away from where I keep my go-bag, I realize that I'm being followed. But because I didn't notice it until now, it's too late for any evasive maneuvers.

So I do the only thing I can do.

I run.

Taking a sharp left, I dart down another road, leading away from my go-bag with all my fake passports and ID cards. If they find those, I will never be able to escape.

The moment I move, so does the man behind me. Boots pound rapidly against the pavement as he gives chase.

Adrenaline pumps through my veins as I hurtle down the street. Right as I round the next corner, I steal a quick look over my shoulder to see Sebastian race after me.

I let out a curse under my breath as I skid onto the next road.

Why couldn't it have been Derek? He's much bigger and bulkier, which makes him slower. But Sebastian is lean and much, much faster.

Empty bottles clink and roll across the uneven stones as I leap over a pile of trash and aim for the other end of the road.

Sebastian rounds the corner behind me.

While trying frantically to call up my mental map of this area, I veer right and sprint down another street. There has to be some place where I can lose him.

The footsteps behind me grow louder. Closer.

Fuck, fuck, fuck.

I throw myself around the next corner.

And come face to face with a dead end.

My heart leaps into my throat, but I don't hesitate.

Picking up speed, I hurtle down the narrow alley and

towards the half-rotten wooden crate halfway down. The building on that side is too tall for me to reach the roof, but I might be able to reach the opposite one.

Sebastian closes in with each second.

I push myself to go as fast as I can.

Sprinting down the alley, I leap up onto the edge of the crate and then use my leg to push myself sideways in a rapid jump.

Air whips around my face and rips at my hair as I shoot up and sideways towards the lower roof on the other side.

Even with all of my power behind the jump, my fingers barely reach the edge of the roof.

The rest of my body slams into the stone wall underneath.

My breath escapes my lungs in a huff at the impact.

I drag air back into my lungs while trying to haul myself up as fast as I can.

A hand wraps around my ankle.

Panic surges through me.

I kick instinctively with my other leg.

Sebastian hisses in pain as my heel slams into his nose, and he loses his grip on my ankle for a second.

Yanking my legs back up, I grit my teeth and use every smidgen of my strength to haul myself up onto the roof.

On the ground, Sebastian is already hurrying to duplicate my move with the crate.

With my heart thundering in my chest, I roll over the edge of the slanting roof and jump to my feet before taking off.

Tiles rattle underneath my boots as I run along the edge and towards the next building. It's the one that makes up the dead end, so if I can just make it there, I should be able to get down to the street on the other side.

A groan sounds behind me. And then the tiles rattle even

more as another set of footsteps pound across them. I pick up speed.

Darting along the edge of the roof, I whip my head from side to side so that I can form some kind of escape plan once I'm on the ground.

There. An open window on street level a short distance from this building. If I can just make it there before Sebastian can reach me, I might be able to lose him.

The roof ends abruptly. Skidding to a halt, I spin around and swing myself down over the side of it. My stomach lurches as I let go of the roof and plummet towards the ground. But I learned long ago how to land properly, so I'm up and running again in a matter of seconds.

Pushing myself with everything I have, I sprint towards that open window.

And then leap through it.

A deserted living room meets me on the other side. As does a hideous orange couch that is much sturdier than it has any right to be.

Pain flares up my shoulder as I slam right into it and come to a very abrupt halt. The sofa grinds against the floor and crashes into the table on the other side, making something topple and clank on the floor.

Someone lets out a surprised yelp from somewhere upstairs.

I leap to my feet and vault across the inconvenient orange furniture before darting out of the living room and into the hallway. Whoever lives here comes pounding down the steps. But by the time they're halfway down, I have already reached the front door. Unlocking it, I shove it open and run out onto the next street.

Air explodes from my lungs.

At first, I can't figure out what happened.

I was running out the door but now I'm staring up at the sky, which means that I must have fallen over and landed on my back. I try to get my limbs to move, but my entire body is just spasming. I try to draw in a breath, but that doesn't seem to work either.

Then I see the source of it.

Derek is standing right outside the still open door. His arm is outstretched and his fist closed. The bastard rammed that right into my solar plexus, using both his own strength and my speed to deliver his blow.

Fuck.

Once again, I try to get my body to obey my orders. But all it does is to just lie there, spasming from the strike to my solar plexus.

Derek flashes me a cold grin as he bends down and jabs a needle into my arm.

The world goes black.

My head pounds and pain pulses through my body when I regain consciousness. I draw in an unsteady breath and blink hard, trying to clear my vision.

"Finally," Derek grunts from somewhere on my left.

"I told you not to give her so much of it," Sebastian says.

"You know I had to. She was one of us. She has a base tolerance for the stuff."

Sebastian lets out a hum in agreement.

I blink again while my surroundings slowly come into focus.

A warehouse. Metal walls. Beams in the ceiling. The

windows on the ground level have been boarded shut, but the smaller ones higher up reveal red and orange light from the setting sun. I must have been out for hours.

I try to move my arms.

It makes a metallic rattling sound fill the air.

Glancing up, I find that I'm wearing handcuffs and that they're secured to a metal hook attached to a chain in the ceiling. My toes barely touch the ground.

So that's why my shoulders ache.

Pain shoots through my cheek, and my head snaps to the side as Derek backhands me while I'm still glancing up at the ceiling.

"Stop looking for ways to escape," he orders. "Because there are none."

I slowly turn my head back so that I'm facing him. He will pay for that strike. Maybe not today. But someday.

He grabs my chin. Hard. His fingers dig into my flesh as he leans closer. I yank against the manacles and the chain that keeps my arms trapped above my head, but it's no use. I can't get him to take his fucking hand off my chin.

"You know the drill, Anna," Derek says, his voice dropping menacingly low. "You tell us what we want to know, and we won't hurt you."

An overwhelming urge to spit in his face crashes over me, but I manage to stifle it. Antagonizing him unnecessarily is just plain stupid. Instead, I just glare back at him.

"Where is Enrico Morelli?" he demands.

I keep my mouth shut.

His fingers tighten on my chin, digging in so hard that I know they will leave bruises. "Where is Enrico Morelli?"

I say nothing.

A jolt shoots through my body, and I suck in a sharp breath between my teeth.

Behind me, Sebastian jabs what feels like a cattle prod into my back again.

Pain pulses through my body and my muscles cramp again.

I grit my teeth.

Derek continues staring me down. "Where is Enrico Morelli?"

I stare right back at him.

Sebastian discharges another electric current into me. Again. And again. My body spasms, but I refuse to make a sound. Refuse to give them the satisfaction of hearing me cry out in pain.

With a snarl, Derek yanks his hand away from my jaw and stalks over to a table. Sebastian uses the cattle prod on me again while Derek picks up a knife and then strides back to me.

Grabbing the hem of my shirt, he slides the knife underneath it and then pulls upwards.

A ripping sound fills the air as he cuts the shirt away from my body.

Light from the flickering lamp above glints in the sharp blade as he holds it up in front of my face.

"Where is Enrico Morelli?"

I keep my eyes locked on his but say nothing.

He flicks his wrist.

Pain sears through my skin as he cuts a shallow wound on my chest.

"Where is Enrico Morelli?"

I clench my jaw, glaring back at him.

He cuts me again and then repeats the question. I refuse to answer.

Gritting my teeth, I block out the pain as Derek opens another half dozen shallow cuts over my stomach and chest. Warm blood runs down my skin. But they're not life-threatening. Because they still need to deliver me alive back to the Master so that he can torture me himself for one hundred days before he finally executes me.

When the knife and the cattle prod doesn't work, they pull me down from the chain and instead strap me to a chair.

Burning pain shoots up my arms as they push long and thin splinters of wood in underneath my fingernails.

But still, I don't scream.

And I don't tell them where Rico is.

Next, they try waterboarding me.

My body shakes and my mind is screaming in panic.

But I still refuse to tell them where he is.

I try to convince myself that it's because it would only doom me further if I confirm that he is indeed still alive. But in my heart, I know that it's a lie. They already know that he is alive. It's why they're here, torturing me, after all.

No, the real reason why I refuse to tell these bastards where Rico is has nothing to do with my own survival. And that realization terrifies me more than the Hands of Peace and the torture I'm being subjected to ever could.

The real reason why I'm protecting Rico is because I feel like he is the other half of my soul that I have been missing.

I felt the first flicker of it that night I was supposed to kill him, and the feeling has only grown stronger these past weeks when I have gotten to know him. He is a part of me. Always has been. A part that the Hands of Peace will never be able to take from me, regardless of how much pain they inflict on my body.

So no matter what these assholes do to me, I will never give them the part of my soul that resides in Rico. I will never give them Rico.

When I pass out for the third time, Derek slaps me awake and curses at me. I just let my head roll to the other side. He raises his fist again, but before he can hit me, Sebastian calls to him from where he's standing in the doorway.

When did he even leave the room?

"It's almost time," Sebastian says, holding up a phone. "He is expecting our call in the next two minutes."

He. The Master. Waiting for his bloodhounds to report back on their progress.

My stomach lurches as Derek frees me from the chair and hauls me up. Dragging me over to a cage that looks like it's meant for large dogs, he throws me into it and then snaps a pair of handcuffs shut around my wrists. I just lie there on the ground as he stalks back out and locks the cage door behind him.

"Alright," he says to Sebastian. "Let's get ready."

Lying on my side, I remain exactly where they left me as I watch them leave.

The moment the door has closed behind them, I push myself up into a sitting position and reach around my body towards where I keep my lockpicks sewn into my pants.

Every muscle in my body screams, and fresh blood wells up from the wounds across my chest and abdomen. My fingers fumble, but I at last manage to get the lockpicks out.

I draw in a steadying breath to clear my swimming vision as I start picking the lock on the handcuffs. They click open.

Casting a quick look towards the door, I get to work on

the lock on the cage. It takes longer than it usually does, but I manage to get it open eventually. After carefully opening the door, I slip out and run towards the hook and chain that is still hanging from the ceiling.

There is no time for second thoughts. This plan I concocted while I was trying to distract myself from the pain earlier has to work. It has to.

Leaping up, I grab the end of the chain and start pulling myself upwards.

An intense burst of pain flashes through my whole body. It's so overwhelming that I almost pass out.

Dropping back to the floor, I have to gasp in a silent breath and pause for a few seconds to block out the waves of pain rolling through my every nerve.

Then I leap up and grab the chain again.

This time, I'm ready for the pain so I manage to brace myself for it.

Gritting my teeth, I use only my arm strength to pull myself up that chain. My muscles are trembling. Screaming at me to stop. Blood runs down my chest and stomach from the wounds that I have yet again opened up. But I don't stop. I can't. Either I escape now, or not at all.

Once I reach the top of the chain, I throw up an arm and grab the edge of the metal beam that it has been secured to. Everything inside me protests violently as I drag myself upwards. I swing a leg up, managing to get it over the side of the beam. Using that as leverage, I at last pull myself the final distance and roll onto the beam.

My head is swimming, and the metal ceiling shifts and blurs like waves above me.

Sucking in desperate breaths, I have to lie there for a little while so that I won't pass out.

Once I'm reasonably confident that I won't just topple over and fall down from the beam, I roll over onto my stomach. And then I crawl towards the end of the beam. There is a window there.

While praying to any god who is willing to listen, I carefully edge it open. The hinges don't squeak. I slip out the window and then pull myself up onto the roof outside.

Straightening on the flat roof, I scan my surroundings.

Shock ripples through me when I realize that we're relatively close to where I keep my go-bag.

I start in that direction.

Getting down from the roof is difficult, and I almost pass out while accomplishing it. But I manage to get to my secret hiding place and grab my go-bag without collapsing.

Slinging it over my shoulder, I stagger back into the deserted alley that smells of spilled alcohol and piss.

My head pounds, my vision swims, and my ragged breaths are so loud that I'm pretty sure people can hear them from halfway across the city. Not to mention that I'm half-naked and covered in blood.

I have to keep one hand on the wall as I stumble out of the alley. Dread washes through me, because I know my own body better than anyone. And I know that it's about to give out.

I won't be able to drive like this. Hell, I won't even be able to make it to my car in this condition. I need to lie down and give my body a chance to recover for a minute.

But where?

My gaze drifts towards that tall building I passed every week without knowing what was on the other side.

At this point, I don't have much of a choice. If there is any place that I can pass out and have even the slightest chance of not being found, it's inside that abandoned park.

Blood pounds in my ears, drowning out everything else as I desperately make my way towards it. My feet drag slightly on the stones as I move. I need to get out of sight. Now. Before Derek and Sebastian finish their report and go back in to find me missing.

Branches claw at my bare arms and snag in my hair as I stagger through the wild underbrush.

Just a little further.

My body spasms, and I have to throw out a hand and brace myself on a tree trunk as my knee buckles. The bark scrapes against my palm. I barely even feel it.

Pushing off from the tree, I force myself to move deeper into the vegetation.

At last, a pond becomes visible between the trees. I stumble the final steps out from the branches.

And then, my body at last gives out.

I hit the grass hard.

But I don't even have enough energy left to roll over on my back. So I just remain like that, my cheek pressed against the ground. It smells of dirt and grass.

My chest heaves.

I suck in a few breaths before my vision starts to fade.

And the last thing I see before I'm dragged into oblivion is that dark blue water covered in glittering silver stars.

36

RICO

It's stupid to come back here. I know that. Especially so soon after last time. But after everything that went down with Isabella in the woods earlier today, I feel off-kilter. Restless. I can't sleep, so instead of lying there in my bed, staring at the ceiling, I drive into the city and head to the last place I should be right now.

I park the car right on the other side of the building, because I can't risk being here for more than a few moments. It was impossible to sneak past the guards my grandfather has now posted around the house, so they insisted on following me. They'll arrive any second, and I just need a few fucking moments to myself to think. And to remember. Remember what it was like to share this place with Isabella. Before everything changed.

Branches rustle as I push them aside while striding towards the pond. Apart from that, the only sound comes from the nocturnal insects humming and chirping in the foliage.

At last, I can see the dark blue water through the trees.

It both makes a sigh of relief escape my throat and sends a pang of pain through my chest. This time, I don't try to block it out. Instead, I feel it all as I walk out of the trees and onto the stretch of grass before the pond.

My heart lurches in my throat.

A person lies slumped on the grass halfway to the water.

My first instinct is that it's some kind of trap, so I let my hand drift to my gun as I carefully move closer.

But then I realize *who* it is.

And my stomach bottoms out.

"Isabella," I blurt out.

Rushing forward, I close the final distance between us in a few quick strides and then drop to my knees next to her.

A terrible clanging echoes inside my skull as I stare at her limp form. She's unconscious, her shirt is missing, and she's covered in blood. There are several cuts across her chest and stomach, and bruises on her jaw and face.

"Isabella," I say, my voice coming out raw, as I place my hands on her cheek and turn her face fully to me.

She doesn't stir.

There is a black duffel bag on the ground next to her. I gently move the strap away from her body and then sling the bag over my shoulder instead.

With my heart pounding, I slide my arms underneath Isabella's unmoving body and lift her up. Holding her to my chest, I spin around and run back out of the park.

My grandfather's guards are waiting outside when I emerge, and they lurch into motion when they see me.

"What happened?"

"Who is she?"

"She's..." I begin while heading straight for my car. "A

friend," is what I finish with at last, because I can't exactly tell them who she really is.

"We'll take her to a hospital."

"No," I immediately reply.

If I take her to a normal hospital, they will have a lot of questions for her when she wakes up. And that will draw attention to her, which will compromise her chances of survival.

"Drive ahead and get the university doctors," I order. "Bring them to our house immediately."

I don't give the guards any other explanation. They don't need to know my reasons. They only need to obey my commands.

And they do.

After inclining their heads, they dart back to their own cars and drive back towards Blackwater.

I carefully place Isabella in the backseat so that she's lying across it. Then I yank open the driver's side door and toss the duffel bag into the passenger seat before I leap inside. The car roars as I speed away.

My hands are shaking slightly, so I grip the steering wheel hard as I drive us back to Blackwater. And every few seconds, my gaze darts up to the rearview mirror to check on Isabella. She's just lying there, her eyes closed.

I squeeze the steering wheel harder.

What the fuck happened?

She was supposed to leave. So why was she lying bleeding inside the park I took her to earlier?

Did those two bastards who killed my parents find her? She has obviously been tortured. But why would they do that?

I force myself to relax my strangling grip on the steering wheel, and flex my fingers.

It doesn't matter why they did it. All that matters is that they are going to die screaming.

The car screeches to a halt as I slam on the breaks outside our house. I have barely turned it off before I'm jumping out and yanking up the door to the backseat.

A short distance away, Jace throws open the front door to our house and hurries out.

"What happened?" he demands.

I gently lift Isabella out of the backseat and cradle her in my arms as I hurry towards him. "She's hurt."

"The doctors—"

"On their way."

Jace scrambles backwards as I reach the door and stride into the hallway. "I'll get the closest spare room ready."

My first instinct is to tell him that I will be taking her to my room. But then I consider how Isabella will be feeling when she wakes up, and decide that Jace is right. One of the spare rooms is a much more neutral location.

I give Jace a nod, and he whirls around and sprints up the stairs. I follow at a slower pace so that I won't jostle Isabella too much when I move.

When I reach the top of the stairs, Kaden appears from his room. He was obviously sleeping, since it's the middle of the night, and is only wearing a pair of pants.

Either Jace has already filled him in, or he was able to piece it together on his own, because he immediately walks past me and towards the stairs while saying, "I'll show the doctors to the right room."

"Thank you," I reply.

But he is already heading down the stairs and I'm halfway to the spare room closest to my bedroom. The door is open, and the sound of rustling fabric comes from inside. I walk across the threshold right as Jace straightens from where he was bent over the bed. There are now fresh sheets, pillows, and a duvet on it.

"Hold on," he says before I can thank him for that.

Running back to the closet by the wall, he pulls out a set of spare towels and places them across the sheets. Good thinking. She's covered in blood, and I don't want her to sleep in a bloodstained bed once the doctors are finished.

Once the dark towels cover the bed, I carefully place Isabella on top of them.

Her brown hair partly covers her face. I draw soft fingers over her forehead, brushing aside the stray locks. My heart aches.

"They're here," Kaden says from the door.

A second later, three doctors hurry across the threshold.

"Out of the way, please," the first one says, her voice full of command.

I quickly step aside to give them space.

They work quickly. I pace restlessly as they examine her, make a plan, set her up with what I assume is some kind of painkiller, and then start stitching up her wounds and tending to her other injuries.

She gasps and shoots up from the bed.

The doctors jerk back in surprise, and then immediately try to make her settle down again while mumbling about how the painkillers should have knocked her out.

I hurry over to her as she weakly tries to push them away.

"Isabella," I say, putting my palms on her shoulders and pushing her back down on the bed. "It's alright. It's—"

"Rico." Her eyes lock directly on mine for a few seconds before sliding out of focus again. "It's okay. You're safe."

The lead doctor gives me a look while increasing Isabella's dose. "She's a bit loopy from the painkiller and the blood loss."

"You're safe," Isabella repeats, her gaze once again zeroing in on me for a few seconds. "I didn't tell them where you are. I didn't tell them."

My blood freezes in my veins.

I can hear my own heart pounding in my ears as I gently place my hands on Isabella's cheeks and turn her head back so that she is looking at me again.

"Is that why they tortured you?" I ask, my pulse thrumming. "Because they wanted you to tell them where I am?"

Her eyes slide out of focus again.

"Isabella," I demand, because I know that this is my only chance to get a truthful answer out of her. She would never admit to anything like this if she wasn't high on painkillers and delirious from blood loss. And I need to know. "Did they torture you like this because you refused to tell them where I am?"

She blinks, and her eyes finally focus on me for another second. "Yes. But I didn't tell them. I didn't tell them where you are. You're safe. You're..."

Her eyes close and she drifts off mid-sentence as the painkillers take effect again.

For a few seconds, all I can do is to just stand there next to the bed, my hands still cupping her cheeks, and stare down at her.

She was tortured. She endured all of this. Endured all of these cuts and bruises and everything else that they did to her that didn't leave a mark. Because she refused to give up my location to the other cult members.

Pain slices through my heart like a burning blade.

Why would she do that? Why didn't she just give me up? She should have given me up! She can't possibly—

"Please give us some space to work," the lead doctor says, her dark eyes meeting mine with a pointed expression.

I take my hands off Isabella's cheeks and step back.

Time seems to both rush by and not move at all as the doctors work on her injuries and then clean the blood off her.

When they're at last finished, they ensure me that she will be fine but that she needs rest. I nod, feeling like I'm in a daze, as they file out the door and go back to the beds that my guards dragged them out of.

Kaden and Jace hover by the door.

"When she said *they*," Jace begins, tearing his eyes from Isabella and instead locking his gaze on me. "Did she mean those two men who killed your parents?"

"Yes," I reply. "They... Fuck!" Panic surges through me, and I hurry towards the door. "I need to call Federico."

After a quick look over my shoulder, to make sure that Isabella is sleeping, I stride into the hallway and then into my room. Closing the door behind me, I slide out my phone and call my grandfather.

He knows that I would never call at this hour unless it's important, so he picks up after only three signals.

I quickly inform him that Derek and Sebastian were spotted close to the park tonight. Just as when I told him the other information about them that Isabella gave me, my grandfather assumes that it comes from an intelligence network that I have set up on campus. It's more or less true, anyway, which was why I was able to convince him of that in the first place.

On the other end of the line, he immediately starts issuing orders for people to comb through that entire part of the city right away. He promises to keep me updated, and then hangs up.

I'm only just sliding my phone back into my pocket when Jace knocks and then opens the door without waiting for an answer.

"You should come quickly," he says.

My heart lurches, and I hurry after him and back to the spare room.

When I reach it, Kaden is trying to keep Isabella from getting out of bed. Even in her weakened and drugged state, she is surprisingly tenacious.

"I need to go," she announces as she practically falls out of bed. "I need to leave."

Kaden backs away as I approach Isabella instead.

Bracing one palm on the mattress, she straightens and then manages to take one whole step before her legs buckle.

I lunge towards her and grab her before she can crash down on the floor.

"I need to leave," she blurts out again, her eyes sliding in and out of focus.

Adjusting my position, I slide my arms underneath her and lift her up. She tries to fight me but only manages to swat weakly at my chest.

"I need to run," she protests. "Before it's too late."

Even through the drugs and the confusion, I can hear the undercurrent of panic in her voice.

"It's okay," I say as I carry her back to bed.

"No. I need to get out."

So as I tuck her in again and brush a few strands of hair out of her face, I tell her the same thing she told me over and over again tonight.

"You're safe."

37

ISABELLA

Bits and pieces of memories swirl through my brain as I regain consciousness. Doctors and needles and a pair of terrified brown eyes staring down at me. But I'm not sure exactly what happened after I passed out in that park, so I keep my eyes shut and instead try to listen to what is going on around me.

There is nothing. No voices. No movement. Nothing.

Since I'm fairly certain that I'm alone, I open my eyes to take in my surroundings.

And find Rico looking straight at me.

I start in surprise.

He is sitting on a chair by the dark wooden wall, watching me. He must have noticed the second I woke up. I suppress the urge to groan. Or maybe laugh. Because of course he did.

Shifting my attention away from him, I sweep my gaze over the rest of the room. It's a bedroom with floorboards and wall panels that are made of what looks like very expensive wood. Apart from the double bed I'm currently occupying, there are two nightstands, a closet, and a desk. Since there is no chair at it, I'm assuming that that's the one Rico is sitting on. There are no decorations or any sort of personal effects inside the room.

I shift my gaze back to Rico. "Where…" The word comes out in a croak, so I have to clear my throat before trying again. "Where am I?"

"In our house on campus," he replies. His brown eyes remain locked on me, but his face betrays none of his emotions. "In one of the spare bedrooms."

Silence falls around us for a few seconds. Then I say, "You found me in the park."

It's more of a statement than a question, but he confirms it anyway. "Yes."

"You didn't take me to a hospital."

"No. I brought you here and then made the university doctors come to you instead."

Another few moments of silence pass as we just watch each other.

"Why?" I ask eventually.

"You know why."

I actually meant, *why did you save me?* Not, *why didn't you take me to a hospital?* Because I already know why he brought the university doctors here instead.

But I can't seem to find the courage to ask that outright, so I don't correct him.

Instead, I swallow and flick a glance towards the closed bedroom door before meeting his gaze again. "Am I a prisoner?"

He holds my gaze in silence for a few seconds before replying, "No."

I sit up, which sends a flare of pain through my whole body. I suppress a wince and instead nod towards the door.

"So if I were to walk up to that door right now, it wouldn't be locked?"

The chair groans as he abruptly pushes himself to his feet. Striding over to the door, he shoves the handle down and throws the door wide open. Then he steps aside and sweeps his arm, gesturing towards it.

"Go ahead," he says. "Leave if you want. But those two people will still be looking for you." His eyes harden as he nods towards the bandages across my torso. "To finish the job. So I would recommend at least waiting until you're not wincing just from sitting up."

Surprise flutters through my chest. He noticed that? I thought I suppressed that wince before he could see it.

With his arm motioning towards the door, he stares me down from across the room. Challenge pulses on his face.

Part of me wants to get up and stalk out of here just to spite him. But the problem is that he is right. Going back out there in this condition would not only be reckless, it would be downright stupid.

So I force out a defeated breath and instead scoot backwards so that I can lean my back against the headboard.

A victorious smirk pulls at his lips.

I ignore the way it makes my heart flip.

After closing the door again, he walks back to the chair and drops down on it. It creaks in alarm underneath his muscular frame.

Another short silence descends over the room.

"We didn't find them," Rico says after a while. "Derek and Sebastian. Our people searched the area around the park all night, but there was no sign of them."

I just nod. I didn't expect there to be. They're too skilled for that.

"Why didn't you tell them where I am?" he suddenly asks.

Alarm crackles down my spine. While gripping the sheets hard on the other side of my leg, where he can't see it, I keep my voice casual as I ask, "What do you mean?"

"They tortured you to get you to give them my location. But you didn't. Why?"

Fuck. I must have accidentally admitted that sometime last night when I was completely out of it.

There is no way that I can tell him the truth, because I barely even want to admit it to myself, so I lie and say, "Because it would've been proof that I let you live six years ago, which would be bad for me."

"Yeah..." he begins, and shoots me a pointed look. "Except, they already know that."

I say nothing, because we both know that he's right and that my answer was a lie.

Thankfully, though, he doesn't push the matter.

"Do you have anyone else?" he asks instead. "Anyone you can call?"

A sudden wave of embarrassment washes over me, and I avert my gaze before admitting, "No."

"Then you're staying."

I snap my gaze back to his. But it wasn't a question. Just a simple statement of facts. And he isn't even waiting around to see if I agree.

Rising to his feet, he starts towards the door without a second look back. I just sit there, watching him in stunned silence as he walks out the door.

Disappointment slithers through my chest and tightens around my heart.

It immediately makes me angry. Because I have no right whatsoever to be disappointed.

Rico and I were done. I had spared his life and he had spared mine. We were even. Finished. So he was under no obligation to save me when he found me unconscious in that park. But he did it anyway.

So I have no right at all to feel a bit disappointed that he just walked out without another word.

And yet, there is a strange ache in my heart as I stare at the door that he left halfway open on his way out.

Cursing myself for a fool, I shake my head and start to slide down from the headboard so that I can lie down again. Each small movement sends a spike of pain through my body, and I pause for a second. Then I grit my teeth and get ready to try again.

Footsteps sound in the hallway outside.

I stop moving and blink in shock as Rico walks back into the bedroom. Frowning, I glance down at the items he is holding. Books. Four of them, to be precise.

He strides up to the side of my bed and then drops the books on the nightstand. They land with a loud thud.

"Romance," he says.

My mind is spinning, so I just stare up at him in complete befuddlement. "What?"

"The genre." Amusement blows across his features briefly before that neutral mask is back again. Then he taps the topmost book. "Romance." He moves his finger to the spine of the book underneath it. "Thriller." Down to the third one. "Fantasy." And the last one. "Horror."

"Uhm..." is all that makes it out of my mouth, because what the hell is going on here?

"Try them and see which one you like." He slides his hands into his pockets and shrugs nonchalantly. "And let me know if you don't like reading at all, and we'll try something else tomorrow."

My entire brain is malfunctioning, so all I do is sit there and stare at the pile of books while his words echo inside my skull.

He knows that I don't know what I like. So he's…

Movement registers at the corner of my eye, and I realize that Rico is walking back to the door. I give my head a quick shake to clear it, which only partly works, and snap my attention back to him.

"The doctors said you need to rest," he says over his shoulder. "Especially today. So just stay in bed and get some rest."

"I'm fine," I blurt out. Because what else am I supposed to say?

He pauses with his hand on the handle and turns back to level a commanding stare on me. "Get some rest, Isabella." A burst of light glitters in his eyes, and the ghost of a sly smile tugs at the corner of his lips, ruining the otherwise perfect mask of hard authority. "Don't make me get the handcuffs."

Then he walks out and closes the door behind him.

I wait for him to lock it. He doesn't.

As I sit there in the soft bed, staring after him, I suddenly want to burst into tears. Or maybe laugh. Or both.

But I can't fall apart. Not here. Not now.

So instead, I reach towards the nightstand and pick up the first book.

38

RICO

An entire week has passed since I brought Isabella home with me. And to my utter amazement, she hasn't tried to sneak out and disappear without a word. Instead, she has done exactly what I was hoping she would. Stayed. Rested. And let her wounds heal.

Thankfully, there were no complications or lasting damage. Her bruises are starting to fade and the cuts on her chest and abdomen are healing nicely. She slept a lot the first few days. But even after that, she has done as the doctors ordered and not moved around too much.

I've skipped all my classes every day since then. I told my guards that it was because I was taking precautions since the two assassins were spotted so close to me, which was an excuse my grandfather happily accepted.

While I tried to convince myself that I was staying in the house solely to prevent Isabella from simply vanishing into thin air one day, deep down I know that the reason is something else entirely. But it's not something I dare to admit. Even to myself.

"How's that pile coming along there?"

I look up from the board to find Isabella grinning at me. There is light in her eyes now, actual *light,* that sparkles when she smiles. I never used to see that in her eyes when we first met. But now, I see it almost every day. It's an absolutely astonishing sight, and it still takes my breath away every time.

Narrowing my eyes, I shoot her a pointed look. "It's coming along just fine, thank you very much."

"Uh-huh." She smirks at me. "Is that why I have already captured half of your pieces while you have…" She makes a show of squinting and leaning forward across the table to count the pieces in my pile. Then she flicks her gaze back up to me and finishes with, "Four of mine?"

I let out a huff. "I was trying to be nice. To go easy on you since this is your first time playing this game."

After the first few days of just letting her rest and get some peace and quiet, I suggested that we could watch something on TV. She agreed, more eagerly than I had anticipated, so we watched an entire season of one of my favorite shows. After that, I suggested that we could try some video games. To my delight, she absolutely sucked at that. Which I teased her about rather mercilessly.

One day at dinner, she mentioned that she has never played board games. We don't own a lot of board games, but I manage to dig one up from the library. So that's what we're playing at the desk in her bedroom now. And she is kicking my fucking ass even though I *am* trying to win.

She flashes me a knowing grin. "Sure you were."

"Cocky, aren't you?"

That incredible light dances in her eyes again. "Well… is it really arrogance if it's true?"

I chuckle.

Warmth spreads through my chest. I love seeing this side of her. The real her. Not once since I brought her here has she played the part of the meek and mediocre girl that she pretended to be for weeks. Every day, she has only been herself. Her true badass, intelligent, and slightly cocky self. And I fucking love it.

"If you really have been going easy on me, then let's up the stakes." Mischief glints in her eyes as she holds my gaze. "From now on, every time someone loses a piece, they have to take off one item of clothing."

My eyebrows shoot up.

Her grin just grows more villainous. "What? You scared?"

I scoff. Shaking my head, I lock eyes with her. "Fine. You're on."

It takes me less than a minute to lose the first piece.

Isabella arches an expectant eyebrow at me. "Well?"

After leveling a sharp look at her, which just makes her laugh, I stand up from my chair and grab the hem of my shirt. With one smooth motion, I pull it off and toss it to the floor beside the desk. We've pulled the desk out from the wall so that we can sit facing each other, and I've brought in a second chair from another room. We were planning on sitting at the kitchen table, but Kaden and Jace came back from campus right as we were about to start. And call me selfish, but I wanted Isabella all to myself.

Now, as she rakes her gaze over my naked chest, I'm suddenly very thankful that we're alone in her bedroom and not where those two troublesome psychos are, because they would never let me live this down.

"That was just me getting warmed up," I say as I sit down again.

Isabella, who of course sees right through the lie, smirks. "Of course."

It takes me another minute to lose the next piece. This time, I take off one of my socks and drop it pointedly on the floor. She chuckles. And then proceeds to capture yet another one of my pieces. I take off the other sock too.

"If you're planning to actually win, you might want to..." She flicks a deliberate look down at my crotch. "Get a move on."

I just shoot her a threatening look back, and then calculate my next move. This time, I do manage to take one of her pieces. But the sly smile that ghosts across her lips as I pluck it from the board and make a show of dropping it on my pile, makes me wonder if she might have *let me* win that one.

She grins like an absolute villain.

I give my head a quick shake. No. She's just messing with me. Trying to get in my head and make me question my own skills.

While licking her lips, she stands up and then slowly pulls her own shirt off.

My heart still constricts painfully when I see those wounds on her skin. But they are healing well, and she doesn't wince when she moves anymore.

Then that treacherous heart of mine lurches when I see the necklace that she was wearing underneath her shirt. The necklace I gave her. She was wearing it when I found her in the park. And she's still wearing it. Every day.

After dropping her shirt on the floor, Isabella slides her hand through her hair and then casually draws it down over her collarbone and towards her tit.

Blood rushes to my cock.

A wicked laugh escapes her lips as she lets her hand drop back to her side while she sits down.

The little menace really is trying to get in my head. And by God, it's working.

Since I'm even more distracted now, I lose the next piece even faster than the other three. Isabella just looks down at my pants expectantly.

Blowing out an exasperated breath, I stand up and start unbuckling my belt. She watches my hands as I take my time with it before undoing the button and then pulling down the zipper.

She licks those wicked lips of hers again, and fire sears through my veins. Slipping my hands underneath the dark fabric, I slowly push my pants down. Her eyes track my every move, and linger a bit longer on the bulge that is now clearly visible against my black boxers. A victorious grin spreads across her lips.

I let out a huff of amusement as I pull my pants off fully and then toss them on top of my shirt. I'm now completely naked except for my underwear, while Isabella is sitting there almost fully clothed.

"Well," she says, a teasing note in her voice, as I take my seat again. "You'd better not lose the next one then."

I give her a flat look before studying the board in front of me again, trying to figure out what she is planning to do and what kind of move I can use to outplay her.

After going through several possibilities, I move my piece into a place that will definitely make me win.

"Ha!" I smirk at her. "How's that?"

"Good." She moves one of her own pieces, capturing mine. "But not good enough."

"What the fuck," I groan. Heaving a deep sigh, I fix her

with a disbelieving look. "I thought you said that you had never played this before."

"I haven't. But it's just about strategy, so it's not really that difficult."

"Uhm, ouch."

She chuckles and then raises an eyebrow at me. "Well? I'm waiting."

I stare back at her. "Have you no mercy, woman?"

"Mercy is for weaklings." She grins and shoots a pointed look down at my cock. "Now, strip."

Incredulity washes through me, and I shake my head in astonishment as I stand up. Because God, this woman is absolutely incredible.

Heaving a resigned sigh, I take off my underwear and then sit down again, completely naked.

Isabella watches me with a sly smile playing over her mouth. Fire burns in her eyes as she rakes her gaze over my body and then bites her lip slightly.

My cock hardens even more.

"You know," she begins, meeting my gaze again. "You could continue to play this game and watch me fuck you over on every turn. Or… you could take me to that bed over there and just… fuck me."

My cock throbs with need at the mental image. But I say, "Didn't the doctor tell you not to engage in any demanding physical activity for a while?"

"Demanding?" She laughs. Standing up, she pushes the desk aside and saunters up to me with a downright devilish smile on her lips. "Oh, little mafia prince, I bet I can make you come without any *demanding physical activity* whatsoever."

Lust pulses through me like searing waves as she places

her hands on my thighs and then lowers herself to her knees between my spread legs.

"Is that a challenge?" I say, but my voice comes out sounding more strained that I had planned.

My whole body thrums with need for her as she slides her hands up my thighs. Lights flicker behind my eyes as she wraps one hand around my cock.

"Yes, it is." She grins up at me. "And after I win, you're going to bend me over that desk and fuck me so hard that it rattles the walls."

Before I can even think of a response to that, she leans forward and takes my cock into her mouth.

A moan rips from my chest, and I throw my head back while gripping the armrest hard.

She lets out a dark chuckle around my cock.

Pleasure flashes through me as she sucks and licks my throbbing shaft.

Another gasp escapes me as she lightly scrapes her teeth over my sensitive skin.

Tightening her grip with her fingers, she slides her hand up and down the base of my cock while her mouth works along the rest of it.

She swirls her tongue over the crown of my cock before taking me deeper.

My hand shoots out, and I draw it through her hair before taking it in a firm grip. She laughs smugly again with my cock halfway down her throat. Then she draws back and flicks my tip with her tongue.

Pleasure crackles through me like lightning.

Bending down, she licks and sucks my length again.

I tighten my grip on her hair as she keeps pushing me closer and closer to the edge.

Fucking hell, she sure knows what she's doing.

Dragging in deep breaths through my nose, I try to hold on to the last slippery strings of my restraint, but she shows me no mercy.

Release explodes through my body.

Isabella keeps her soft lips around my pulsing cock as I come down her throat.

My heart pounds in my chest.

I release my grip on her hair, flexing my fingers and sucking in a shuddering breath, while I try to piece my mind back together.

Isabella slides her lips off my cock and then wipes the corner of her mouth with her thumb. Even though I have literally just come with that perfect mouth around me, my cock immediately throbs and begins to harden again, because that small move is so fucking erotic that I can barely think straight.

With a victorious grin on her lips, she wiggles her eyebrows at me. "Told you."

A breath of amusement rips from my lungs, and I slowly shake my head at her. "You really are a bloody menace, aren't you?"

She just smirks back at me.

Bracing her palms on my thighs, she stands up again and then gives me an expectant look. "Well? I think you owe me one hell of a fuck."

I rise to my feet as well so that I'm towering over her. After brushing my fingers along her jaw, I take her chin between my thumb and forefinger. "The doctor still said that you should be taking it easy."

"Don't worry." She reaches up and gives me a brisk pat on the cheek. "You'll be doing all the hard work this time."

I chuckle. "Fine." Letting my hand drop down again, I flick a commanding look up and down her body. "Then strip while I move the table."

"Why are you moving the table?" she asks while she starts to slide her pants down her toned legs.

"Because you wanted rattling walls." I grin at her over my shoulder as I shove the desk across the floor until one short side is pressed against the wood panels. Then I sweep my arm over it, making the board game and all the pieces clatter to the floor. "So I'll give you rattling walls."

Desire burns in her eyes like dark flames as she strips out of the rest of her clothes. I twitch two fingers at her. I can tell that she both loves and hates to be bossed around, which is why I love doing it.

Walking up to me, she puts her hands on her hips in a defiant move.

I jerk my chin towards the table. "Bend over."

Her eyes narrow, but that lust burns hotter in her eyes.

"You said that I would be doing all the hard work," I remind her. "Then that means that I will also be issuing all the orders. So..." I smirk at her and raise my eyebrows. "Bend. Over."

A shudder rolls down her spine. With that desire swirling in her eyes, she moves so that she is standing in front of the desk's other short side. Then she braces her forearms on the tabletop and bends over.

My heart skips a beat. Fuck, she's gorgeous.

"Spread your legs," I command.

She casts a look at me over her shoulder. I just arch an expectant brow. Amusement flits across her features as she turns back to face the wall, but she does spread her legs wider.

I move up behind her.

For a few seconds, I don't do anything. Just let her stand bent over the table like that with me behind her as she waits to see what I'm going to do next.

Right when I feel she's about to lose patience and turn around to snap at me to fuck her already, I draw my fingers up the inside of her thigh.

She sucks in a sharp breath.

I trace teasing circles over her skin, making her shift her weight and wiggle her hips as I slowly move upwards. But right before I can reach her cunt, I draw my hand back.

"What are you—"

Before she can finish speaking, I slip my hand between her hip and the edge of the table, and draw my fingers right over her clit.

Another gasp rips from her. Followed by a moan as I rub my fingers over her clit while I move up closer behind her.

"Didn't I tell you that I was calling the shots?" I demand while I continue to tease that sensitive spot. "So stop questioning me and just *feel*."

She curls her fingers into fists on the table as another moan spills from her lips. Her hips move, and she tries to push her cunt harder against my hand.

I grab her hip, forcing her to remain in place. "What did I just say?"

Only another moan and a shudder answer me as I roll her clit between my fingers.

Her breathing grows heavier as I work her clit until she's squirming on the desk. I smirk. I love seeing her like that. Seeing her pant and moan and squirm from all the pleasure that I can draw from her perfect body. Everything that I can make her feel.

"Rico," she gasps out.

I know that she's right there on the edge, but I haven't let her fall over it yet.

"Yes, Isabella?"

A violent shudder courses through her body. It often does whenever I say her name. And I love seeing *that* even more than her squirming.

Instead of replying, she just flexes her fingers on the table and drags in unsteady breaths. I keep torturing her until she tries again.

"Rico," she repeats.

"Yes, Isabella?"

"Please," she stammers. Her entire body is practically vibrating with pent-up need.

A dark chuckle rolls from my throat. Because I do love hearing her beg too.

I slide my hand from her clit and instead wrap it around her other hip. With a firm grip, I angle her ass upwards so that I can reach her cunt better.

She whimpers on the tabletop as I drag my hard cock along her soaked cunt. I do it again, just to torment her some more.

Then I shove my cock inside her.

Her head snaps up from the table, and she lets out a grunt as I settle deep inside her. I draw out slightly and then ram into her again. Another moan spills from her lips.

With that firm grip still on her hips, I start up a hard pace.

And just like she asked for, the wall rattles as the table slams into it with every thrust.

I pound into her. She wiggles on the tabletop and moans even more as the pleasure mounts. Which only makes it increase even more inside my own soul as well. Fucking hell, I love watching her writhe in pleasure like this.

The table thuds against the wall as I rail her.

Her chest heaves, and she clenches and unclenches her hands faster. She presses her forehead against the desk as a series of whimpering pleas drip from her lips.

I slam into her.

She gasps.

Her cunt tightens around my cock, her inner walls fluttering, as release sweeps through her body.

I keep my grip on her hips, helping to hold her steady through the orgasm while I continue pounding into her until I climax as well.

A groan tears from deep within my chest as I come inside her.

Pleasure ricochets through my entire body.

God, I could do this every day. I could spend every day for the rest of my life with Isabella. Playing stupid games that I will lose, fucking each other's brains out, mocking and teasing each other, eating waffles, and *living*.

This past week while she has been recovering from her injuries has been like a dream. A place where time stands still and nothing exists except for the two of us.

But she will be fully healed soon.

And where does that leave us?

39

ISABELLA

The floorboards creak faintly as I pace back and forth across my room. Around me, the rest of the house is blessedly silent. Kaden and Jace are presumably in class, or whatever else it is that they do in the middle of a normal weekday. And Rico is away getting us some food. I'm thankful for that, because intense panic has been growing inside me every day for the past week.

Raking my fingers through my hair, I stalk across the smooth floorboards yet again while that pulsing panic in my chest reaches critical levels.

Because this week and a half has been the best ten days of my life.

I love being here. I love trying out different books. I love playing board games. I love watching Rico mess with his cousins. And *I* love messing with Rico. I love hearing him laugh. I love watching his eyes glint with mischief. I love hearing him moan and seeing pleasure flood his features when we fuck. I love spending time with him. I love… him.

All the air is sucked right out of my lungs as that last thought passes through my brain.

Staggering a step sideways, I sit down hard on the bed. The mattress shifts underneath me. I just stare at the wall ahead, feeling shellshocked.

I love Rico Morelli.

The realization makes warmth spread through my chest and sends a surge of hope through me. I want this life. I want *him*. Desperately. I want it so badly that my chest aches. And for a moment, I let myself believe that I can. That this can all be real. That *we* can be real.

But then that searing panic comes crashing down over me again.

I was a part of the group that murdered his parents.

And even if he could somehow love me despite that, I am still a walking death sentence. The Hands of Peace will never stop hunting me. They will chase me to the ends of the earth, because if they let my betrayal go unpunished, it will open the door for more disobedience from the other members. Which means that anyone close to me will always be in danger as well.

If I were to stay with Rico, the Hands of Peace would just come at him even harder. It would be a death sentence for him.

In the face of all that, how could there ever be a future for us?

The answer is simple.

There can't.

Because I can never have a normal life. And certainly not with the man I was sent to kill. The incredible man who sees right through my soul and who understands me in a way that no one else does. The one who understands what it's like to feel lonely even when you're surrounded by people. The man who took a ruthless lying killer and gave her a taste of what a real life is like. A small taste that I will cherish for as long as I live.

A sob threatens to escape my throat, so I snap my mouth shut and swallow hard.

I can't believe I almost killed him. I can't believe that I almost snuffed out the radiant light that is Rico Morelli.

Shooting to my feet, I squeeze my hand into a fist and make a decision.

I have to make sure that he lives.

No matter what, I have to make sure that Rico lives.

The moment I have made the decision, I feel a sense of peace. A sense of absolute clarity. This is how it's supposed to be. This is how it's supposed to end. Because I know now, without a doubt, that my love for him is greater than my need for survival.

I walk over to the black duffel bag on the floor. My go-bag. Another burst of pain stabs through my heart as I think about what it means that Rico just gave it back to me, guns and all, and trusted me enough not to use it against him.

Forcing all those emotions aside, I pull out my secure cellphone and turn it on. This one might be a heavily encrypted one with a blocked number that no one knows about, but I still know all of *their* numbers. After punching in the correct one, I hit dial and bring it to my ear.

Five signals pass before the person on the other end picks up. However, he doesn't say anything. As expected.

"It's me," I say.

Another few seconds of silence. Then Derek's voice sounds on the other end. "Anna. Well, isn't this a surprise."

"I want to make a deal."

More silence. Then, he replies, "It's a bit too late for that. Your betrayal has created quite the mess for the Master. No matter what you do, no matter what you try to bargain with, you will suffer through the hundred days of torture and then be executed."

"I know. That's not what I meant."

"Oh?"

"I want to make a deal for Enrico Morelli's life."

This time, I can almost hear the stunned surprise pulsing through the phone. Eventually, he answers, "What kind of deal?"

"My life for his."

"What exactly are you suggesting, Anna? Spell it out."

"I'm saying that I will give myself up to you and then take his punishment too. I will take his one hundred days of torture on top of mine. And after those two hundred days, I will beg the Master for forgiveness in front of everyone and make sure that they all know how wrong I was to disobey him. And then I will let you execute me without fighting back." My voice hardens. "And in exchange, you will let Enrico Morelli live. You will take him off the hit list and you will let him go."

Even more silence from the other end.

Closing my eyes, I blow out a soft breath before opening them again. My heart is pattering in my chest. I need to convince him to take this deal. There is no other alternative. But getting him to agree will require a flawless argument.

"And why would I agree to that?" Derek asks. "Why would I settle for just you when I can get him too?"

"Because you're running out of time. You don't have me, and you don't have him. And every day you waste trying to find us is another day where more unrest spreads through the

Hands of Peace. Where more people start to wonder if they really need to obey the Master's every order without question. Wonder if they too might get away with doing what I did. It has been months already since I made a fool of you all and escaped. How long before a true rebellion starts?"

He doesn't reply. I strain my ears, trying to read the silence. But it's impossible.

"Call back in five minutes," Derek says at last, and then hangs up.

I check the time and then walk over to the duffel bag.

After folding up the other clothes I had pulled out of it, I put them back in along with my normal burner phone that I have been using while on campus. My eyes linger on the guns and the passports. But in the end, I just heave a sigh and zip the bag closed before placing it on the bed.

Once five minutes have passed, I use my encrypted phone to call Derek back.

"Well?" I say as soon as he picks up. "Have you talked to the Master? Did he accept my deal?"

"Yes."

Relief washes over me.

"With one condition," Derek adds.

I narrow my eyes. "What condition?"

"He wants you to put on a show when we bring you back with us too."

"Let me guess? He wants me to grovel and beg and convince everyone that resisting him is futile even before the two hundred days of torture, so that it will stop the unrest right away."

"Correct."

"Fine. Done." I heave another sigh. "So, do we have a deal?"

"Yes, we have a deal."

"Good. I'll meet you at that deserted parking lot behind the old textile factory."

"We'll be there. And Anna? If I see one single weapon on you, the deal is off."

"Understood."

Before he can reply, I hang up.

For a few moments, I just stand there in the middle of the room, taking it all in. Memorizing what happened in here. The happiness I experienced here. I will need it for what's to come.

Once I'm ready, I drag in a deep breath and then stride towards the door, leaving my go-bag with the guns and the passports on the bed. I glance out the windows as I reach the ground floor. There are guards stationed around the house. But they're here to protect Rico, not to prevent me from leaving, so they won't stop me.

Air smelling of warm stone and pine trees envelop me as I open the front door and step outside.

Just as I expected, the undercover guards don't challenge me as I simply walk away from the house and down the street. I head back to the parking lot behind my apartment building, where Rico left my car after retrieving it from downtown.

My heart squeezes in agony as I slip into the car and drive away, because I know that there is still one thing left to do.

As I drive out of the residential area, I pull out my encrypted phone and call Rico.

"Who is this?" he answers, his voice hard and suspicious since the number I'm calling from is blocked.

"It's me," I reply.

"Isabella?" He sounds surprised.

"Yes. I'm just calling to tell you that I'm leaving."

"What? What are you talking about?"

"I'm leaving the country."

"No, you're not."

"This isn't a discussion, Rico. It's a courtesy call because of your hospitality this past week. I am leaving."

"What—"

"And I have left all of the passports that you saw in the duffel bag, so don't bother tracking them because I'm using a new one. In fact, you won't be able to track me at all. After this, you will never see or hear from me again."

"Stop. Just fucking stop! What the hell is going on, Isabella?"

Cracks spread through my heart at the hurt and confusion in his voice. But I need him to let me go and just move on with his life, so that he can live for the both of us. It's the only way that I will be able to get through the next two hundred days and my impending execution. As long as I know that he is out there, living a real life at last, I will be able to bear it all.

So I make my voice hard, *cruel,* as I echo, "What's going on? You ruined my fucking life, that's what's going on. Because I spared your life, I forfeited my own. I will never know one single day of peace for as long as I live. Not one moment. And it's all your fault."

"I—"

"Don't ever try to find me again."

"Isabella, I…"

Gripping the steering wheel hard, I try to block out the pain in his voice. The agony. The desperation.

My throat is closing up, but I spit my next sentence at him with as much venom as I can muster.

"I wish I had killed you and your grandfather along with your stupid parents and your entire fucking family that night."

On the other end of the line, Rico sucks in a sharp breath.

But I don't wait for him to reply. I just hang up and then toss the phone out the window.

Something breaks inside my heart. Violently. It sends spears of pain shooting out through my entire body.

Clenching my jaw, I try to physically stop a broken sob from bursting out of me. But I can't stop the tears that stream down my cheeks.

It's better that he hates me, because that way, he won't find out what I really did.

I give myself time to cry until I'm three streets away from the parking lot. Then I swallow and wipe my wet cheeks as I park my car along the road. After dragging in a deep breath to steady myself, I get out of the car and walk the final distance to the parking lot.

When I reach the far end, Derek and Sebastian appear on the other side. The main building of the large textile factory that is no longer in use looms on my left, while the other three sides are boxed in by abandoned annexes that belonged to the factory. All of them are built by red brick, but the façade is now stained with dirt and grime after years of disuse.

I raise my hands, palms out, as I slowly start towards my two former colleagues. Only four cars are parked on this flat stretch of asphalt, and they're all at the edges of it, so there is nothing blocking Derek and Sebastian's view of me as I approach them. They keep a gun in their hands anyway.

I walk until I'm only a few steps away from them, and then I come to a halt with my hands still raised.

"You came," Sebastian says, his gray eyes flicking up and down my body as if searching for weapons.

"You sound surprised," I reply.

"Why did you make this deal?" Derek cuts in. His brown eyes study my face intently. "Why give yourself up? For him."

"That's none of your business," I reply. "The Master has accepted the deal, so the reason is irrelevant."

Both of them study my face in silence for a few seconds.

Then Sebastian's eyes widen. "Don't tell me you fell for—"

Gunshots tear through the air.

I jerk back, throwing myself sideways. But the shots didn't come from my former colleagues.

Blood sprays into the air as bullets tear through Derek and Sebastian's wrists, making their guns clatter to the ground.

Panic blares inside my skull.

I whip my head from side to side, trying to spot the shooters. But before I can, voices boom across the parking lot.

"Get down on the ground!"

"On the ground!"

"Now!"

Sebastian reaches for another gun with his uninjured hand, but he just cries out in pain as another bullet tears through that wrist as well.

Red dots appear on my chest and arms.

A fucking *mass* of red dots.

"ON THE GROUND!" a man bellows again.

I drop to my knees, bringing my hands up behind my head.

"You set us up," Derek hisses as he and Sebastian quickly kneel on the ground as well.

Utter shock clangs through me as people swarm in from all sides, so all I manage to press out is, "No."

Because whoever these men are, they're not with me.

There are red dots on Derek and Sebastian's chests, backs,

foreheads, and the backs of their heads, so I assume I have sniper rifles pointed at me from all directions as well.

I remain perfectly still as the host of men rush up to us with weapons drawn. About half of them are wearing black combat clothes, but the others are in civilian clothing.

Something tugs at my memory.

But before I can connect the pieces, someone plants a boot between my shoulder blades and shoves me face down on the ground. I slide my hands away from the back of my head and instead rest them on the ground beside me, but I keep my forehead pressed against the warm asphalt. The boot that shoved me down remains on my back, keeping me pinned to the ground.

And then suddenly, the final piece clicks into place in my mind.

The people in civilian clothing.

I know who they are.

They're—

"I knew it," a hard voice says. Authority and hatred and smug victory all pulse from that dark rumbling voice. "I knew that if I followed one rat, it would lead me to the others."

My blood freezes to ice at the sound of it.

Slowly, I twist my head to the side so that my cheek is pressed against the ground instead.

Polished black shoes and the hem of a pair of impeccably tailored black pants become visible. I resist the urge to swallow.

"He might think that he can keep things from me," the man continues. "But I knew that a rat has been living right underneath my grandson's nose for weeks now."

I glance up at the man towering over me and meet the merciless gaze of Federico Morelli.

40

RICO

It feels as if someone has ripped my heart out of my chest, leaving a jagged and bloody hole behind. No, not *someone.* Isabella.

Sitting on her bed, I just stare at the opposite wall while I try to figure out what the hell happened. Isabella's duffel bag sits beside me on the smooth sheets. She left everything. Her extra sets of clothes. Her money. Her passports. Her guns. Everything.

She just… left.

What the hell happened?

I thought we had reached a point where we enjoyed spending time together. A point where we didn't lie to each other.

But it seems like I underestimated her and her ability to lie without me seeing it.

You ruined my fucking life. I wish I had killed you and your grandfather along with your stupid parents and your entire fucking family that night.

Pain rips through my already shredded chest as those

words echo inside my skull. All this time, *that* was what she was really thinking. When we talked and played games and fucked, she was actually thinking about how much she hates me and my entire family.

And the worst part is that I understand it. I understand why she hates me. She *should* hate me. Just like I *should* hate her for her involvement in my parents' death. But I just thought that we—

My phone vibrates. Again.

I glance down to see that it's Kaden calling me for what has to be the tenth time. Deep inside, I know that I should pick up. But I saw the entire Petrov clan when I drove back here, so I know that he's not calling because he needs help. And I just can't handle talking to him about something else right now because I know that he will see straight through me.

Heaving a deep sigh, I decline his call and go back to staring at the wall.

My mind is at war with itself. Or maybe it's at war with that bloody pulp that used to be my heart.

Part of me wants to go after Isabella. To try to track her down and… I don't know. Confront her or something. Or find her at least.

The other part of me is starting to think that maybe she was right. Maybe we have too much history. Too many complicated things between us that we will never be able to truly let go of. So maybe it's better this way. She leaves, and I move on with my life.

A sharp ache pulses through my chest at just the thought of that.

Even from all the way up here, I can hear the front door being yanked open violently.

"RICO!" Kaden bellows a second later.

I sink down on the bed again since I now know that it's not an attacker. A groan escapes me as I hear Kaden's footsteps pounding up the stairs. I can hear from just the way he's walking, or rather running, that he is angry. And I don't feel like dealing with it right now.

The door to Isabella's bedroom is yanked open, revealing a furious-looking Kaden.

"So, your hands *are* working," he snaps as he stalks towards me.

It was not what I had been expecting him to say, so I just frown at him and reply, "What?"

He reaches the bed.

My stomach lurches as he grabs me by the collar, hauls me to my feet, and then slams me up against the nearest wall so hard that my teeth rattle.

"Unless you want me to break your hands for you so that you have an actual excuse," he growls in my face. "The next time I call you, you fucking pick up. Is that clear?"

I just stare back at him, my eyes wide, for a second before trying to push him off me. "What the hell—"

"I said, is that clear?" he cuts me off, his brown eyes crackling with fury.

"Uhm..." I begin, suddenly feeling like I'm missing half of the conversation we're having. "Yes."

"Good. Now that we've established that, shut the fuck up and listen to what I've been trying to tell you."

Stunned shock still pulses through me, so I just nod. Kaden doesn't back off. He keeps his hands buried in my collar, pinning me to the wall.

"Isabella is in deep shit," he says.

My heart stalls, but I force the flash of panic aside and

instead reply, "I know. She called me and told me that she's leaving the country to get away from the cult. And she said that right before she told me to fuck off and that she wishes that she had killed me. So whatever trouble she's in is her business."

"And you believed her. Oh, you fucking moron. Is that why you haven't been picking up your phone? Because you've been moping around heartbroken over her mean words?"

"Fuck you," I snap, once again trying to shove him off me. "I—"

He slams me against the wall again, so hard that my breath rips out of me in a huff.

"Enough," he barks. "And *listen* to me."

His eyes bore into mine, and I find myself closing my mouth instead of snapping back at him.

"Isabella made a deal with that cult of hers," he says when he's satisfied that I won't fight him again. "To give herself up in exchange for your life."

My heart stalls. Eyes wide, I barely manage to press out, "What?"

"She didn't know that I was right outside her door when she made the call. She told them that she would give herself up to them, take your punishment too, which apparently is one hundred days of torture, on top of her own one hundred days, and then publicly grovel before their Master, after which she will let them execute her without fighting back." His eyes are locked on mine. "In exchange for them letting you live and taking you off their hit list."

I open my mouth, but no sound makes it out.

"She was the one who decided the location, which means that I heard it too," Kaden continues. "I followed her, thinking it was the perfect opportunity to catch those two bastards who killed your parents. I called you, but you were already on the phone with someone else. And after that, you didn't pick up at all. So I went alone."

Closing my eyes, I let my head thump back against the wall while a tidal wave of regret crashes into me.

"I watched her walk up and surrender to them," he continues.

With that terrible regret clawing its way up my throat, I open my eyes and meet Kaden's gaze. It's not a victorious gaze, which means that his plan didn't work. It might have, if I had been there. But I wasn't. And now, we've lost the opportunity. And her.

"So, they have her now." It's more of a statement than a question.

But Kaden shakes his head. "No."

My eyebrows shoot up.

He holds my gaze. "Your grandfather does."

Ice seeps through my veins. I snap my head to the side, staring towards the window and finally seeing what I didn't notice when I arrived. All of the guards in civilian clothing who are supposed to be posted around the house are no longer there.

"He showed up with a ton of his people," Kaden says as I turn my head back to meet his gaze again. "Which means that his guards must have been following her as well. They ambushed her and those two other assassins, handcuffed them all, and shoved them into vans before driving off."

"Oh fuck..."

"You know your grandfather best, but I'm guessing he's not taking them out for a picnic." At last, he releases his grip on my collar and steps back. "So, like I said, Isabella is in deep shit."

I stagger away from the wall, feeling like someone just blew the entire floor out from underneath my feet.

Then I'm running.

Darting into my bedroom, I snatch up my own gun before sprinting downstairs.

"Do you want me to come with you?" Kaden asks, following me as I hurry towards the front door.

"No. If you're with me, they might not let us through. But if it's just me, I have a better chance of forcing the guards to let me into the room."

He nods.

After shoving open the door, I pause for a second and turn back to him. "Thank you. And I'm sorry."

A small smile blows across his face, and he jerks his chin. "Just go get your girl, brother."

I give him one last grateful nod.

Then I throw myself into my car and floor it.

41

ISABELLA

The coldness from the hard floor seeps into my legs and chills my whole body even more. I'm on my knees, my wrists and ankles shackled. Those manacles are in turn secured to a thick metal ring set into the concrete floor behind my back, trapping me in a kneeling position. And since I picked the lock on the handcuffs while I was in the van earlier, they also decided to remove most of my clothes to make sure that I didn't have any other lockpicks sewn into them.

So I kneel there in the cold basement, in only my underwear, while Federico Morelli begins to torture Derek.

Sebastian is kneeling a short distance from me, also shackled and wearing only his underwear. Six muscular men stand guard around the room, guns in their hands.

There are four rooms on the other side of the empty space. That entire wall is made of what I assume to be one-way glass, so that the people in this room can watch what happens in the other smaller rooms.

Only the room on the left is occupied. Derek is tied to a

chair there, while Federico stands before him like the devil himself. A truly impressive set of torture instruments are laid out on the table beside them.

I drop my gaze to the floor.

The moment my eyes are no longer on the room ahead, the guard next to me pushes his gun against my temple.

"Mr. Morelli ordered you to watch," he growls. "So, watch."

Raising my head again, I do as I'm told and continue watching as Federico tortures Derek.

It takes less time than I had expected for the screaming to start. Derek is well-trained. We all are. But apparently, Federico is a skilled torturer.

Once that stubborn silence has been broken, the patriarch of the Morelli family sets his tools down and leaves the room. Derek slumps back into his chair, his chest heaving. I keep my eyes on him, as instructed, while Federico walks back into our room.

He stops between me and Sebastian.

My heart slams against my ribs.

"Him," Mr. Morelli says. "Put him in the next room."

I flick a glance towards Sebastian, who clenches his jaw to suppress the brief flash of dread on his face, as two of the guards remove the chain that locks him to the floor and then drag him towards the room next to Derek's.

Federico's hard eyes land on me for a second.

And I suddenly realize what he's doing.

Not only is he trying to increase our fear by making us watch the others' torture, he is also trying to break our pride. Our will. Our souls. He will torture Sebastian until he screams for the first time too. Then he will come back and put me in the third room, and then torture me until I scream. Once I have broken down and screamed, he will go back to

Derek. And only when he screams, will Federico move on to Sebastian.

The only way to get a brief respite from his torture is to scream and acknowledge the pain he is inflicting and the power that he has over us.

He will no doubt keep increasing that threshold. At first, he will stop when we scream. Then we might need to cry too. Then beg. And then outright grovel. Until he has ground our spirits underneath his heel and broken us completely.

Fuck.

Panic clangs inside me, growing more intense with every second as I watch them shackle Sebastian to the chair in the second room.

My silver necklace shifts around my neck as a shiver courses through me.

It was one thing to meet this fate of torture and death when I knew that I was doing it to save Rico's life. But now, the Master will think that I have betrayed him and will put Rico back at the top of his hit list. So I will just be tortured and executed without it even accomplishing anything.

I will die for nothing.

I will… die.

My entire mind rebels at the thought. And I must have jerked back physically too, because the chain to my manacles rattles behind me.

A gun appears against my temple immediately.

"Watch," the guard orders yet again.

Dragging my gaze back to the room before me, I watch as Mr. Morelli picks up a set of tools and gets to work on Sebastian. Soon, blood runs down Sebastian's skin. His body shakes, but he keeps his jaw clenched, not making a sound. Just like we have been trained.

And right now, I'm grateful for that. Because I only have until he starts screaming before it's my turn.

I don't want to be here. I want to go home. I want to *have a home* to go home to.

All my life, I have been an emotionless ghost who simply killed on command. I have faced death more times than I can count, and I have never begged. Never pleaded for mercy. But right now, I'm on the verge of begging for my life.

Because now, I've gotten a taste of it. I know what it would feel like to have a life. A real life. And I want it more than anything.

My body trembles, but it's not from the cold.

On the other side of the glass, Federico continues torturing Sebastian.

A scream shatters through the room.

My heart drops.

Sucking in short shallow breaths, I watch Mr. Morelli drag one more scream from Sebastian's throat. Then he sets his instruments down and turns towards the door.

Everything inside me is screaming as the mafia king stalks towards me.

My heart thrashes behind my ribs.

I don't want to die. I don't want to die. I don't want to die.

Because now, after twenty-two years of being a ghost, I finally know.

I know that I like thrillers but not romance books. I know that I like board games more than video games. I know what kind of toppings I like on my waffles. I even know how to watch something on TV.

That last thought threatens to make a broken sob rip from my throat.

I know what it's like to own something. To own a necklace

that was bought specifically for me and that is mine and mine alone.

And I know what it's like to want to protect someone. What it's like to care about someone so much that I would willingly give up my life for him. What it's like to love someone.

My heart aches.

If I could've had that life, if Rico and I could've had that life together that I let myself dream of, then I would've protected it with everything I have. I would've faced hell itself for a chance to have that life with him.

"You," Mr. Morelli says as he comes to a halt in front of me.

Desperation crashes over me as I stare up into his merciless eyes.

Please. I don't want to die.

The words are right there on my tongue. But I can't bring myself to say them. I am going to die. There is no question about it. But I will face it the same way that I have faced everything in my life.

By staring death right in the eyes, and waiting for death to blink first.

Federico Morelli lets out a huff, and I can't tell if it's amusement or approval or disgust.

Then a cold smile stretches his lips.

"Take her."

42

RICO

Stalking through the hallway, I approach the door that leads down to the basement. Two of my grandfather's guards are standing outside. They exchange a hesitant glance.

"Stand aside," I command as I close the final distance.

"Sir, Mr. Morelli has—"

"That was an order." My voice, pulsing with utter authority, seems to echo down the hall.

The guards exchange another glance, but then quickly move aside as I reach the door. I shove it open and then stride down the steps. My boots thud against the concrete floor as I reach the corridor beyond. I know exactly where Federico will have taken them, so I head straight for one of the doors at the end. Shoving this one open as well, I stalk into the large concrete room beyond.

Six guards whip towards me, raising their guns, before they realize who I am and lower their weapons again. Two men are tied to chairs in the rooms on the other side of the glass walls ahead. The two men who murdered my parents.

But I barely notice any of them, because my eyes are fixed on two people by the wall.

Isabella, in only her underwear, is kneeling on the cold hard floor. Her wrists and ankles are shackled and locked to one of the thick metal rings that have been set into the floor behind her. She was glaring up at my grandfather when I burst through the door, but the moment I walked in, she snapped her gaze to me. Her eyes widen in shock as she stares at me.

I drag my gaze up to Federico, who is standing before her.

Rage roars through me.

"Let her go," I say. It's not a request.

"Enrico," my grandfather says. There is a hard expression on his face, but his eyes soften a little when he looks at me. "I was going to send for you later, because I was anticipating this kind of reaction." He flicks a venomous look down at Isabella. "This snake has managed to fool you into—"

"Do not," I growl. "Talk about her like that."

He heaves a sigh. "You're just proving my point, Enrico."

With my eyes locked on his, I hold out my hand. "Give me the keys."

"No. My guards here are going to unlock her chain and then they are going to shackle her to that chair in there." He nods towards the third room before meeting my gaze again. And when he speaks, his voice takes on a hard edge full of absolute authority. "And then you are going to stand here and watch as I torture her and her two colleagues for *murdering your parents*. Unless, of course, you want to help me torture them. Which is an acceptable adjustment to the plan."

"She—"

"Six years, Enrico," he snaps, cutting me off. His dark eyes flash with both anger and pain as he stares me down. "We have waited six *years* for this! Six years to get our revenge. And I am going to carve that vengeance from their flesh and make them bleed for every second of that." He snaps his fingers at his guards. "Take her."

I react purely on instinct.

Yanking out my gun, I level it at my grandfather's head.

The six guards around me immediately point their own guns at me.

I don't even look at them. All of my attention is focused solely on my grandfather as I lock hard eyes on him.

"Don't. Touch her." Power and threats drip from each word as I speak. "Don't you dare touch her."

On the floor, Isabella sucks in a sharp breath of surprise. I can feel her staring at me with wide eyes, but I can't break eye contact with Federico right now.

He is also staring at me. But he doesn't look angry. With his eyebrows raised, he just looks genuinely stunned.

Waving a hand, he motions for his guards to lower their weapons. They do. I, on the other hand, keep mine right where it is.

"You would really pull a gun on me?" Federico asks. "Your own grandfather. For *her*."

"Yes," I reply without hesitation.

"Why?"

This time, I do break eye contact. My gaze darts down to Isabella as I reply, "Because I love her."

A small gasp escapes her lips, and emotions flood her features.

I shift my gaze back to my grandfather, who heaves an exasperated sigh.

"Love makes fools of us all," he says, almost wistfully. Then his expression hardens again and utter certainty creeps into his voice. "But this is not it. This is an illusion. A lie. She is a liar and a killer and she is only using you for her own survival."

"Yes, she is a liar and a killer," I reply. "But not with me."

At last, Federico's patience seems to snap. Fury flares up in his eyes. "Enough! Lower your gun and get out if you can't stomach it, but I am going to torture all three of them to death right now."

"You are making a mistake."

"They are the reason my son is dead!" The words rip out of him, full of agony and rage.

It only ignites the anger inside me as well. Raising my other hand, I stab it towards the two men behind the glass walls. "*They* are the reason your son is dead." I shift my hand, pointing down at Isabella. "*She* is the reason why your grandson *isn't*."

"She's one of them."

"She spared my life."

"Because she chickened out."

"She didn't chicken out. She made a choice. She chose to let me live even though she knew that she forfeited her own life in doing so. And she has saved my life two more times after that too."

"She has you fooled."

"Look at her!" I scream, stabbing my hand down at Isabella again. "Where do you think she got all of those injuries? All of those cuts and bruises?" With my eyes locked on Federico's, I swing my arm around and motion towards Derek and Sebastian. "They tortured her to get her to tell them where I was. They *tortured* her. And still she didn't sell me out."

A brief hint of hesitation flickers in his eyes before he sets his jaw again. "It could've been to protect herself."

"Protect herself? By getting tortured?"

"It's—"

"Fine, then how about this? Do you know why she went to that parking lot to meet them today?"

My grandfather just looks back at me in silence.

"She went there because she had made a deal with them," I begin. "A deal that involved Isabella publicly groveling before their fucking master, enduring two hundred days of torture, and then letting them execute her in exchange for them taking me off their hit list and letting me live."

Surprise flits across Federico's features, and he casts a glance down at Isabella.

I look down at her too, and find her staring at me in shock. She obviously didn't expect me to know that.

"Kaden was in the house," I explain to her softly. "He overheard you when you made that phone call."

"She could've staged that," Federico protests. But he sounds uncertain now. "She could've just said all of that into an empty phone because she knew that Kaden was listening."

"Ask *them*." I flick my wrist towards where Derek and Sebastian are shackled in the other rooms. "Ask them about the deal. And about the torture. They'll confirm it."

For a few seconds, he doesn't move. Only stands there, watching me while thoughts swirl in his eyes. I just look back at him, keeping my gun pointed at his head.

At last, he jerks his chin.

Two of the guards walk into the other rooms.

The screaming starts quickly. They aren't playing around, dragging things out to torment them. They just want answers. Fast. And since this is information that has no value to the Hands of Peace, I'm fairly certain that they will give it up quickly.

I'm proved right when the guards eventually return and give my grandfather a nod, informing him that both Derek and Sebastian independently confirmed what I told him.

He clears his throat, almost a bit self-consciously, as he turns back to me.

"The keys," I say, holding his gaze.

Reaching into his suit jacket, he pulls out the keys to Isabella's manacles and hands them to me.

I take them. And then, at long last, I lower the gun from his head. Sliding the weapon into the back of my pants, I turn around and then crouch beside Isabella.

"Are you okay?" I ask as I unlock her handcuffs and the shackles around her ankles.

She glances between me and Federico before replying, "Yes."

The locks click open. Metallic rattling fills the gray concrete basement as I pull the manacles off her and drop them on the floor. She rolls her wrists and shoulders. I hold out a hand, helping her to her feet.

Once she is standing again, I turn to the closest guard. "You. Give me your suit jacket."

He glances questioningly towards Federico.

"That wasn't a request," I snap.

His gaze darts back to me, and he immediately begins shrugging off his jacket. I take it from his outstretched hand and then drape it around Isabella's shoulders. I would have given her mine, if I could, but I'm only wearing a t-shirt.

Isabella doesn't seem to mind. She lets me put the jacket on her and then wraps it over her stomach, covering herself up.

"Where are her clothes?" I demand.

The guard exchanges a glance with one of the others, who replies, "In the van."

I stare them down in silence.

"I'll go get them right away and bring them to a room upstairs, sir," the second one hurriedly adds.

On my other side, Federico watches me while two guards scramble out the door. There is a small approving smile on his lips.

I shift my attention back to Isabella. She's just standing there, wearing that oversized black jacket and staring at me with an uncertain expression on her beautiful features. Her hair is slightly messy and those stunning eyes of hers look more hesitant than I have ever seen. As if she doesn't know what to say or do now. I, on the other hand, know exactly what I want to do while we wait for them to bring her clothes.

"Which one of them tortured you?" I ask her, jerking my chin towards where Derek and Sebastian are still trapped.

Her gaze slides to them, and a hardness sweeps over her features. "Both of them." She nods towards Derek. "But mostly him. He is also the one who shot your mother. Sebastian killed your father."

I nod before shifting my gaze back to her again. "Would you mind terribly if I tortured him to death?"

A surprised laugh rips from her lips. Then she clears her throat and gives me a knowing smile. "Not at all. Please do."

I flash her a matching grin back.

Then I slide my hand around the back of her neck, and pull her towards me, claiming her lips in a possessive kiss. She melts against my body.

"I will never let anyone hurt you ever again," I whisper against her lips as we break the kiss.

She smiles against my mouth. "Likewise."

A warm chuckle escapes my chest. I kiss her one more time before drawing back.

"I'll take her upstairs and make sure that she gets her clothes back," my grandfather says.

I glance towards Isabella. She nods, signaling that she's fine with that.

"I'll come back down here and help you afterwards," she promises as a savage grin curls her lips.

The smile on my own mouth is equally vicious. "I look forward to it."

After giving both her and Federico a nod, I turn around and stalk towards Derek's room. Behind me, I swear I can hear my grandfather speak softly under his breath.

"I knew you would make a great king."

With that savage smile still on my lips, I stride into the smaller room on the other side of the one-way glass and take up position in front of Derek.

He pales visibly when he takes in the expression on my face.

There will be no mercy here.

This man murdered my mom, ruined my life, and tortured my girl.

And he will pay for that with every excruciating slice of my blade. I pick up a knife. A knife meant to be used for skinning animals.

Vengeance, long and bloody and brutal vengeance, burns in my eyes as I raise it.

A dark stain spreads across the front of Derek's underwear.

I grin down at him.

And then I get to work.

43

ISABELLA

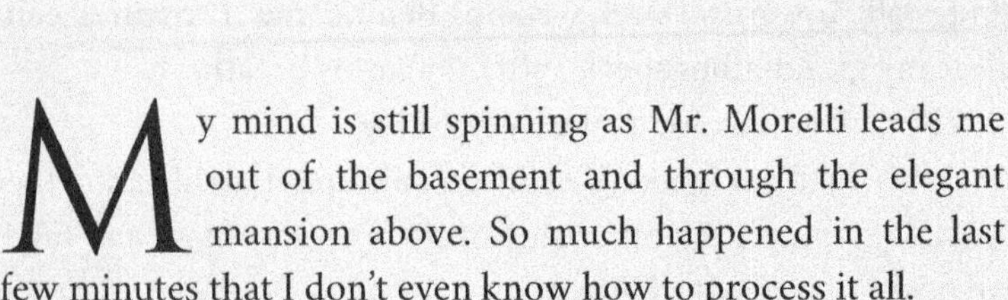

My mind is still spinning as Mr. Morelli leads me out of the basement and through the elegant mansion above. So much happened in the last few minutes that I don't even know how to process it all.

Rico came for me.

And he put a gun to his grandfather's head. Put a gun to the head of the reigning monarch of the Morelli mafia family. For me.

Because he…

Because he loves me.

The thought makes my head swim with a sudden surge of vertigo.

Rico Morelli loves me.

The man I was sent to kill six years ago loves me, and he is willing to go against his own family for my sake.

Warmth, fizzy sparkling warmth, spreads through my chest and envelops my soul. Never in my life have I ever been put first. No one has ever chosen me above everything else.

But now I know, without a doubt, that Rico will always have my back. Just like I will always have his.

"Your clothes are in there," Federico says, and nods towards the door to our right.

Since I'm not sure what to say, I just nod back and reach for the handle.

"Before you go back down, come and see me, would you?"

It's phrased as a request, but I know that it's not. It's an order.

"Of course," I reply in a neutral voice.

"Good. I will be in the room at the end of the hall."

Before I can reply, he walks off. I just blow out a long breath and open the door.

Just like he said, my clothes are there. They are folded neatly on top of a chair in what looks to be some kind of study or reading room or something. There is also a hairbrush atop the pile.

A tired laugh escapes my throat.

We were just about to torture you to death, but hey, here's a hairbrush to make up for it.

Shaking my head, I walk up to the pile of clothes and start getting dressed.

I do, however, understand Federico Morelli. His son, his only child and heir, was murdered in his own bed along with his wife, and he has been searching for the killers for six long years. Technically, I was a part of that assassination squad, so his anger and hatred towards me is entirely justified.

If Rico and I ever have a child of our own, I would be equally protective of…

Blinking, I draw upright halfway through buttoning my pants.

If Rico and I have a child.

Gods above, what am I thinking? He told me that he loves me, yes. But now I'm definitely getting ahead of myself.

I doubt Rico would even be allowed to marry me. After all, isn't the heir to the most powerful mafia family in the state supposed to marry someone equally powerful? And I'm no one. An ex-cult member who doesn't even have a last name. Why would we be allowed to marry? Let alone have a child? Federico might have let me live, but he will never accept me as a part of the family.

Gritting my teeth, I angrily finish buttoning my pants.

Because who the hell cares what Federico Morelli thinks? I told myself that I would face hell itself for a chance to have that real life with Rico. And I will. I will fucking fight for him regardless of how much his grandfather disapproves of me.

A small burst of agony flickers through me, because it would have been nice to be a part of a family. Rico is all that matters, but by all the gods in all religions, I can't deny that my heart aches when I consider what it will be like to always feel his grandfather's disapproval and hatred following me everywhere I go.

Shaking my head, I push the thought aside.

After dragging that brush through my hair a couple of times, I head back into the hallway.

To my surprise, there are no guards outside my room. If I wanted to, I could just walk back down to the basement where Rico is. But I told his grandfather that I would see him first, so I start towards the room at the end of the hall.

A dark wooden door, carved with subtle yet elegant shapes, awaits me there.

I raise my hand and knock.

"Come in," Federico answers from the other side.

Pulling the door open, I walk across the threshold and into

the room. It's another study, though this one is larger. I sweep my gaze through it.

Either this isn't his real study, or he prefers a very open space.

There is a desk, also made of dark wood, on the other side of the room, facing the door. Federico sits behind it. Bookshelves line the walls, but apart from that, there is nothing in here. It leaves a fairly large bit of floor space empty in the middle.

I move closer to the desk.

Four guards stand by the walls, watching me.

Coming to a halt a few steps from the desk, I meet Federico's eyes. "You wanted to speak to me."

"Yes," he replies.

Silence falls. For a few seconds, we just watch each other. Outside the windows, the afternoon sunlight illuminates some of the other elegant buildings that make up the vast Morelli compound.

"I will not apologize for what I did," Mr. Morelli says.

"I don't expect you to." I hold his gaze. "I understand why you hate me, and I would have done the same thing, if I were in your position."

He seems surprised by that answer. But he recovers quickly, and instead slides a checkbook across the desk. The topmost one is signed, but there is no amount filled in.

I raise my eyebrows in silent question.

"Fill it in," he says.

"Why?"

"Because I would like you to leave." He nods towards the checkbook. "So fill in whatever amount you want, take it, and then go wherever you want to start a new life."

My reply is immediate. "No."

He narrows his eyes. "Think this through properly before you refuse."

"I don't need to. The answer will always be no."

"You would really turn down the chance to have a life, a real life, without having to worry about anything?"

A laugh spills from my lips.

Federico's gaze sharpens.

"I apologize," I say. "I meant no offense. It's just… I have a real life now. Here. With Rico."

"It's a blank check. A blank check can buy you another life. Away from all of this violence and death."

"Mr. Morelli," I begin, feeling my patience dwindling. "It doesn't matter what you offer me. I will never leave Rico."

I expect him to get angry. Or at least frustrated. But he only cocks his head, looking pensive.

Standing there on the other side of the desk, I simply hold his stare with determined eyes.

"Why?" Federico asks at last. He sounds genuinely curious. "Why would you turn down this money? And why did you endure torture at the hands of your former colleagues instead of giving up Enrico's location?"

Yet again, my answer is immediate. "Because I love him."

For the briefest of moments, I swear I can see a small smile ghost across his lips. But then that stern mask is back on his face, and he gives me an appraising look.

"I will not be trusting just anyone with my only grandson and heir," he declares.

Keeping my chin raised, I just stare back at him.

"But if you can prove yourself against four of my elite guards," he continues, and flicks his wrist at the four men standing by the walls. "I might change my mind."

He watches me as if he expects me to object. I don't.

Instead, I just move back from the desk and towards the middle of the room.

"Don't hold back," Mr. Morelli says to his guards in Italian. "I want to see what she's truly made of."

"I think that sounds like a wise strategy," I reply in flawless Italian as well. "Since it would otherwise be difficult to assess my skills."

Shock pulses across his features.

It's so satisfying that I nearly let a victorious grin spread across my lips. But I thankfully manage to stifle it and instead keep the cool expression on my features.

"You speak Italian?" Federico asks, still in that beautiful language of his ancestors, as he stares at me with wide eyes.

"Yes," I reply, also in Italian. "And Russian. And Chinese."

That ghost of a smile blows across his face again for a fraction of a second. Then he waves his hand at his guards.

They immediately descend on me.

I duck underneath the first fist, twisting and driving the heel of my hand into the second guard's stomach. A satisfying huff escapes his chest. I draw my foot along the floor, forcing the third one to jump back. Then I yank up my forearm to block the strike from the fourth one.

Pain vibrates through my bones as his fist connects, but I'm already moving again.

The stitches on my wounds pull against my skin as I twist and duck and punch and kick, but I ignore the flickers of pain. Because I am going to win this. I'm not just going to prove myself. I'm going to win.

I land several punches and kicks, making the guards stagger back and lose their breath. And I manage to keep them from grabbing me.

But even with my lifetime of being trained as an elite

assassin, I can't simultaneously knock out *four* grown men, who not only have an entire head and about a hundred pounds on me, but also have their own elite training to rely on.

However, I refuse to lose.

So once I have shown off my hand-to-hand skills, I go in for the kill.

Feinting a strike to the right, I duck and twist in the other direction while swiping the gun that the guard kept underneath his suit jacket.

In one fluid motion, I straighten and level the gun straight at Mr. Morelli's head.

"Don't," I snap at the other three guards, who were reaching for their own weapons in a sudden flurry of panic.

Surprise and quite a lot of curiosity swirl in Federico's eyes as he watches me.

"Tell them to take out their guns and slide them across the floor towards the other wall," I tell him.

He watches me for another few seconds before giving his guards a nod.

The guns make a faint scraping noise as they slide along the floor before coming to a halt by the opposite wall.

"Now tell them to back up to the other wall and get down on their knees," I continue.

Yet again, Federico gives them a nod.

I watch as the four men back up and then lower themselves to the polished wooden floorboards. Once they're kneeling, I turn back to Mr. Morelli and flash him a smile.

Releasing my grip on the gun, I let it spin around so that it's only hanging on my finger with the handle facing Federico. I keep it like that, offering him the gun. With his gaze locked on mine, he stands up from his chair and takes it.

I let my hand drop back down to my side, but I say nothing. Only keep holding his gaze.

"You're not only very skilled in close combat," Mr. Morelli says eventually. He glances down at the gun in his hand before meeting my eyes once more. "You're also intelligent. Not many people understand the difference between fighting hard and fighting smart."

A soft thud sounds as he puts the gun down on his desk. Twitching his fingers, he motions for his guards to get to their feet again. Their dark suits rustle faintly behind me as they no doubt rise from the floor, but I keep my eyes on the mafia king before me.

My heart patters in my chest as Mr. Morelli straightens his spine, standing taller. Judgement is about to be passed now.

"You're an exceptionally skilled fighter," he says, his serious eyes locked on mine. "You're intelligent. And you're loyal."

I swear I can hear my own heart pounding in my ears as Federico pauses for a few moments and lets the silence stretch.

Then a smile breaks across his features, and light glints in his brown eyes. "I knew that Enrico would someday find someone who matches him so perfectly."

A small gasp escapes me. It's followed by a flood of emotions so intense that I can feel tears prickling behind my eyes.

Federico holds out his hand to me, that warm smile still on his lips.

"Welcome to the family, Isabella."

44

RICO

The cardboard box lets out a huff as I drop it on the floor in the middle of the spacious living room. Polished oak floorboards stretch out towards the tall windows on my right, and there is a fireplace along the wall on the other side. Apart from that, and the small pile of cardboard boxes that I have just dumped in the middle of the floor, the room is completely empty. Just like the rest of the house.

Leaving my stack of boxes behind, I walk over to the glass balcony doors and push them aside. Warm air smelling of pine trees and clear water washes into the silent house. I wander out onto the balcony.

It faces a glittering lake, with lush forests on both sides. The sun is setting over the water, painting it with gold and red light.

The house, along with the massive garden around it, is technically situated within our family's vast compound. But it's secluded enough to make it feel private. Secret, almost. Hidden like a gem here at the edge of the woods and the lake.

Tilting my head back, I watch the sky.

I will be able to see the stars from here.

A smile spreads across my lips.

She really picked the best house of them all.

After drawing in a deep breath of clear afternoon air, I walk back into the living room. Since I didn't have that much stuff to bring, I didn't bother marking any of the boxes. I bend down and open the first one. It's full of clothes. Pushing it aside, I open the flaps of the next one. More clothes. I straighten again.

And feel the barrel of a gun against the back of my neck.

"You really should be more careful," a smug voice says. "Leaving the balcony door open like that. Who knows what kind of wicked person might climb inside."

A grin curves my lips. "And what if that was my intention?"

"Then I would say that you accomplished your mission, little mafia prince."

The gun disappears from my head, and I turn around to face a smirking Isabella. She tosses her gun down on one of the cardboard boxes. It lands with a thud.

"Hello, Rico," she says.

"Hello, Isabella."

A small shiver rolls down her spine when I say her name. It makes warmth wash through my chest. Almost subconsciously, she lifts her hand and fingers the necklace I gave her. I watch her until she seems to realize what she's doing and instead shifts her hand to the straps of her backpack. Sliding it off her shoulders, she lets it drop to the floor next to my boxes.

I raise my eyebrows. "That's it?"

She shrugs and nudges the backpack with her shoe.

"Everything else belongs to Isabella Johnson. These clothes were the only ones that I felt belonged to Isabella..." She trails off, and her eyes go distant for a second, as if she's trying to come up with a new last name for herself. Her hand once again drifts to the necklace, fidgeting with the thin silver circle. Then she lets it drop and shrugs again. "Just Isabella."

Since I can tell that not having a real last name is still a little painful for her, and not something that she wants to talk about right now, I quickly change the subject. "So, I hear that my grandfather tried to pay you off to get you to leave."

Relief washes over her features at the change in topic. Then she chuckles. "Yeah. With a blank check too." Mischief glitters in her eyes as she advances on me, backing me up against the wall. She reaches up and draws her fingers along my jaw while a brilliant smile decorates her lips. "Imagine the amount of waffles I could've bought with that."

I slide my fingers through her hair, hooking it behind her ear. "I will buy you all the waffles you like. As many and as often as you want."

"You'd better."

A soft laugh escapes me. She opens her mouth to no doubt continue her mock threats. I use that opportunity to flip us around. Her back hits the wall with a thud while she blinks at me in surprise. I press closer, slanting my lips over hers for a second before drawing back.

"And I hear you speak fluent Italian," I say, raising my eyebrows at her.

Tilting her head back, she grins up at me. "I do."

"That would've been nice to know before I cursed you out in Italian, thinking you didn't understand a word of it," I say in Italian.

"Well, it was a very creative and colorful curse, I'll give you that," she replies in absolutely flawless Italian as well.

I laugh in amazement before switching back to English. "I also hear that you outmaneuvered four elite guards and that you put a gun to my grandfather's head."

"I did."

"God, you're ballsy." Leaning closer, I skim my lips over hers. "And fucking incredible."

She lets out a shuddering breath as my words caress her lips. Closing my eyes, I rest my forehead against hers for a few seconds. Just breathing her in and reminding myself that she is here. That *we* are here.

After I finished skinning Derek alive, Federico and I showed his body to Sebastian. The blond hitman pissed his pants and then spilled everything about the Hands of Peace. Their current location, which Isabella didn't know since they had moved after she escaped. Their security systems. Everything.

After my grandfather had finished torturing Sebastian to death too, he immediately sent a strike team big enough to conquer a decent-sized country to take out their entire cult. And they did. Everyone who belonged to the Hands of Peace are now either dead or in custody. Isabella even flew there with us to personally identify the Master's body. He turned out to be a brute of a man who looked as vicious as Isabella had told us he was. But now he is dead. And the threat both to her and to me has been neutralized.

After that, Federico once more suggested that I should stop pretending to be Rico Hunter and return to the Morelli empire as the rightful heir. And this time, I agreed.

I know who I am now.

I am not the Enrico Morelli who I was before I officially died six years ago.

And I am not Rico Hunter who I have been pretending to be for six years either.

I'm a mix of them both. With some new bits that have been added since I met Isabella. Rico Morelli. A new person. Someone who finally feels like me.

So I dropped out of Blackwater, reclaimed the name Morelli, and at long last returned home. Isabella dropped out too, since the only reason she enrolled was to hide from the Hands of Peace. And when I asked her to move in with me, she thankfully said yes.

Since this is her first home, I wanted her to choose it. So I let her check out all the houses spread out across the massive land area we own. And she picked this one, because she said that it felt like home. Our home.

And by God, I agree.

This will be *our* home. And we will slowly fill it with things that fit us both. Our real personalities. Not the people we have been pretending to be for years.

A real home. For us.

"What did you tell my grandfather?" I ask as I draw back again, meeting her gaze with serious eyes. "When he asked you why you didn't take the money? And why you endured the torture instead of telling them where I was? He refused to tell me that part. Said that I should ask you directly instead."

Golden light from the setting sun reflects in those storm-swept blue-gray eyes of hers, making them glitter. Like water blanketed with gilded sparkles.

"The truth," she replies, holding my gaze. "That I love you."

My heart skips several beats, and an unsteady breath escapes my lungs.

"Can I ask you something?" She traces her fingers over my cheekbone and then down along my jaw while a wistful smile blows across her lips.

Everything inside me is thrumming with heat. With life. With love. I drag in a steadying breath and nod. "Of course."

"Why didn't you kill me that day in the forest? After I had told you everything you wanted to know?" She lets her hand drop back down and instead cocks her head, her gaze curious. "The only logical reaction would have been to kill me, or to hand me over to your grandfather after that. But you didn't. Why?"

"Because when I looked into your eyes, I saw the other half of my soul that I have been missing."

Her breath hitches.

I cup her cheeks, kissing her deeply. Then I rest my forehead against hers and whisper against her lips, "I love you, Isabella."

"I love you too," she whispers back, her voice raw. "You are the soul I didn't even know I possessed."

Bracing one arm against the wall, I slide the other hand around the back of her neck as I press my lips to hers. She locks her hands around the back of my neck too, pulling me closer. I rest my knee against the wall between her legs.

She kisses me back fiercely. Passionately.

And there in the golden light inside the house that will be our home, we lose ourselves in each other with our souls thrumming. Finally whole. Now and forever.

EPILOGUE

ONE YEAR LATER

The crowd parts before us as we walk through the room. Rico, wearing an impeccable black suit, moves like he owns the place. Like he expects everything and everyone to back up and bow before his unflinching power. And they do.

Men and women from rich, influential families incline their heads in respect as we pass. I drink in the feeling. Relishing in the fact that I no longer have to hide in the shadows. No longer have to hide behind a mask.

Now, I'm walking with my spine straight and my chin up. And when I scan the crowd, people quickly drop their gazes for me too.

Everyone has heard of me by now.

The elite assassin who captured the heart of a mafia prince.

Or rather, the heart of the de facto mafia king.

Since Federico's health has been getting worse, Rico has stepped up to fill his role. And gods above, he does it well. *We* do it well.

With the two of us side by side, no one dares to oppose us.

I casually brush my hand over the skirt of my dress. It's silver, looking like melted metal flowing around me. And underneath it, I have a gun strapped to one thigh and a knife to the other.

Rico follows the subtle movement of my hand from the corner of his eye, and a smirk tilts his lips.

All around us, people continue dipping their chins in respect as we leave the extravagant party behind and stride out towards where our car is waiting. It was a party for the Morelli family's numerous business partners, so we needed to make an appearance.

Now we have, which means that we will finally be heading home to the surprise that Rico promised me.

I don't like surprises. An old assassin mentality that is hard to reprogram. So I almost considered sneaking away from the party and back to our house to check what the surprise was before we returned together.

But that would've meant leaving Rico alone at the party, and I don't do that. I protect him. And he protects me.

So I had to stifle my curiosity and wariness the entire evening. But now, as we slide into the car that the valet brought out for us, I can't contain myself anymore.

"So," I begin as Rico starts the car and drives us away from the glittering building where the party will continue for several hours still. "Are you going to tell me what the surprise is?"

His lips curve in that troublesome smirk of his as he casts me a glance from the corner of his eye. "Wouldn't be much of a surprise then, would it?"

I narrow my eyes at him. "I could always *make you* tell me."

His smirk widens to a devilish grin. Reaching over with

his right hand, he slides it over my thigh. My skin prickles as he pushes the silk fabric aside until he exposes the knife strapped to my thigh. He traces the edges of the strap and flashes me another smile.

"I'm sure you could," he says.

I open my mouth to retort, but right then, he dips his fingers down between my thighs and brushes them over my pussy.

A gasp escapes my lips instead.

Gripping the silk fabric of my skirt, I squeeze it hard as Rico slides his fingers underneath the thin seam of my panties and nonchalantly starts playing with my clit.

"Rico," I press out, throwing my head back against the headrest.

"Yes, Isabella?"

But I forget what I was about to say as he rolls my clit between his fingers, drawing a moan from my mouth and a shudder from my body. He shifts his hand.

Another gasp rips from me as he pushes two fingers inside me while his thumb rubs over my clit. I whimper, crushing the silver fabric harder in my grip as Rico starts pumping his fingers.

With one hand on the steering wheel and the other drawing pleasure from my body, he drives us back home while pushing me closer and closer to the edge of an orgasm.

Pent-up tension vibrates inside my soul as his clever fingers move across my sensitive skin. I can barely concentrate on where we are, let alone on what I had planned to make him tell me earlier, as he fucks me with his fingers.

My chest heaves and lights flicker behind my eyes as I soar towards that sweet release.

He curls his fingers on the way out.

Pleasure crackles through me.

I cry out and then gasp into the ceiling of the car as release shoots through my limbs like lightning strikes. Moans drip from my lips.

The car swerves slightly.

"Fuck," Rico mutters.

But his fingers continue pumping into me, drawing out the orgasm and prolonging the pleasure.

Once the last of it has receded, Rico pulls his hand back. I suck in a shuddering breath and tilt my head to the side, resting my cheek against the headrest.

"Why did you curse?" I ask, my voice coming out breathless.

Amusement tugs at his lips as he casts me a sideways glance while turning into our driveway. "Because you looked so fucking stunning when you climaxed around my fingers that I almost drove off the road."

A laugh rips from my chest. Followed by smug satisfaction.

"And what are you looking so smug about?" he teases as he parks the car. "When I'm the one who managed to distract you enough that you forgot to threaten me into telling you what the surprise is."

Raising my eyebrows, I look between him and the house in front of us. Our house. Then I narrow my eyes at him. "Oh, you cunning bastard."

He lets out a dark chuckle. Opening his door, he gets out of the car while saying, "Come on."

I follow him.

Stars shine in the dark blue heavens above, and they reflect against the still lake, making it look like a piece of the night sky. I know how much Rico loves that. It's one of the reasons why I picked this house for us.

After unlocking the front door, he opens it for me.

I walk inside while saying, "Whatever the surprise is, it's going to have to wait for ten minutes."

"Oh?" he asks while following me into the hallway.

Looking over my shoulder, I give him a pointed glance. "I need to take a shower first. Since someone decided to ruin my dress and make me all sticky."

"I didn't hear you complaining in the car." He grins back at me, but then nods. "Join me on the balcony when you're done."

While he heads into the kitchen, I go up to our bedroom and take a quick shower before changing into another dress. This one is blue, one that matches my eyes, and has silver gems sewn into the bodice like glittering stars.

When I walk back down to the living room, a heavenly scent drifts through the air. It gets even stronger as I walk out onto the balcony.

A wide smile spreads across my lips as I find the table out there packed with waffles and dozens of toppings.

"Okay," I say, shifting my gaze to Rico, who is standing by the railing. "I might have to revise my opinion on surprises. *This* is a very nice one."

He smiles as I walk over and join him by the railing. For a few seconds, I just gaze out at the lake. The trees around it rustle faintly in the wind. The gentle breeze sweeps across the star-dusted water, making the surface ripple slightly.

Next to me, I can feel Rico watching my face, as if memorizing it.

I turn towards him.

"There is something I want to ask you," he says.

My heart stutters at the sudden intensity in his eyes and the seriousness of his voice, so all I manage is a nod.

"You haunted my dreams for six years." A smile blows across his lips as he traces his fingers over my cheekbone. "I dreamt of your beautiful eyes. Of the emotions I saw in them. And then when I finally met you again, I knew that there was no turning back. We are, and always have been, two bodies with one soul. You are mine, Isabella. And I am yours."

Emotions well up inside me, and I draw in an unsteady breath.

His eyes glitter in the starlight as he watches me. As he drinks in the sight of me.

My heart leaps in my chest as Rico lowers himself to one knee. Everything inside my head goes silent, so silent that I can hear the erratic pounding of my own heart, as he reaches into his black suit jacket and pulls out a small box.

A jagged breath escapes my lungs as he opens the box to reveal a breathtaking silver ring with a sapphire in the exact color of my eyes.

"I know that you don't have a last name of your own," he says, looking up at me. "So I would like to give you mine. If you'll have it."

My heart bursts and the whole world tilts on its axis. And at the center of it all is the kneeling mafia prince before me. Offering me a ring. A name. A home. And a life. Everything I have ever wanted.

"Yes," I gasp out.

His eyes light up like the stars themselves, and he slips the ring onto my finger. Rising to his feet, he slides his hands through my hair, which is now back to its natural auburn color.

My soul flutters and my toes curl as Rico claims my lips the way he has just claimed my heart.

"Well then, Isabella Morelli," he says when he draws back.

There is a brilliant smile on his face. "Would you like some waffles to celebrate?"

The name sends a pleasant shudder coursing through my body, leaving a sparkling warmth in its wake.

Starlight glints in Rico's eyes as he watches me.

I smile back up at him, feeling so light that I could float away to join the clouds.

Isabella Morelli.

Neither name was mine from birth. But they are the names that I have chosen for myself. The only ones that have ever felt right.

This life is the only one that has ever felt right.

Here. With him.

Because it's real.

We are real.

We have fought our past and our enemies and even our own families to have this life together. We have carved out our own happiness from a complicated world full of violence and blood. We have found our own path. Our future. Our place in this beautiful and lethal life of ours.

And now, we are going to do what both of us have been dreaming about for years.

We are going to live.

BONUS SCENE

Do you want one more spicy scene between Isabella and Rico? Then scan the QR code to download the exclusive bonus scene:

Made in United States
Orlando, FL
20 July 2025

63124543R00208